THE
WITCH'S
PET

TIANA WARNER

ROGUE CANNON PUBLISHING

Content Warnings

This Dark Romance contains sexual content (exclusively f/f), magical coercion, power imbalance in a relationship, and death. For a detailed list of warnings, please visit tianawarner.com/thewitchspet

Copyright © 2026 by Tiana Warner

All rights reserved. No portion of this book may be reproduced in any form without written permission from the author.

Cover design by Artscandare.

978-1-0690967-8-4 (paperback)

978-1-0690967-9-1 (ebook)

ALSO BY TIANA WARNER

How to Flirt with a Witch
From Fan to Forever
The Road Trip Agreement
Snowed In With Summer
Striking Gold

Get a free Sapphic Cozy Fantasy novelette when you sign up for Tiana Warner's newsletter:

tianawarner.com/newsletter

I

HANNAH

THE BONFIRE BURNS HOTTER as I toss another piece of Riley into the flames. I mean, not *her*, specifically, but memories of her. I have no idea where *she* is, and to hell if I care.

The fire warms my front while the late October chill drags its fingers down my spine, the temperature dropping as the sun dips below the horizon. I've reduced three boxes of Riley's belongings to ash, from clothes to love notes to the toothbrush she kept in my bathroom, and I still can't figure out why she dumped me.

My whole body wants to sink into the earth as her soccer jersey ignites. The memory of her wearing it, grass-stained and sweaty as she picked me up and spun me around after her last game, barges into my mind. Then the smell of her lilac detergent dissolves into the acrid scent of burnt material. My eyes water—from the smoke, obviously—and I blink to clear them.

"Don't take this the wrong way, Han, but this isn't the most conventional way to process your feelings," Dean says from his perch on my back steps. His long legs are folded awkwardly, and his pale face is rosy from the cold. He sips the pumpkin spice latte he brought me, which is probably iced after sitting in the wintry air for an hour.

I shrug. "This is cheaper than therapy."

And more effective. One cathartic night of burning everything, and then I'll move on.

Anyway, between my pitiful wage at Book Nook and saving for university, I don't have the budget for therapy. Believe me, I looked into it long ago.

The flames swell, casting writhing shadows across my flat, square yard. The world looks extra dreary and colorless tonight, with the gray sky pressing down like a wet blanket and the forest behind the fence, where I've spent countless hours alone since I learned to walk, buried in decaying brown maple leaves. The neighbors have gone into hibernation for the winter, leaving the dead-end street so quiet that all you can hear are crows.

Perfect night for burning the last of my ties to the girl who pulverized my heart, I guess.

"And I'm not just randomly torching things." I poke the crumbling logs with a metal broom handle. "I'm conducting an investigation."

"Into...which materials burn the fastest?" Dean asks.

"Into why Riley started acting like I had the plague before dumping me via text." I shake back the sleeves of my oversized black hoodie and pick up the book she left behind, *The Encyclopedia of Herbs.* "Something was going on with her in the last couple of weeks."

Dean's footsteps squelch closer on the wet grass. "What d'you mean?"

"She changed. For starters, she suddenly became interested in stuff she didn't care about before. Asked me to dig up books from work about folklore, local history, and..." I show him the encyclopedia. "She started collecting herbs and crystals. It made her bedroom smell like the forest. One night, she showed up with scars on her hands and arms. She said they were from work, but..."

Dean furrows his brow. His many piercings glint in the firelight. "But she works at a coffee shop."

"Exactly. The most dangerous thing there is the espresso machine."

"Steam burns?"

I lift a shoulder, at a loss.

I can still feel the texture of those dark scars under my fingertips, raised and rough against the smooth brown skin I'd memorized. When I'd traced them, asking what happened, she pulled away so fast I was left grasping at nothing. And when I offered to help, she rolled her eyes and snapped, "You're overreacting to a few little bumps. Stop making everything a big deal."

Her cold dismissal still stings. She acted like I was a nuisance for caring.

"The thing is, the scars looked old," I tell Dean, "like they'd been there for years. But..." But I knew her intimately. I licked and kissed her from head to toe every night. "Those scars weren't there before," I finish simply.

"Okay, that is pretty weird." Dean's breath mists, and he wraps his scarf one more time around his neck, hiding the lower half of his face so I can only see his narrowed brown eyes.

I flip through the book, scanning one last time for anything strange. No hand-written notes, highlighted text, or dog-eared pages. So I chuck it onto the flames, where it lands with a heavy *thump* and begins to smolder.

A shame. I liked that book. But I want to move on properly, which means I can't keep anything that reminds me of her.

As the pages curl and blacken, my heart flutters nervously. What was Riley hiding from me? Did she meet someone else who's into herbs and folklore? Or is she just changing as we get older, getting bored with the girl who was nothing more than a post high school fling?

My stomach clenches at the prospect that that's all I was to her.

I nudge the final box with my foot, rattling its dwindling contents. "I'm giving myself until this is empty, and then I'm going to stop analyzing what happened. No more caring about her and trying to figure her out. No more torturing myself over someone who didn't think I was worth a real explanation."

In my periphery, Dean studies my face. "It's okay to feel hurt—"

"I'm more confused than anything," I snap. *And frustrated, and angry...* Nothing about this breakup makes sense. The not-knowing gnaws at me, an ache so deep I can't remember ever feeling anything else.

When I look back at the fire, the sky behind it is darker than a moment ago. I cross my arms to suppress a shiver. My leggings offer zero warmth in this weather, and my socks are soaking up the lawn's dampness through my Birkenstocks. My hair is a mess, blonde tresses falling loose from my bun and sticking to my tear-streaked face. I must look like as much of a wreck as I feel.

"Sounds like she was going through something," Dean says. "People get into weird hobbies when they're stressed. Remember soap carving during finals?"

I huff. "Whatever this was, it's not as simple as taking up soap carving to get through exam stress. And why wouldn't she confide in me if..." My throat gets painfully tight, so I shut my mouth and shake my head.

The fire pops, sending sparks into the darkening sky.

"Or," Dean says gently, "we're overthinking this."

I pick up a box of Riley's favorite chocolates that she left in my pantry: dark with lemon creme filling. The remainders rattle inside. "What's the straightforward answer, then?"

"We're only twenty. Maybe she wasn't ready for something serious."

I restrain myself from throwing the chocolates at him. "We were together for two years. Her toothbrush lived in my bathroom for long enough that it had to be replaced a couple times."

"People change. Especially at our age."

My eyes prickle all over again. We might be young in the grand scheme of things, but when I was with her, it didn't feel that way. I felt like a woman in love, ready for commitment, and I never thought of our relationship as temporary and disposable.

But maybe Dean is right, and I'm looking for clues to something simple: she changed, and she just doesn't love me anymore.

I hurl the chocolates into the fire, trying not to think of the time I fed one to Riley on the couch, and she'd sucked on my fingers with that playful look in her eyes. *These taste better when you feed them to me.*

God, I'm going to miss her. I already miss the sweet taste of her lips, the melody of her voice, her ability to make my whole day better with a smile... I'll miss the way she wrapped her strong arms around me and made me feel safe. Not to mention how she made me feel *desired*—waking me up by sliding her hand between my legs, pinning my wrists above my head when she climbed on top of me...

I shake away the memories and pull out the last item from the box—the thing I've been avoiding.

"I think you should keep that one," Dean says softly.

I snort. "Why?"

"Because one day you'll want to remember the good parts, even if it hurts now."

I scowl at him. Is he right? Should I hold onto some proof that what we had mattered, even if it ended in a way that makes me want to throw the whole planet into this fire?

"Maybe," I say, my voice hollow.

I stare down at it—the leather-bound journal of handwritten poems that Riley gave me for our one-year anniversary. My traitorous eyes sting.

All these poems she poured onto the pages for me, and one short text message ended it all: *I can't be with you anymore. I'm sorry.* No explanation. No conversation. She blocked me and everything.

I clutch the book tighter, as if hoping I can squeeze it to dust in my fists. How can someone who meant so much to me, who changed my entire world, disappear so quickly? She came into my life when I needed love the most, swooping in to fill the hole my parents left behind. She made me feel like there was nothing wrong with me and made this empty house less lonely.

The crumbling logs blur as the unwanted memory crashes over me: the night she went from best friend to girlfriend. It will live forever in my brain, a memory no bonfire can reduce to ash. The air shifted as we looked into each other's eyes on my couch, both of us knowing what we wanted but afraid to say it. Next thing I knew, her athletic legs were straddling my lap, and her warm hands were pushing me back on the cushions. The cool air raised goosebumps on my freckled, sun-kissed skin as she untied my bikini top. She paused, gave me a chance to change my mind. But I was ready. I remember her breasts as she peeled off her shirt, the dips in her waist under my hands, and my heart pounding as, tentatively, I leaned forward to lick a trail along her throat.

Then she shimmied down, and suddenly her lips and tongue were between my legs, licking and sucking and making the most tantalizing sounds. In that moment, all our flirty, casual hangouts became something more. I gripped the couch with white knuckles, reduced to a barely coherent string of "oh my God" as her tongue drew circles and her hands pushed my thighs apart. She'd moaned loudly. Told me I tasted good. Said dirty things I'd never heard before except in movies.

Gazing into the fire, I can almost feel her tongue again, and her lips moving hungrily against me. Heat pools in my belly, and I hate that my body still responds to memories of her.

But nothing in my life had ever felt so amazing. From that day on, every moment we spent together was a dream.

Until...

Until she stopped smiling at me the same way two weeks ago. Until she began scowling every time she thought I wasn't looking, flexing her fingers and clenching her fists like she was antsy, flinching when I touched her.

Until she stopped coming over and became someone I didn't recognize, who abruptly ended years of love with a text.

I shake my head and open the journal, flipping through pages covered in Riley's handwriting. Over the last year, she added a new poem every few weeks, with the most recent one being a month ago.

The inside cover always baffled me—some verse written in another language, maybe Latin, and not even in her handwriting.

Hic anima tenetur vincta
Donec victima libens
Se tradat toto corde
Vinculo quod infernum facit
Sic somnus frangetur.

The love poems overshadowed it, so I never asked what it meant. Probably meaningless decorative text, and anyway, it doesn't matter anymore.

I fold my arms across the book, holding it to my chest. "I should get to bed. I'm exhausted."

Dean nods. "Call me if you can't sleep. We can watch a slasher movie or whatever you want."

"Thanks."

He strides over and wraps me in a hug, and I stiffen, not ready for the contact.

When he pulls back, he has that worried expression I've been seeing a lot lately. "You sure you're okay? I can stay."

"I'm fine. Just tired."

He hesitates, then nods again.

I should be grateful he came over to support me through a breakup, but I just want to be alone. Opening my heart to other people never seems to end well, and I'm not particularly interested in doing it again, even for my best friend.

The moment he leaves through the side gate, a tear slides down my cheek like it's been waiting there all evening. I wipe it away angrily.

I have to stop getting abandoned. If I keep letting people matter this much, if I keep giving them the power to destroy me, eventually there won't be anything left of me. I should've learned this lesson two years ago when my parents chose traveling over their daughter, but here we are.

Never again. Nobody is allowed to make me feel this weak and vulnerable anymore.

I hold the journal out over the flames—these poems that meant the world to me. *"Promise me you'll always keep this close, no matter what,"* Riley had said. *"Even if we fight. Even if you're mad at me. I know it's just poems, but...they're* our *poems."*

Fuck that. Maybe Dean is right that this book could mean something again one day, but right now, all it represents is an emotional tie I don't need. Once I get rid of it, I'll be free from her. I can move on and become a new person, and I'm never going to make the same mistake again.

Drop it. Just do it.

Every memory of her has to go. Every picture, every video, the smell of her clothes, the taste of her chocolates, the inner workings of her brain that she poured onto these pages.

"Good riddance," I mutter, as if the words are an incantation that will sever whatever still connects us.

My hands shake as I hold the journal over the flames. The leather is warm from the fire's heat, just like Riley's body used to be when she'd curl against me.

"I love you so much it scares me," she said one night that wasn't so long ago. *"I didn't know I could feel like this."*

A sob bursts from my throat before I can stop it, raw and ugly in the quiet night.

I suck it back, holding my breath like I'm about to jump off a cliff...and drop my last and most meaningful piece of Riley into the fire.

It lands on a crumbling log with a *crack*. The noise echoes, filling the sky. Through a haze of ash and flames, I swear I see dark wisps of smoke curl around it like ghostly fingers rising from the earth.

And the fact that I'm now hallucinating is definitely my cue that it's time to pack it in.

I rub my tired eyes and toss the empty box after it, waiting for the relief and freedom to hit me.

The sun has set, dusk turning everything gray, and my breath mists. The Walshes' lights are on next door, their TV flickering through drawn curtains. The faint sound of their baby crying carries through the closed windows. The reminder of familiar people nearby should be comforting, but it only makes me lonelier.

As the journal disintegrates into dying embers, I grab the broom I used as a poker and turn away, ready to get inside and warm up by the old wood-burning fireplace that's been by my side since I was born. At least my house can't abandon me, even if everyone in it has.

I take one step when the flame flares in my periphery. A blast of heat washes over me.

My breath catches, and I spin back to the bonfire.

It's roared back to life, bright and blazing hot. It hisses and crackles, drowning out the distant cawing of crows.

My heart jumps, and I step back. Did I accidentally toss in something dangerous? Should I get the fire extinguisher?

With another whoosh of light, the flames turn green. The air shimmers around them, forming a haze between me and the treeline.

I cover my mouth and scramble backward. Shit, is the fire reacting to something toxic? Maybe it's the ink in the poetry book or... Could there be traces of gasoline at the bottom of the cardboard box?

The flames reach higher, casting a green glow across the yard. The haze spreads, and a thick, earthy smell meets my nose. Strands of my hair lift in a gust of wind.

Oh God. Something tells me no household extinguisher or garden hose is going to smother this thing. I have to call the fire department.

But before I can race to the house to get my phone, the fire goes out like someone flipped a switch.

I freeze, holding the broom out as if it can protect me.

Smoke billows.

Silence engulfs me, so absolute that my ears ring.

Then, a rumble. It grows louder, sending a shiver up my spine.

The ground trembles. It spreads outward, rattling the chain link fence and making dead leaves dance across the grass.

A crack appears in the earth beneath the firepit, widening into a jagged line that splits the yard from the fire to the back fence. Smoke pours into the sky, the smell drying my throat and making me cough.

Run. Run. Run.

But my feet won't move. My chest is tight, my breaths coming fast.

Forget the fire department. Something weird is going on, and this isn't an ordinary toxic flame.

The smoke thickens, swirling upward in a column that gradually takes shape. It's the outline of a woman.

In my next panicked breath, she solidifies, stepping out of the firepit. Her presence seems to fill the entire world. She must be about forty, with light skin and wavy brunette hair that catches the moonlight as it falls past her breasts. She's wearing a long coat that billows open, its dark fabric like a black hole in the twilight.

When she opens her eyes, they're full of an intensity that makes my pulse quicken. I feel stripped bare, standing alone on the lawn with nothing but a broom. I can't move. I can't even tear my eyes away from her. I'm trapped in a nightmare, my legs shaking so hard I'm afraid they'll give out.

Of all the confusion rocketing around in my brain and all the frantic questions I have, two facts are clear:

First, that thing I burned was not an ordinary journal.

Second...I've just unleashed something supernatural in my backyard.

2

JULIA

M Y MAGIC IS A rabid animal inside my chest, clawing and desperate to feed. The hunger is all-consuming, a pain worse than anything I have known.

I gasp, drawing in air that's all wrong—thick, heavy, and bitter. My vision swims as I try to focus on my surroundings. Like waking from a deep sleep, everything eludes me. What day is it? Where am I? *Who am I?*

I take two unsteady steps before I have to stop and catch my balance.

Beneath the haze and swirling ash, my body tingles. I rake my fingers through my hair, which is unusually tangled, then down my throat, where my pulse beats rapidly. I continue downward, running my palms over my white blouse, feeling my chest rise and fall, then down over my bodice and hips.

I'm all here.

A wintry wind makes my cloak flap against my calves and my hair whip around my face. I curl my toes. Beneath the hem of my brown trousers, my bare feet are on hot, dry ash, looking pale in the gathering darkness. Wet grass surrounds the ash.

Did...did someone attempt to burn me at the stake?

My hands fly back to my waist, checking for burns, for rope marks, for any evidence of what was done to me.

But no. There's no stake. Just me standing in crumbling debris.

Indignation tightens my chest. *Where* are my boots? And *why* is my hair in this untamed state instead of its usual chignon? As a cold breeze sweeps over me, I tug my cloak shut and fasten the button to reclaim some control.

Heavy breathing comes to my attention, and it's not my own.

The back of my neck prickles.

I snap my gaze to the source and raise my hands, ready to defend myself.

A young woman stands strides away on the grass—and if I thought I was dressed improperly, she puts me to shame. Her hair, the warm-gold color of autumn leaves, is so disheveled that I'm surprised birds have not taken up residence in it. And her garments! The fabric is like nothing I have seen, the material clinging to her legs as tightly as a second skin. She's pretty in a delicate, breakable way, with soft features and a pale, freckled complexion. Her pink lips are open as she stares at me, her blue eyes wide with terror.

I curl my fingers, ready to feed. But my magic can wait a moment. Getting answers is more important.

"Who are you?" I demand, my voice surprisingly strong.

"I—I was going to ask the same!" Her words come out high-pitched and tremulous. She huffs and clenches her fists. "What are you doing in my yard?"

She's inching backward as if she thinks she can sneak away.

I raise my hand, summoning my magic so I can stop her and force her to talk. "Leaving already?"

I ask the ground behind her to rise and bring her closer, but my power is sluggish, the effort of moving even a bit of dirt sending black spots across my vision. I create no more than a bump in the grass, which she trips over.

She catches her balance and looks down. "What the fuck was that?"

Hot frustration wells inside me, and I ball my fists, snarling. "What spell have you cast upon me?"

Her face is pale with fear, and she continues backing toward the house. "Nothing! I was just burning some stuff, and..."

I pause, searching her face. The tremor in her voice and her genuine confusion tell me she's being truthful. She's certainly no witch, and she's fragile even for an ordinary human. I could snap her like a twig.

But my power is so weak I can barely feel it. It's like my veins are filled with broken glass, each heartbeat sending shards through my body. My entrails have been replaced with a hollow ache as my essence cries out for sustenance. Every breath feels thin, like drowning in air.

I need a life force to feed on, and soon.

"This is not the Fort." I take in the plain, gray houses all lined up. They're strangely uniform, with excessively bright lights that sting the eyes.

Where is the riverbank? The wall?

A distant hum I cannot place nags at my ears, like harsh wind or a roaring sea. Even the air is unfamiliar, foul-smelling and sour. It burns my throat and makes my stomach queasy.

I gesture at everything and nothing. "Where am I?"

"My house?" the girl says uncertainly.

"Yes, but where?" I bark, the hunger making me snappy.

"Um, 3866 Belvedere Court." She shifts, as if she's unsure if this is the answer I'm looking for. When I continue to stare, she adds, "In Burnaby, BC, Canada. Why?"

My heart beats faster. How did I get so far from Fort Langley, and why don't I recall how I came to be here? "And your name?"

"Hannah Schmidt. Will you tell me what's going on?"

Schmidt. Germanic. No one I know by that surname. No relation to my coven.

Another question rises to my lips, one I'm afraid to ask. "And…what is the date?"

Hannah hesitates, looking at me warily. "It's October 28, 2009."

The earth seems to jolt beneath my feet. I sway, dizzy with the impossibility of her words. The year begins with a *two*?

I press a hand to my throat, where my pulse ticks rapidly.

"That's…no." I try to calculate how long it's been, but my brain will not cooperate. "It's… 1891 was…"

"1891?" Hannah repeats, as if she's never heard of such a number.

"Yes," I snap, growing impatient. "How many years ago was that?"

She pulls something rectangular out of her pocket and taps it with her thumbs. "Hundred eighteen."

"I've been gone for *118 years*?" I roar.

"Okay, um—a little quieter, please." Hannah puts her hands out. "My neighbors are probably putting their baby to bed, and… Look, I'm going to get someone to come pick you up and bring you back to your caretaker, okay?"

My heart slams against my ribs. *Over a century.* God, this cannot be! The number feels impossible, yet the strange world around me confirms it. Do any of my coven sisters remain, or has everyone I knew turned to bones? Did anyone mourn me when I vanished? Did they wonder about my fate or cast a tracking spell to find me? Or did they move on and assume I chose to disappear?

My chest tightens unbearably with a loneliness I have not felt since my mother passed. The utter terror of having no one who cares where I am or what happens to me. Of having no one who knows my face, my name, my soul.

My breaths come quick and tremulous, and I clamp my jaw shut before the girl notices. I am Julia Moreau, and I do not break.

Instinctively, I lift my hands to cast a kinship spell. I must know if anybody I can trust is near.

"*Sorores, voces vestras nunc exquiro...*" I murmur, but it's clear from the first word that it's no use. Dark wisps of magic sprout feebly between my fingers, too weak for a complex spell. My hands tremble, and I curl them into fists. The void inside me pulsates, my power desperate to be replenished.

"Is there a phone number I can call?" Hannah asks. "Your family or caretaker?"

Drawing deep breaths, I take in the houses with the colored lights flashing in the windows, the putrid air, the uniform grass under my bare feet... No wonder everything looks foreign. The world has undergone generations of change since...

A shiver rolls through me. Since *what*? What happened to me?

My memories are hazy, like trying to see through fog. What is the last thing I remember?

Warmth. The scent of sage and jasmine and sweat. Rebecca's lips grazing my throat as her blonde hair spilled through my fingers.

We were on the floor of her sanctum, the pentagram beneath us, candles casting moving shadows on the stone walls. I'd gone there to help her with a spell, but we never finished the chant. As we knelt and joined hands, sharing our breath to strengthen the enchantment...she leaned in.

In the next beat of my heart, we were kissing hard, both of us finally giving in after weeks of wanting. I pushed her onto her back, scattering our carefully placed herbs. The candles snuffed out, leaving us in darkness while the wind howled outside.

"I want to feel your power, Julia," she'd whispered.

The words sparked a fire in me. Of course that's what this was about: her desire to feel what it was like to be fed on by a sanguine witch.

So I'd pressed my body against hers, and she moaned under me, parting her legs. I teased her lips with mine and plunged my tongue into her mouth. Lifted her skirts. Slid my fingers between her thighs. Her teeth stung my bottom lip. My hair came undone beneath her frantic fingers, cascading down and caressing her face. She came apart at my touch, arching her back beneath me.

I'd just begun to recite the feeding incantation when...

Darkness. Sleep. Nothing.

I place a hand over my frantic heart, the truth crashing over me.

Rebecca did this to me.

The pentagram, the spell... It was a setup. She lured me there so she could curse me to an enchanted sleep. I should have known when she seemed nervous and wouldn't meet my eyes.

I cannot believe I trusted her. I let myself kiss her, lick her, thrust my fingers inside her. And she used my desire against me. Turned my moment of weakness into a trap.

Molten anger bubbles up within me, making me tremble, before Hannah's uncertain voice yanks me out of the memory. "Excuse me? Can you hear me?"

I snap my gaze to her, fury pulsing so hot my vision blurs. "Where are my coven sisters? Are they still alive?"

"I don't know any...covens...but if you tell me your name and where you came from, I—"

I stalk closer, pointing at her with my fingers curled into claws. "Then how did you wake me?"

"It was..." She glances at the ash under my feet, her eyes widening.

There, among the charred wood and fabric, is a lump of something that might have been a book.

"Were you...*in* the journal?" she asks, then makes a face, as if she's confused by her own words.

I pick it up, and it crumbles further between my fingers.

A *book*? My prison was a *book*? The indignity boils my blood. To be trapped in something so mundane and so easily destroyed is the sort of cruel irony Rebecca would find amusing.

If that bitch is still alive—and it's possible, as I have known witches to live past two hundred—she's going to regret this. She cursed me for 118 damned years, and I'm going to make her repent for every single day I lost.

Hannah wraps her arms around herself, shivering as she backs toward the house. "Well, if there's no one I can call, do you mind letting yourself out the side gate?"

I narrow my eyes and raise both hands. "Not until I'm done with you."

If she can't give me answers, she can at least give me what I crave. My magic is weakening with each second I stand here, and this young woman's life force is strong, beckoning me like a honey-sweet aura. Draining her should buy me enough time to find Rebecca.

At my command, ash and debris from the fire lift and swirl around her, pushing her closer.

"Wait—what's happening?" she cries, ducking.

Panic I've heard a thousand times. It's never stopped me.

Manipulating the elements is the simplest form of magic, and yet, sweat beads at my hairline as I summon the last drops of power left inside me.

The air crackles, charged with energy that makes my hair stand on end. As the debris pushes her forward, I step in to meet her, my pulse racing in anticipation.

My lips part. My chest heaves. My mind might not have perceived the lost time, but my body has, and my magic is *starving*.

When the girl is right in front of me, I reach for her, tangling my fingers in her hair.

"Let go!" she cries, struggling. But the moment I make contact with her scalp, she stops, gasping like a drowning swimmer breaking the surface.

I recite the incantation.

"*Tua essentia mea fit*

Per contactum animam bibo

Quod tuum est, meum erit

Usque ad finem huius ritus."

Her life force begins to flow into me, thick, warm, and sweet.

She lets out a soft, "*Oh,*" and shivers, the fight leaving her.

I can taste her energy, feel it flowing into my core. It fills my senses, my soul, every hollow space that a century of dormancy has carved out.

A moan tears from my throat. *God,* she tastes good. Has feeding always been this good, or is my hunger making her extra sweet?

I keep murmuring the incantation, drinking in her essence, intent on consuming everything she has until my power is full and satisfied.

And then...

Something shifts.

Before I can drain her, a resistance hits me, like pulling against a tether. A sharp pain shoots through my chest, and I gasp, clutching my ribs.

I stand frozen, hands pressed to my sides. Feeding is supposed to strengthen me. It always has. But pain throbs with each heartbeat, foreign and impossible, and for the first time in my life, my body—my *magic*—betrays me.

Hannah coughs and sinks to her knees on the grass. "What's...happening..."

I turn my hands over. My fingers have blackened from the feeding, which is normal... So what was that about?

Perhaps my body is ill adjusted after a century of sleep.

I shake out my arms and place a hand on either side of her head to keep draining her.

"Get—off—" she says between gasps, trying to push me away.

The pain surges back harder, making me gasp and stumble back.

The connection between us dies, leaving me gulping down air. The interruption leaves me aching and unsatisfied. The deep well inside me is still dry, holding barely enough magic for a couple of spells.

I turn my back to her and ball my hands into fists, leaving her on her knees.

This isn't right. Feeding has never hurt me. I have drained people to fill my power every lunar cycle since I was thirteen. What differs this time?

A chill ripples through me. Is this Rebecca's doing? Either I can't drink my fill of magic anymore, or I can't drink my fill from this girl who broke the spell.

Which is it? And *why*?

The idea of being doomed to live the rest of my life hungry, never being able to feed to satisfaction, sends an icy feeling through me. I've never been so vulnerable.

I square my shoulders. I have to find my coven. I need answers—and I need to make Rebecca pay.

I stride away from Hannah and the firepit, looking for this supposed gate that will let me out of here. *How* I will find my coven in this unfamiliar world is a mystery, but maybe with luck, Fort Langley will still exist. I can start there.

As my numb feet squelch over the grass, I wrinkle my nose. Maybe I can also find shoes along the way.

But as I push through the gate and leave Hannah behind, a strange sensation washes over me, like a tightening in my chest and an unbearable weight crushing me. My thighs quake as I fight to stay standing.

I force one foot in front of the other, my cloak catching the wind as I fight this invisible barrier. Each step feels like walking through thick mud, my muscles screaming in protest.

I reach the front of the house and march down the road, pain stabbing my chest more insistently. I clutch it, gasping for breath.

My knees buckle. I cry out as I hit the ground, my kneecaps cracking against the road that's as hard as stone.

Something must be holding me here, tethering me to the yard, or the book, or...

My jaw tightens.

To *her*.

I summon every drop of strength and limp back toward the house. The weight lifts, and by the time I storm through the gate, the tightness in my chest eases. "What have you done to me?" I snarl.

"*Me*? You just attacked me!" Hannah, too, sounds out of breath. She waves her arms, looking as pale and exhausted as one would expect of someone who nearly had her life force drained.

I hum. No, of course this isn't her doing. She is too weak and powerless to be doing dark magic.

Which means...

Hannah sways on her feet, her teeth gritted. "Look, I don't know what the hell you just did, but—"

I throw my hand out toward her. "Silence! I need to think."

I step closer, and the pulling sensation eases, my strength returning like water rushing back through a drought-stricken riverbed.

"Don't tell me..."

I back away. A threatening pang returns to my chest.

No. Rebecca wouldn't... She couldn't have.

To be certain, I take two more steps back. The pain tightens like a noose.

The truth crashes over me in a cold wave.

Damn you, Rebecca.

Fists clenched, I stalk forward again, circling Hannah. The pain ebbs at once. I breathe more easily. And as my pulse steadies in her proximity, her breath hitches. She feels this invisible tether too, and she's afraid to say it.

I clench my teeth so hard that my temples throb. Rebecca, that bitch, put a binding spell on me. Not only am I forced to stay close to a fragile, unremarkable human, but I must also keep her alive—because if she dies, so do I.

I cannot drain her to fill my magic, but I cannot leave her either. I'm stuck with her.

I can almost hear Rebecca taunting me. *The most powerful witch in the region, perpetually dependent on an ordinary human...*

But that hag made a crucial mistake: she left me alive. And if she's still alive too, then I have until I find her to plan my revenge.

Hannah's lips part as she catches her breath. She's not running, just glaring at me with fire in her eyes.

"It appears," I say, my voice dripping with disdain, "that when you broke the curse that kept me asleep, you unwittingly bound yourself to me."

3

HANNAH

S o I burned Riley's poetry book to cut emotional ties forever, but apparently, 'forever' lasted about thirty seconds before I bound myself to someone infinitely more dangerous than my ex-girlfriend.

Bound. The word settles like a block of ice in my gut.

That *can't* be true.

I turn and sprint away from this terrifying woman, and this time, she lets me go. I burst into the warmth of my home and slam the back door, my hands shaking as I fumble to lock it. As if running from someone who levitated bits of earth with a fucking hand gesture will make a difference.

"Wake up... This has to be a nightmare," I murmur.

My brain scrambles for rational explanations. Gas leak. Hallucination. Some kind of elaborate prank my coworkers set up, though they'd never go this far. A stroke? Is this what a stroke feels like? Maybe I'm having a breakdown. God knows I'm due for one.

But she's so real and solid, and when she touched me...

I run my fingers through my hair, still feeling the phantom sensation of her hands on me.

The adjoining living room and kitchen are behind me, lit by soft lamp-light and the wood-burning fireplace. It's all too bright, like spotlights that will let this woman watch me through the large windows.

Breathing fast, I kick off my shoes and peel off my wet socks. The invisible rope around my ribs tightens with every step away from the woman. I shudder like a dog shaking off water, trying to force the sensation away.

My cold, damp feet stick to the hardwood as I race to shut all the blinds. I can see her standing by the back door, arms crossed, fingers tapping her biceps as she stares out into the darkness. Waiting? Plotting?

The heat from the fireplace tingles through me, fighting off the bone-deep chill. My head is throbbing and my vision is wonky, like a migraine is threatening to come on.

I grab my phone off the coffee table, chewing my lip. I should call the police and tell them there's an unhinged woman trespassing, and she tried to kill me.

Except...

"Dammit," I whisper, rubbing my chest.

As much as I want to make her leave, I can't deny the painful tightening in my core when we're apart and the easing when we're close. When she grabbed me, it was...not exactly a bad feeling.

Okay, fine, it felt *good*, and that's what's scary. The sensation was over fast, bookended by terror as I caught the dangerous flash in her eyes. But in the middle...

God, those few seconds in the middle felt incredible.

My face burns. I shouldn't be dwelling on this. But when her fingers tangled in my hair and brushed my scalp, it was like a gulp of wine easing down my throat and hitting my bloodstream, making my brain fuzzy and my whole body relaxed. It was intimate in a way I'd never experienced, like the raw connection at the moment of climax. Like she was touching my soul. Stroking it. And when the connection broke, a hollowness filled me, leaving me so empty that it was like part of me had been ripped away. I almost asked her to keep doing whatever she was doing.

Heat stirs in my belly, and my face burns hotter. I hate that my body is responding this way to something that clearly just about killed me.

A power I don't understand is at play, and I think she's telling the truth when she says a supernatural force is binding us together.

What was it she said? Her *coven*?

My heartbeat quickens as the pieces slide into place. The Latin verse. The way she levitated the ash. The intoxicating sensations that flowed through my body.

A word surges into my mind, which I can't argue: *witch*.

My knees weaken. I sway, grabbing the couch for support.

No way. Witches—are not—real. This must be a hallucination from inhaling toxic smoke. Or a nightmare.

Yes, a nightmare. I squeeze my eyes shut. Any second, I'm going to wake up in the back room of Book Nook with our latest shipment scattered around me.

But the fire keeps crackling, and my feet stay on the floor of my living room, and I don't wake up.

My phone buzzes in my hand, and I jump, snapping my eyes open.

It's a text from Dean: *How are you holding up? Want me to come back over?*

I stare at the message, the words taking a moment to absorb. How do I explain that I accidentally freed a witch from an enchanted book and now we're supernaturally bound? That she tried to kill me but couldn't? That part of me *enjoyed* the feel of her fingers drawing the life out of me, or whatever the hell that was?

I can't. So I type back: *I'm fine. Thanks boo.*

Another lie to add to the collection I've been building for years. I was fine when my parents abandoned me the day I turned eighteen. I was fine when Riley disappeared without explanation.

The lock clicks, and the back door swings open. The woman steps inside with the confidence of someone who's been, you know, *invited* in. She sweeps her hand to shut the door behind her without touching it.

Fuck, I guess locks mean nothing to a woman who can control anything with telekinesis.

As I back away, she unbuttons her cloak, revealing a white blouse and bodice that hugs her curves. Her thick brown hair falls past her breasts, and she tosses it back over her shoulders. Her nostrils flare as she rakes her gaze over every corner of the house—TV, microwave, laptop, vinyl kitchen floor.

"I never introduced myself." She turns her winter-blue eyes onto me. Her voice is silky, not at all as sharp as a moment ago. "I'm Julia Moreau, Sanguine Witch."

I grab the fireplace poker and point it at her. "I kinda figured you were a witch when you tried to kill me with magic."

The words *witch* and *magic* sound strange coming from my lips. This can't be happening.

"*Tried*," she says, as if that makes it fine. "I stopped, didn't I? A little forgiveness would go a long way, love."

"I don't think I'm ready for that," I step forward, keeping the point level with her chest. "New rule. You don't use magic on me or my property. I may be stuck with you, but I'm not your puppet."

Julia raises an eyebrow, amused. "And what will you do with that little stick?"

"Iron," I say, remembering the folklore I read in one of Riley's books. "Want to test if the stories about iron and magic are true?"

There's a flicker of surprise in her eyes. Then her lip curls, and she steps forward until her bodice is pressed against the tip of the iron. "Go ahead."

Shit.

She grabs the end of the poker with her bare hand—so much for that theory—and rips it out of my grasp. It hits the couch, then bounces to the floor with a clatter, and I scramble back.

My heart jumps. *Yeah, poke her with a stick, Hannah. Brilliant survival instincts.* Now I've pissed off someone who can kill me with a twitch of her fingers.

I step behind the round kitchen table, keeping it between us, and curl my fingers over the back of a wooden chair. I need to figure out how to reverse whatever this is, and fast. "How do we unbind?"

"Not by brandishing sharp implements at one another, I assure you."

She stalks around the table toward me. I step sideways to keep it between us. Though she's only a few inches taller than me, it feels like she's taking up all the space in the kitchen.

"But it *can* be fixed?" I ask. "I'm not stuck with you forever?"

"Every lock has a key. We just need to find the witch who cast the spell."

I freeze, bile rising in my throat.

Here's the question: what in the living hell was Riley doing with a journal that held an ancient witch trapped inside? And why did she give it to me under the guise of being a book of love poems?

"Promise me you'll always keep this close, no matter what..."

Ice shoots through my veins. Holy fuck, did Riley get involved in something darker than I realized? The mysterious books, the scars, the way she'd been acting...

Is she a witch?

I've only known her for a couple of years. Maybe she dumped me before I realized she's secretly five hundred years old and...

No. This doesn't fit with the Riley I know. She isn't evil or dangerous. Besides, her strange behavior only started happening in the last two weeks. Wouldn't she have known this about herself long ago?

"Do you know who cast it?" I ask, my mouth dry.

"I do," Julia says, "and we'd best find her quickly."

The hardwood creaks under our feet as we move in this dance around the table, predator stalking prey. The house feels too small, the air too thick.

I'm hyperaware of her movements, the way her hips sway as she stalks me, the grace in her steps. My skin prickles like I'm being hunted, and the worst part is that each time her steps bring her closer, the ache in my temples eases and I breathe a little easier. There's a pull low inside me, like my body wants to stop fleeing and move closer despite my terror.

I ignore what my body wants, stepping sideways to keep her opposite to me.

"What's her name?" I ask, trying not to sound terrified of the answer.

"Rebecca, and she's a formidable celestial witch, which means the spell will become permanent when the moon sets." Julia looks out the window, her nostrils flaring. "What phase is the moon tonight?"

My relief that she didn't say "Riley" is immediately smothered by a flood of dread. My stomach plummets through the floor. *Permanent?*

"It—it's full," I say, my voice coming out squeaky.

"So we have until sunrise, more or less," Julia says tightly.

Sunrise. That's it. Then we're bound forever.

God, I'm supposed to start university next year! Faculty of Arts. My acceptance letter is on the fridge. I've been working my ass off, saving every dollar, so I can get a real degree and a real career that will pay the very real bills Mom and Dad left me with.

I picture myself trying to go to class, make friends, and live a normal life while tethered to this witch. Always weak and helpless, trailing behind her like her obedient familiar.

Nope. Not an option.

"Let's go, then," I say through my teeth, checking the time on the stove. 6:33 p.m. If I have any fucking say in this matter, we're going to break this spell before bedtime.

"First thing's first." Julia strokes the air with her fingers as if to beckon some invisible force toward her. "I require power. I'm depleted."

"Fine. How do you get more power?"

"A sanguine witch must feed." She tilts her head. Her gaze lingers on my throat before moving down the rest of my body.

A tremor ripples through me. "What do you mean, *feed*?"

She sighs, like I'm asking too many questions. "A person's life force typically sustains me for a lunar cycle."

My blood runs cold. Is that what she tried to do to me outside? Feed on my life force to replenish her magic?

I grip the chair in front of me, trying not to let my hands shake.

"Oh, stop acting like a scared little bunny," she coos. "The binding spell protects you. I can't drain you without sacrificing my own life too, and I'm not in the mood to die."

"How comforting," I say dryly.

"It should be. I need you alive, which makes you the safest person in the world when you're with me."

I scoff. Safe? I've never felt more in danger than I do right now. But I refuse to give her the satisfaction of admitting that. She's probably the type of sicko who gets an inflated ego over being feared.

She hums, squinting past me out the window over the kitchen sink. "If I can't feed on *you*, then I'll need another source."

I follow her gaze, my skin prickling. The Walshes' TV is still flickering through their drawn curtains. "What happens to a person you feed on?"

Julia walks toward the back door, looking over her shoulder at me with a raised eyebrow. "It's tidier if I don't leave them alive to ask questions and send the pitchforks after me."

Jesus Christ. I've bound myself to a serial killer.

My heart thuds against my ribs in time with her steps as she approaches the door. *Thump. Thump.*

I can't let this happen. As scared as I am, and though I know nothing about magic, one thing is certain: I would rather die than let her murder innocent people. I'm the one who unleashed a monster, and she's my responsibility now.

4

HANNAH

Summoning every drop of bravery I have, I run past Julia and launch myself between her and the door, blocking her with my arms crossed. "You are *not* going to murder anyone tonight."

A flash of surprise crosses her face, but she regains her composure quickly and opens her arms. "Then by what means do you propose I restore my magic?"

"You don't. As long as we're *bound* or whatever, I'm not letting you kill anyone. You can find some other way to refill your magic—or lose your power. I don't care."

She laughs, loud and unrestrained, tipping her head back to expose her elegant jawline and throat. The sound ripples up my spine. "Never mind the fact that we'll *need* magic in order to locate my coven and break the binding spell... Magic will keep us both alive. Don't you feel it? This weakening energy?"

I furrow my brow. When I focus on something other than trying to put distance between us, there it is: the ache in my temple and a swelling pain behind my ribs. Each pump of my heart sends a jolt down my left arm, like it's struggling to keep beating.

My breath catches. This spell really is going to take me down with her.

Julia looks even worse than I feel. There's a sheen of sweat on her forehead and chest. Her skin is paler than before, and her breathing is labored. Her hands have a subtle tremor, and she keeps clenching and unclenching her fists like she's fighting off pain. She reminds me of someone in the grip of a fever—or withdrawal. And between the desperation in her eyes and her wild hair spilling over her shoulders, she looks borderline rabid.

Still. This witch will *not* be murdering anyone on my watch.

"Every month? And you don't feel guilty?" I snap.

"Lions don't feel guilty about gazelles."

"People aren't gazelles!"

She raises an eyebrow. "Shall we discuss the value of life while we both waste away?"

I roll my eyes. "You're doing a great job of getting me to like you."

The way she smiles, with that curve in her lips and the gleam in her eyes, makes my stomach flip.

Yeah, fine, she's attractive. Whatever. That doesn't mean I like her.

"You're too innocent to understand that power requires sacrifice," Julia says.

"And you're too out-of-touch to understand how wrong you are."

She scoffs. "In my day, young women showed proper respect to their elders."

"In my day, we don't let murderers lecture us about manners."

She rubs her forehead as if this conversation is becoming exhausting.

Finally, she drops her hand. "Miss Schmidt," she says slowly, like she's tasting my name. "If you won't let me feed, we're going to be bound forever."

Both options are terrible, but I stay put.

She waves her hand, and a cold draft hits my back as the door flies open.

I close my fingers over her wrist to stop her from passing. "Julia, don't."

A pleasant sensation rushes up my arm when I touch her, so intense that my breath hitches. It's a shadow of whatever happened when her fingers were on my scalp, but it's enough to make heat stir in my belly. For a moment, I forget why I'm trying to stop her. I just let this feeling trickle into every gap in my soul.

Her nostrils flare as she glares down at me. She's so close that I catch her scent—something warm and intoxicating, like woodsmoke and apple cinnamon tea.

I release her, ignoring the tingling in my hand.

She inclines her head, peering down at my face like she's searching for something.

"If you're done being noble," she says at last, "let's stop wasting time."

She shoves me aside hard.

I stumble and hit the wall, pain erupting in my shoulder. "Ow! Hey! Julia, wait!"

She strides into the darkness as if she didn't hear me. I sprint after her in my bare feet, the cold slamming into me.

She stalks around the side of the house, and as we reach the front yard, I cut over to block her from going to the Walshes' house—but her attention is elsewhere. Headlights illuminate the street as a car approaches.

Julia jerks back, shielding her eyes from the lights. "What manner of beast..."

"It's a car!" I cry. "Like—a horseless carriage? Now would you please come back inside and—"

"Just what I need." She raises both hands, and the sedan screeches to a halt as if hitting an invisible wall, its tires smoking against the asphalt. The engine roars in protest.

"No!" I change course back to her, slipping on the wet grass.

Dammit, why didn't I tell her the car was a flaming hellhound that would kill us unless we turned around and went back inside?

Julia is panting, her breaths rasping as she forces the car to stay still. She takes labored steps closer, as if using magic is draining the life out of her.

With another sweep of her arm, the driver's side window explodes in a shower of glass. The man inside cries out in fear.

No, no, no...

Julia reaches through the shattered window and hauls him out with a grunt of effort. His body hits the pavement hard.

Oh God, it's Nick from three houses down! He looks younger suddenly, just a twentysomething college graduate who welcomed a daughter into the world last year.

A cold sweat breaks out beneath my hoodie. What have I unleashed?

"What the hell—" Nick's words cut off as Julia's hand closes around his throat.

"Julia, stop!" I slam into her and seize her cloak, afraid to touch her skin in case the contact unleashes whatever effect she seems to have on me.

She keeps squeezing, and before my eyes, her fingers blacken as if consumed by shadows. Her eyes, too, darken at the edges like bruises.

My throat constricts. I gulp down air, dizzy.

Though I pull hard, trying to pry her away, she doesn't move. Nick's eyes bulge and redden, his body convulsing.

Throwing caution aside, I claw at Julia's arm. "Let him go!"

She shoves me back without looking. I stumble off-balance and fall, hitting the asphalt hard. Pain explodes in my hip, and the ground scrapes my palms.

I prop myself up, wheezing, my palms stinging. I can't move, terror locking my muscles. What the hell am I supposed to do?

As she murmurs the incantation and her fingers and eyes darken, an energy I don't understand fills the air. Her hair lifts, and her open cloak billows in the wind. Nick struggles, but she holds him easily by the throat.

A sick fascination freezes me in place. The way she stopped a car, shattered the glass, and pulled a grown man through the window... The sight of her standing before me with power radiating from her whole body... She's as magnificent as she is terrible. How much power does she really have?

Then Nick makes an awful choking sound, jolting me back to reality. His body is going limp, and his eyes are bulging grotesquely.

I have to stop this.

I scramble back to my feet and throw myself at Julia again, grabbing her arm with both hands. "Feed on me instead!"

Julia releases Nick, who drops to the ground with a sickening thud, gasping and coughing.

She spins to face me, and I barely recognize her behind the feral look in her eyes.

My heart jumps as the offer hangs between us. For a moment, I want to take it back. But no. I meant what I said. I have the power to prevent this woman from killing people, and this is how I wield it.

Her brow furrows. "We established I can't do that."

"We established you can't *kill* me. But as long as you don't drain me completely, I can sustain you."

As the implication registers, a cold sensation crashes through me. This is my worst nightmare. As if being bound to a witch wasn't dangerous enough, now I'm offering to let her feed on my essence over and over, making myself so vulnerable that she could kill me if she goes too far.

Julia cocks an eyebrow. "You would let me feed on you to stop me from killing someone else?"

When she puts it like that, the choice is obvious. I won't let others die because I'm too afraid.

I nod firmly.

Her eyes flick down my body, and I clench my fists so she doesn't see my hands shaking.

Nick seizes the chance to heave himself back into his car, wheezing and coughing. Julia sweeps a hand toward him, her fingers moving as if etching symbols in the air. She murmurs words I don't understand.

I open my mouth to tell her to stop whatever she's doing, but she whispers, "Memory charm."

I bite my lip.

Nick's eyes glaze over as he sits in the driver's seat, his expression going blank.

Julia drops her hand, still studying me with her brow pinched. Standing this close to her, I can barely breathe.

Then she grabs me by the wrist with enough force to make me gasp and drags me back toward the house. I follow her on clumsy feet, fear gripping my throat so hard I can't make a sound.

Back inside, it's suffocatingly quiet except for the crackling fireplace. Julia lets go and steps back to study me. The shadows staining her fingers have faded, and her eyes are back to normal, piercing and wintry.

"A partial feeding won't be enough to fill my magic," she says. "I will have to feed on you frequently."

I hesitate. Letting her repeatedly siphon my life force sounds like a slow death. "There's no other option? No spell or meditation or...crystal ritual that you can do?"

Julia's laugh is sharp and cold. "I'm not some amateur practitioner who sells rocks to superstitious commoners, Miss Schmidt."

"Right." I shift, wracking my brain for other possibilities. "And you can't feed on something other than a human? A bug or whatever?"

Her nose wrinkles. "No."

"And we can't, like, go to a blood bank?"

"*Blood*? What do you think I am, a vampire?" she snarls.

I put my hands out to calm her. "Okay, okay. Fine. So the repeated feedings won't kill me?"

"Not in the short term."

Good enough, I guess, if we're going to break this spell by morning.

I nod. "Then do whatever you want to me."

Her gaze sweeps up and down me, and if this were *any* other scenario, I would swear she was checking me out. Which is probably why my body reacts the way it does, a flutter sweeping through me and heat erupting in my face. It's completely at odds with the terror pumping through my veins, making me even more disoriented.

She shifts, and I tense. A tremor runs through me. I can't believe this woman is in my kitchen. Again.

She backs up, holding my gaze with a blazing intensity until she reaches the wood-burning fireplace. There, she sinks to her knees and extends her hands to me, palms up.

"Right now?" My voice comes out as a squeak.

She sighs. "Would you rather have a nap first? Yes, a slow start to finding my coven is a lovely idea. We have all the way until sunrise, after all."

I clench my fists, my heart pounding. Am I ready to do this again?

"Fine. But if I'm going to be your personal battery, it's going to be on my terms. You ask when you want to feed on me. You only take what you need. You stop if I tell you to stop."

A pause.

"Very well," she says.

The knowing look in her eyes makes my cheeks burn. Is she aware of how good it feels to be fed on? Does she sense my shameful fascination with it?

She's sitting elegantly on her knees, her thighs parted. The fire crackles in the silence. Its warm light flickers across her face, illuminating the sweat and ash, casting moving shadows under her eyes.

I break our gaze, unwilling to let her see the conflicting feelings inside me.

Her outstretched hands hover, waiting for me to take them.

I can do this. It's the first step to leaving this mess behind and getting on with my life.

I walk over on unsteady legs.

"Brave girl," she says.

"You're insufferable," I grumble.

"And you're stuck with me, sweetheart."

I kneel in front of her, trying not to think about how I'm offering my life force to a murderous witch.

Time to feed the monster I've unleashed.

5

JULIA

HANNAH SINKS TO HER knees before me, offering her essence despite knowing how easily I could destroy her.

What a strange, reckless girl. In spite of her obvious terror, she doesn't waver. There's steel beneath that soft exterior, unexpected and intriguing. When was the last time someone surprised me?

In all my years of feeding, through hundreds of victims across decades of hunting, they all responded the same way: begging, bargaining, trying to escape. They've offered me money, possessions, livestock, loved ones...anything but themselves.

But Hannah? She chose self-sacrifice to protect strangers.

Not since Charlotte has anyone willingly given themselves to me. But unlike Charlotte, Hannah will have to stay alive. At least until we're unbound.

The memory of Charlotte's last moments tries to surface—her trembling body, the adoration in her eyes, and then that absolute, final stillness—but I shove it down. Now's not the time to think about her.

With our knees almost touching, I shake loose my shoulders, ready to begin.

The crackle of settling logs fills the silence, and the scent of smoke and something sweet hovers between us. The firelight dances over the crease between her eyebrows, the determined set of her jaw, and her narrowed blue eyes.

I can't help it: my lips curl into a satisfied grin.

Oh, Rebecca. You put a binding spell on me to weaken me and force me into dependency, and instead, you've handed me a girl who willingly offers herself to me.

The irony is delicious. I look forward to watching her realize how badly her plan failed. How she gifted me with a source of power that I don't have to hunt for. Granted, I will have to feed on her energy frequently since I cannot fully drain her, but that won't be a problem given that we're bound.

"What do I need to do?" Hannah asks.

I flex my fingers, my gnawing hunger making me desperate to grab her. "Feeding requires physical contact with the victim."

"I understand that much," she says coldly. She smooths her hair, which is undone and tangled from when I knotted my fingers in it.

I wiggle my fingers, still waiting for her to place her hands in mine. "A simple skin-contact ritual will suffice."

The pinch in her brow tells me she's wondering what other kinds of rituals there are. But there's no sense in scaring her off.

Hesitantly, she reaches out and lays her palms over mine. Her essence pulsates eagerly, rich and vibrant. But it's not just her essence flooding my awareness—it's the flutter of her pulse, the coolness of her skin, the little hitch in her breath. Her hands are so delicate that I might shatter her fingers if I squeeze too hard. As her skin warms under my touch, it's like holding onto silk.

Focus. I've fed on hundreds without getting distracted by the mechanics of their bodies.

I close my eyes and begin the incantation, drawing her energy into me like a deep swig of ale.

"Tua essentia mea fit..."

The sensation is immediate and intoxicating, like warm honey flowing through my soul. And oh, the *feel* of her. Unlike a life force stolen from an unwilling victim, hers is offered freely, and it tastes sweeter than anything I've ever experienced. Her flavor, her texture, the way she settles into my bones...

Hannah sucks in a sharp breath, and I open my eyes to find her gaze locked onto me. In the firelight, her eyes are molten. Her cheeks are flushed, her full lips parted. The way she's looking at me makes heat coil deep inside me, pleasure rushing through my core.

As I continue reciting, her breaths become fast and shallow, and her fingers tighten over mine. She's enjoying this, as she should.

But her life force is...resisting. Perhaps she's stronger than I thought.

I push up her sleeves, exposing her wrists and forearms so I can access more of her. When I press my palms to her bare skin, she makes a small sound in the back of her throat, like she's surprised by the sensation.

I recite the incantation again, louder this time.

My fingers darken. Her life force flows into me in waves, each pulse sending an intoxicating rush through me. I tip my head back, my breaths quickening as power fills me.

God, has feeding always been this good? Have I forgotten after spending so many years dormant? Her taste is better than anything I can remember, and the sensation of her in my veins is better than what any mouth or fingers could do to me.

Hannah's hands twitch in my grasp, but she doesn't pull away. If anything, she leans closer.

My magic wants to keep going. It wants me to push her onto her back and pin her hands above her head, to thoroughly drain her, to take every drop of energy she has until...

Her eyelids flutter, and the rosy color in her cheeks drains. She begins to tremble, weakening.

No. If I don't stop, the binding spell will ensure I die right along with her.

Hannah might be mine to feed on, but she's also mine to protect, whether I like it or not.

My hands might as well have turned to stone, given how hard it is to let go of her. But I grit my teeth and force my grip to loosen. As my darkened fingers uncurl from her forearms, the connection snaps, leaving me breathless.

My insides burn, left wanting and unsatisfied. Like drinking a single drop of water after being parched. Or like stopping right at the moment of climax, denying myself the full release. Spikes of pain pulse through my veins, and I have to clench my fists to keep from reaching for her again.

That's enough, I tell myself firmly.

I wipe my arm across my clammy forehead. My magic coils tighter, yearning to take a little more.

So this is where Rebecca gets me: leaving me perpetually unsatisfied and unable to drink my fill.

Hannah pulls her hands in, cradling them against her chest. She blinks and looks around. The color has returned to her face, which is reddening as a flush creeps up her neck. Her fingers tremble as she touches her forearms, tracing the path my hands took as if trying to understand what happened to her. She looks thoroughly ravaged—lips parted, pupils dilated, sweat glistening at the base of her throat. When her gaze darts to mine, quick and uncertain, the look in her eyes is not fear or disgust, but something like curiosity about a feeling she doesn't know what to do with.

Interesting.

She has no idea what she's invited into her life.

I tear my gaze away and flex my fingers, my restored power tingling beneath my skin.

At my gesture, the kettle rumbles, and steam billows from the spout. I guide it to the coffee table and pour boiling water into Hannah's mug.

"Much better." I set the kettle back onto the stove, sighing with the satisfaction of having my magic respond properly. At least it's enough to sustain me for now. I'll be able to perform basic magic and maybe a complex spell or two before I need to feed again.

"Now we can find the witch who cursed us?" Hannah says, her voice hoarse.

I stand and dust off my sleeves, pleased with how steady I feel despite the incomplete feeding. "Yes. We will start by finding what's left of my coven."

"And...where are they?"

"Before my *sleep*—" I huff. "—we lived in cottages on the outskirts of Fort Langley. Does that still exist?"

Confusion creases Hannah's brow. "Yes. But I think the people who live there would've noticed a coven of witches living in town."

"You would be surprised by how easily we can hide." The thought of finding Rebecca makes my blood sing with anticipation.

Hannah pushes to her feet, swaying. "Okay. Let's go."

I peer out the window, but it's too dark to see outside. "By what conveyance will we travel? Have you horses?"

She stares at me, then lets out a short, incredulous laugh. "Um, no. But there's a bus that runs to Fort Langley."

I narrow my eyes. "An omnibus? Like a stagecoach?"

"No, it's motorized, like...the car you...earlier..." She shifts, hugging herself.

Ah, the man I tried to kill. How efficient. "Wonderful. Take me to this *bus*. And I'll need shoes."

Minutes later, my feet are encased in something she called *Birkenstocks*, and I'm questioning humanity's decision to do away with horses. The bus is a hulking metal beast that wheezes and groans as it lurches through the dark streets, moving faster than any horse I've seen. It belches smoke into the already foul air, and the interior smells faintly rotten. Ghastly lights flicker overhead, casting a yellow glow over the other passengers. Through the grimy windows, more lights streak past. Every surface is sticky, but I have no choice but to grip the seat beneath me for balance as we sway around a corner.

"They let anyone ride these things?" I ask, eyeing the handful of other people on board.

A woman is speaking into a small black object, laughing at someone who isn't there. Is she mad? Possessed? But no one else seems concerned.

Near the front, an older man keeps turning back to look at Hannah. Even when he's facing away, his reflection in the dark window shows him still watching us. It makes me want to curse his eyes right out of his head.

"Anyone with fare." Hannah sinks deeper into her seat, either oblivious to the man's stares or purposely ignoring him. "You'll need me to get around since you don't have money."

How inconvenient. But I suppose it's not like I could leave her side even if I wanted to.

I reach for my magic, testing its edges. Normally, I could compel, curse, shield, hex, and strike my way out of any problem. I could crack the earth beneath us or crush this entire structure to dust. But the incomplete feeding has given me limited power, which I will need to carefully conserve. The idea puts a strange twist in my gut.

Out the window, the world has changed beyond recognition. Everything is huge and sprawling. Buildings stretch skyward like glass and metal mountains. Where there were dirt roads and wooden walkways, there are now smooth stone paths marked with painted lines. Instead of gas lamps, towering poles are topped with harsh lights so bright they turn night into day. The sights drive a cold, hollow feeling into my soul. Did Rebecca know how cruel it would be to make me powerless in a world I don't recognize?

"You okay?" Hannah asks.

Her tone is surprisingly concerned. When was the last time anyone asked how I'm faring?

"I'm quite well," I lie, watching another metal beast roar past mere inches away. "The world is simply different from what I remember."

"I bet. 118 years is a long time."

Her reminder of the number of years that have passed churns my stomach. I've been trying not to think of it, but I will soon have to face the truth: how many of my coven sisters are still alive? Old age would not have come for them yet, but that's not to say other forces didn't.

As the night darkens and we weave through the streets, I study Hannah's profile in the glow of the passing lamps. She has recovered from our feeding session, showing more resilience than I expected from such a delicate creature. But there is tension in her shoulders and tightness around her eyes that suggests she's not as unaffected as she's trying to appear.

Good. I need her to stay motivated to break this infuriating spell—and strong enough to withstand what comes next. I will need to do a more powerful feeding ritual with her soon, whether she can take it or not.

But there are so many unknowns about her. How did that journal end up in her possession? What role does she play in Rebecca's larger design?

The curse may have made me weak, but I cannot let Hannah see how desperate I am for answers, for power, and for any connection to the world I knew. Though the binding spell has forced us together, that doesn't mean I must trust her. Not when the journal that imprisoned me found its way into her hands.

6

HANNAH

As THE BUS TAKES us down the highway toward what I hope to God is Julia's old coven, Julia grips her seat like the driver is about to hit an Eject button. When a semi-truck roars past, she flinches.

I must be smiling because she says through her teeth, "Does something amuse you?"

I lift a shoulder. "Just interesting to see an all-powerful witch afraid of public transportation."

"I'm not afraid," she snaps.

"Right. There must be some other reason you're leaving finger dents in the seat."

I probably shouldn't be teasing someone who tried to kill my neighbor an hour ago, but watching her white-knuckle the bus seat makes her seem less like a threat and more like an ordinary human who is out of her depth—which is almost worse because it makes her harder to hate. Anyway, I'd rather joke than think about how completely my life has derailed. Sarcasm I can handle. Existential terror, not so much.

She releases her death grip, smoothing her cloak with dignity. "In my time, if something moved this fast, it was trying to kill you."

"Welcome to the future. Everything moves fast and nothing makes sense."

"Finally, something we agree on."

My lip quirks. "You can relax, though. I've been riding the bus since I was a kid and it's safe. I mean, we've never crashed."

Safe might be a generous word, especially at night, but she doesn't need to know that.

Julia makes a sound somewhere between disgust and resignation, watching the dark landscape blur past. "This speed just seems excessive."

"What's *excessive* is you murdering people for breakfast."

"Breakfast, supper, the timing is irrelevant." She waves a dismissive hand. "But I do not *eat* them. I feed on essence, not flesh."

"How civilized of you."

She studies me, her gaze burning the side of my face. The silence that follows is not quite comfortable but not hostile either.

I drum my fingers on the empty seat in front of me, glancing out at the full moon. We're in a row of three seats at the back of the bus, away from the other passengers' listening ears, but I still keep my voice low. "Why did this Rebecca person bind us, anyway?"

Julia is looking away from me, but her reflection in the window shows a flicker of surprise. "Why are you asking?"

"Why *wouldn't* I ask?"

She shifts to face me, though her hands stay anchored to the seat. "What?"

"I need to know what I'm dealing with. How magic works." Anything Julia can share about what the hell is happening and how we plan to get out of this mess would be super helpful.

She scowls. "I suspect she wanted to ensure nobody would want to free me. Why would someone wake me knowing they'd be subject to a binding spell, right?"

"Things that would've been nice to know earlier," I mumble.

Her laugh is low and rich, sending a shiver down my spine. I have the sudden urge to say something clever just to hear it again. Which is ridiculous. I don't care what she thinks of me.

"But *why* did she do this to you?"

Julia is quiet, watching the dark landscape and flowing traffic. Finally, she says, "My turn to ask a question. Where did you get that journal?"

The question hits me like a knife in the heart. "Someone gave it to me."

"Who?"

"A girl."

"What girl?"

I chew my lip. I can't tell her my theory about Riley being a witch. If she thinks Riley had anything to do with her curse, she'll want to hunt her down. And as much as I hate Riley right now...

Well, you can't fall out of love in a blink. I refuse to put Riley in this woman's crosshairs.

But I guess there's no harm in mentioning that I got it from her. "My ex," I say begrudgingly.

Julia traces her index finger through the fog building on the window. "Forgive me for being a century out of touch, but what do you mean by *ex*?"

Heat floods my cheeks. "Former...lover." The word feels strange on my tongue, too intimate for a conversation with this woman I just met.

Her hands go perfectly still.

Wait, why am I staring at her hands?

I drop my gaze.

Finally, she says, "I see. And why is she your *ex* lover and not your current one?"

The knife in my heart twists deeper, reopening the wound I've been trying to cauterize. The silence stretches, and something about the darkness outside, or maybe just the turbulent day catching up with me, makes me too exhausted to keep my walls up. "She was just done with me, I guess."

"She gave you the journal and disappeared?" Julia asks, her tone sharpening. "Tell me more about this girl."

"She gave it to me a long time ago," I say quickly. "She knows I love old books, so she probably thought..." I lift a shoulder. Who the hell knows what Riley thought? Apparently, I didn't know her as well as I thought I did.

"And when she broke your heart, you burned it?" Julia asks.

"Yeah." My eyes sting as I hear those words spoken aloud. "The way she broke up with me was so juvenile that I wonder if she never realized how deeply I fell for her. Like she thought we were kids holding hands at the movies instead of women in a real relationship."

There's a pause. Okay, so I'm discussing my love life with someone who had her hands on me earlier. Someone who, through magic I don't understand, makes me feel more at-ease than I did with Riley in the last few days. But these feelings are from the spell, right? It's not real. Not like what I had with Riley.

"Where did you meet?" Julia asks.

My cheeks heat up as I force my brain back to the conversation. Her tone is clinical and emotionless—she's trying to solve a mystery while I'm vomiting my deepest feelings like this is therapy.

"A park," I reply. "The summer after high school, I was on the grass, reading, and Riley was doing the same a few feet over. We started talking."

"Hm."

I can practically see the gears turning in Julia's head, cataloging every detail about Riley. Maybe I shouldn't have brought her up.

"Why does any of this matter?" I ask.

"Because people don't just stumble across cursed objects by acci-dent. And it so happens that witches mature into their craft around the time they reach womanhood."

My blood runs cold. If Riley really is a witch, this would explain a hell of a lot. But it also makes the breakup hurt in an entirely new way. If she was struggling with discovering something about herself, why didn't she tell me? I would have supported her and loved her through it.

"My turn to ask another question," I say before this conversation gets any closer to Julia suggesting that we hunt down Riley. "Why does the spell become permanent when the moon sets?"

She sighs. I prepare to deflect again, to insist that Riley is just a normal girl with a sappy side, but then Julia says, "Because spells are tied to natural cycles. The moon, the seasons, the body, flora and fauna. Magic takes time to plan, to cast, and to root."

"How poetic."

She waves a dismissive hand. "Merely facts."

"So this binding spell is linked to the moon?"

"Rebecca is particularly skilled with time-based spells and curses."

"You said she's a celestial witch, right? Like how you're a sanguine witch?"

She dips her chin. "We're named for how we draw our power."

So Rebecca draws from celestial bodies, Julia draws from others' life forces... "Any other types of witches I should be worried about?"

"My coven had all kinds. Green witches, sea witches...and there are certainly more I haven't met." She pauses, watching me. "A sanguine witch is the most powerful, and there are—*were*—only a few of us in the world, in case you're wondering."

The thought of even one other witch like Julia is enough to make me shiver.

If Riley really is a witch, I wonder what kind she is. Not that she should matter to me anymore.

"How many were in your coven before your, um...nap?" I ask.

She shoots me a glare at my word choice. "Nine, but it fluctuated as members came and went."

The unknown state of her coven hangs between us. Over a hundred years of comings and goings. Even for a murderous witch, that has to hurt.

"How long do witches live?"

The bus stops, and the doors hiss open. An old woman wearing a lot of layers and carrying two shopping bags hobbles aboard.

"Hundreds of years, if we're prudent," Julia replies. "Most aren't. Violence finds us more often than old age."

Another silence. In other words, almost everyone she knew is probably gone, one way or another.

As much as this is literally the worst thing to ever happen to me, it's clear that this is even worse for Julia. At least I haven't woken up in a different time period, unsure if everyone I know is dead or alive.

"I'm sorry," I say quietly.

She scoffs. "For what?"

"I'm just sorry for what you're going through."

She doesn't respond.

Another semi-truck roars past, and this time, she doesn't flinch. Progress.

"Thanks for telling me all this," I say, oddly touched by her honesty.

She lets out a low laugh, watching me with those unsettling eyes. "A word of warning, Hannah. In matters of witches and magic, be careful what you dig into. The more you learn about our world, the harder it becomes to pretend you're still innocent."

I scoff. "I was never innocent."

I'm not sure why I said it. I guess I don't want her to think I'm some sheltered little flower who can't handle whatever we're up against.

"No?" Her tone is amused. "You threw yourself between me and a stranger tonight. That's either innocent or incredibly foolish."

"It's called having a conscience."

"Hm, a luxury I can't afford. Neither can you, if you want to survive what's coming."

We turn a corner, and the force bumps me against Julia. I keep my gaze ahead, ignoring the tingle under my skin.

"I'll take my chances with my moral compass, thanks."

"How noble. Tell me, does your moral compass account for the fact that you enjoyed it?"

My hands tighten on the back of the seat in front of me. "Enjoyed what?"

"You know what I'm talking about."

"That was—" It's suddenly way too hot in here. I shift, keeping a few inches of space between us. "It's the binding spell."

"Sure," she says flatly.

Dammit, should I be worried about how incredible it felt to have her hands on me? How I kind of liked being at her mercy?

"You held back during the last feeding," she says, examining her nails. "I couldn't consume enough to sustain me."

I let out an indignant gasp. "I did not! Do you really think I'd even know *how* to hold back? I have no idea how any of this works!"

She scrutinizes me. After an uncomfortably long minute, she says, "Then let me deepen the feeding ritual when we get to Fort Langley. I need more power."

My heart lurches. "Already? Now you're being greedy."

"You agreed to feed me, and this is what it entails." She drops her hand, her tone shifting to something more serious. "*I—need—more.*"

"*Not—yet*," I say, flinging that tone right back at her.

Something about thinking of Riley and then imagining having Julia's hands on me again, even *deepening* the ritual, makes my insides twist. I've barely recovered from the last ritual and... I don't know. This is all confusing.

I still love Riley. I can't just shut that off. But when I look at Julia, all beautiful and confident and more interesting than anyone I've ever met... I don't know if I'm ready to feel her hands on me again.

Movement in my periphery jolts me back to reality.

The older man who was staring at me has stood up, though the bus is still moving. He sways and stumbles as he makes his way toward the back. My heart misses a beat as his destination becomes clear—he's coming to *us*.

His eyes are bloodshot, and the scent of alcohol wafts from him as he motions to the empty seat beside me. "This spot taken, doll?"

I look pointedly at all the other empty seats on the bus. How am I supposed to respond to this? If I say yes, will he get violent? If I say no, will he sit and bother us?

Before I can figure out how to respond, Julia stands, her cloak brushing my legs.

The man's pupils dilate as she meets his gaze.

"You should return to the seat you came from," she says quietly. Her voice is calm, but underneath it runs a current that raises the hair on the back of my neck.

The sudden quiet feels heavy, as if the air is too thick to breathe. My skin prickles like we've driven into a storm cloud. The yellow lights flicker.

The man opens his mouth, but no sound comes out. His eyes go wide and vacant, as though he's seeing something no one else can. His face drains of color. Then, he backs away so fast he trips over his own feet. "S-sorry to bother you. I'll..." His words dissolve into mumbles as he scrambles away.

Julia waits until he's back at the front of the bus before sitting again.

The air returns to normal. The prickling on my skin fades.

I stare at her. "What did you do?"

"Nothing harmful." She smooths her cloak, composed except for a sheen of sweat on her chest. "He'll have nightmares for a few days, but he'll live."

"Oh." The sound barely comes out.

She turns her gaze back out the grimy window. "I told you you were safe with me."

My cheeks tug into a reluctant smile.

Something loosens in my chest. She's right. She just *defended* me. The realization settles over me like a warm blanket.

It's insane, considering who she is. *Should* I feel safe when I'm with her? Or should I be afraid that I'm magically bound to the most dangerous person on the bus—and probably in the whole city?

I shift, trying to get rid of this weird flutter. It doesn't go away.

The scariest part is that I don't know which feelings are real. The comfort when she's close, the pull toward her, this warmth inside me... How much of this is me, and how much is the spell responding to her proximity?

It must be the spell. It's the reason she protected me too—she has to keep me safe in order to stay alive. That's all it is.

7

JULIA

THE FORT LANGLEY I remember was rough timber and mud, with palisade walls weathered silver by rain. Wagon wheels carved deep ruts into the dirt streets, and the air was thick with the smell of sawdust, horses, and ash. Wisps of chimney smoke once rose from the trees at dusk, the only sign that witches lived in the forest. Now, we enter a town of painted storefronts, gleaming signage, and unnaturally smooth streets. Rather than men in wool coats and mud-caked boots bartering outside the general store, a smattering of people mill about in their strange modern attire, looking down at small glowing rectangles as if divining the future. The town and wilderness I knew are buried under a century of progress, along with any trace of the life I once had.

My throat tightens at the possibility that the place I knew has vanished forever. That I'm a relic in a world that no longer knows or respects me.

As we finally step off the bus, I exhale in relief. What an unpleasant conveyance. Between the lurching corners and the stench, my stomach was ready to revolt.

Hannah turns to face me, hugging herself in the blast of cold night air. "Where do we start looking?"

I glare at the town I once called home. "If my coven is still alive, there will be traces. Hidden signs, magical residue, even intentional clues to tell other witches they're here."

As I lead the way to the heart of Fort Langley, Hannah stays close to my side. Whether it's the binding spell pulling her toward me or fear of whatever dangers we might find, I'm not sure.

I run my hand along a rough brick wall, searching. It's unremarkable under my fingers—no familiar surge of energy, nothing but the mundane, shallow hum of ordinary life. I pull back when I reach a large window, which displays trinkets that are supposedly useful in the kitchen.

"Anything?" Hannah asks, hovering beside me with her arms wrapped around herself. The night air has turned bitter, and her breath mists.

I ignore her and walk onward.

What if Rebecca and my entire coven are dead? What if I can't break this spell before the moon sets and end up trapped with this girl forever?

No. Rebecca will *not* win, even if she is dead.

We continue down the street, and I brush my fingers along every wall and window, feeling for the slightest hint of magic.

"*Vestigia magica revela*," I say, the tracking incantation rolling off my tongue.

The spell sends a pulse of energy outward. But before it gains traction, it sputters and dies like a blown-out candle.

Dammit. Frustration twists my gut. I used what remnants of magic I had to compel that man away from Hannah. Was that foolish?

I try again, pouring more intention into it. Sharp pain shoots through my veins as my power fights to stay alive. Once again, the spell dies before gaining traction.

"What's—" Hannah begins.

"Quiet!"

Humiliation burns hotter than the hunger. I was once powerful enough to flatten houses and make men weep with fear. I could command the earth like an extension of my body. Now I can barely cast a simple tracking spell. I'm reduced to this pathetic half strength, dependent on an ordinary girl for survival.

What if I'm broken? What if a century of sleep has permanently damaged my connection to magic? If I can no longer manage a basic spell… The thought makes me want to scream, but I swallow it down. The girl cannot see me so weak.

Movement catches my eye—a man across the street walking in the other direction. He's alone.

My hunger has become unbearable, making my hands shake and my vision blur at the edges. This weak spark of power I got from feeding on Hannah isn't enough to sustain me.

To hell with her stubbornness. If she will not hold up her end of our agreement and let me feed again, then she forces me to do this.

"Wait here," I tell her, already moving.

"Where are you—Julia!"

I walk faster, my body tingling in anticipation of the hunt. After hundreds of kills over decades, the routine is carved into my bones—following at a distance, letting them get comfortable, slowly creating isolation until it's too late to run. This is perhaps the only thing since I awoke that still feels easy.

The man is looking down at his glowing device, his shoulders relaxed, his gait unhurried. Oblivious. His life force calls to me, rich and healthy. My muscles coil as I gain ground.

With a subtle gesture, I encourage a barrel sitting in front of a pub to roll across the man's path. The wooden thump splits the quiet air. He looks up, startled, lowering his device.

I flick my fingers, and with a *pop*, the streetlamps extinguish. We're plunged into shadow, the only light coming from the full moon overhead.

The man's silhouette goes rigid. His head swivels.

"Julia," Hannah hisses behind me, her footsteps racing to catch up.

When the man's gaze lands on me, I'm already closing the distance.

"Can I help you?" His voice aims for confidence, but there's a tremor underneath—that first inkling that something's not right. His free hand forms a fist.

Too late. My power gathers like a storm beneath my skin, ready to feed. I reach out to command the barrel to bring him closer and—

"No!" Hannah's body crashes into mine from behind, her arms locking around my waist with surprising strength. Her warmth presses against my back as she digs her heels into the ground, using her full weight to drag me backward. "You said you wouldn't!"

"I made no such promise." I snarl and twist, trying to shake her off, but her grip is fierce. The man's survival instincts finally kick in, and he stumbles back, tripping over the barrel before catching himself.

His eyes go wide, reflecting the moonlight. "What's—"

"Sorry," Hannah grits out, struggling. "This woman—thinks it's 1891. She's escaped from the care home."

"Oh, um…" The man stammers, looking torn over whether to be afraid.

"Go!" Hannah barks at him.

He pauses for half a second, then spins and walks away at a fast clip, his footsteps fading down the empty street.

Fury boils in my veins as he disappears into the night.

I push Hannah back, and she lets go this time.

"Clever little pest," I growl.

"Murderous antique," she shoots back.

"I require more power. That tracking spell—"

She gestures wildly to herself. "So feed on me! That was the deal!"

The hunger claws at my insides, making me want to pin her against the brick wall and drain her dry, binding spell be damned. My fingers twitch with the urge. "You refused. You left me no choice."

Hannah scoffs. "Your medieval approach to problem-solving is showing."

"My *approach* kept me alive when other witches were being hunted and killed."

She studies me up and down, her jaw working. In the darkness, the angles of her face are soft, making her look so innocent. So naive.

I step closer, dropping my voice. "You said earlier that you have no idea how any of this works. And you're right. So I suggest you quiet down and let me do what needs to be done."

A snarl curls Hannah's lips, and her eyes flash furiously. "No. And if you try to hurt anyone else again, you're going to regret it."

I laugh. "What are you going to do, exactly?"

She opens her arms. "You need me more than you'd like to admit. You don't know how to drive, use a phone, or even buy food. You have no idea how anything works in 2009."

This stings more than it should. I draw myself up taller. "I have survived plagues, fires, and witch hunts. I can manage a few modern inconveniences."

"Can you?" She tilts her head. "Because from where I'm standing, you can barely cast a spell."

I snarl. How dare she—

"*More importantly...*" She steps closer, clenching her fists. "If you try to kill anyone again, I will jump off a bridge and let the binding spell take you down with me."

Is she mad or bluffing? This girl is as infuriating as she is intriguing.

I peer down at her. "You wouldn't."

"I released you, so the deaths would be on my conscience. So either you agree to feed on me and leave everyone else alone, or we both die."

Hm. I've managed to fire her up. Does she really have leverage over me? Would she kill us both to save a stranger? The fierce light in her eyes tells me she means it.

"Why are you so determined to protect people you don't know?" I ask.

"It's called empathy. You should try it sometime."

"I prefer efficiency." I step even closer, and to my delight, she falters and steps back. So I keep going, backing her against the wall to show her who is in control. When she bumps into it with a hitched breath, I flatten my palms on the rough brick on either side of her head, caging her in. "You'd best not let your stubborn nobility get in the way of what needs to be done tonight, Hannah."

"If you're trying to scare me, it's not working," she whispers.

I bend closer, staring into her wide eyes that betray how afraid she is. "Liar. I could end you with a thought, and you know it."

"But you won't."

The binding spell relaxes in my chest as we stand so close, and I breathe easier. A warm sensation starts in my core and spreads outward until my lips tingle.

The way Hannah bites her lip is distracting, making me forget what I'm supposed to be doing.

Then something hits my senses, and I spin.

There. A flutter, as faint as a moth's wing, brushes my skin from the south. The tracking spell, pitiful as it was, actually caught something.

My fury dissipates like smoke.

"This way." I stride back the way we came, following the invisible trail.

"What? Do you sense someone?" Hannah asks, running to keep up.

I don't respond, staying focused. My heart pounds. After 118 years, my coven is still leaving traces. Could that mean they are alive and well, right where I left them? It would be unusual for a coven to stay put for so many decades, but not unheard of.

Hannah hurries to keep up, her footsteps crunching on fallen leaves. "Where are you going?"

I don't know, so I don't answer.

After a long moment, we arrive at an iron fence.

On the other side, visible among the swirling white fog, are headstones.

My breath hitches.

Wet earth and rotting leaves fill my nostrils, the same smell that clung to Elizabeth's skirts after we buried Eloise in this very cemetery in 1885. We stood in a circle that night, holding hands while we sang the old death songs.

And if the spell is leading me here...

My insides plummet, leaving a cold void. *Are they all dead?*

God, if Rebecca died and took the secret of her binding spell to the grave... If I'm the last person alive who knows any of us ever mattered...

No. I can't give up hope. The tracking spell could be leading me to anyone.

I push the iron gate open, and it groans on its hinges, the sound echoing through the night. The trees, much taller and thicker after a century of growth, cast twisted shadows across the grass.

I step through the gate and walk on, following the faint brush of magic against my skin.

My boots crunch on rock that wasn't here before. The paths were mud and grass when I knew this place, but now, everything is too orderly. The wild tangle of blackberry bushes where Celeste and I picked berries during funerals is gone, replaced by trees that are unnaturally even. I can still taste those berries. Still hear Celeste's laugh.

But if she is dead—if they are *all* dead—am I the only one who remembers the sound of her laugh, and that she always found the best berry bushes and made the best jams? Am I the only person who knows she existed as anything more than a name on a stone?

"*Ducite me ad eas*," I murmur, urging the tracking spell to stay alive. It keeps caressing me like a gentle touch, taking me further into the graveyard.

My heart beats faster, and I lead us onward, deeper into the fog that drifts between the graves like the ghosts of everyone I once knew.

8

HANNAH

WHEN I AGREED TO track down Julia's coven, I did *not* think it would involve stomping through a graveyard at night. But it's not like I signed up for any of this in the first place, so all I can do is stay close and hope that whatever we're here for is over quickly.

The fog wraps around me like cold fingers, creeping into my bones as we swish through the damp grass. The hair on the back of my neck stands up, like it's warning me that something is hiding in the dark pools beneath the trees.

Every survival instinct is telling me to wait until morning and do this when it's light out, but there's no time for that. The full moon taunts us as it climbs higher, and I refuse to let the binding spell become permanent and be stuck as Julia's shadow forever—no matter how much my traitorous body seems to like being near her.

Infuriatingly, I'm way more comfortable the closer I am to her because of the blasted binding spell. And considering we're in a literal graveyard on a chilly October night, her presence is the only thing keeping me from straight-up panicking right now. I'm walking so shamelessly close that her cloak brushes my legs. It almost feels like a touch, and a weird urge to hold her hand for reassurance overcomes me. Which is absurd because a whole other part of my brain is screaming at me to keep my distance.

"What are we looking for?" I ask, my voice carrying in the eerie silence.

Julia slinks gracefully between the headstones, following whatever invisible trail her magic is showing her. "Gravestones from the late 1800s, if my hunch is correct."

I take out my phone and turn on the flashlight. Particles swirl in the beam, which hits a wall of fog a few paces ahead.

Julia does a double-take at the light.

"I have magic too," I say, wiggling my fingers at the phone.

She sighs and keeps walking.

For someone who woke up a hundred years in the future, she's not freaking out as badly as I would be. But considering she's a witch who seems to kill people without a second thought, there's probably not a lot that rattles her.

Some passing graves look clean and new, with adornments like flowers and belongings sitting in front of them, while others are crumbling and grimy. I shine my light on the old ones, staying as close to Julia as I can.

I try to ignore the way my heart flutters every time her cloak touches me. Binding spell aside, it's impossible not to notice that she's attractive, and it was impossible not to react when she pushed me up against that wall. And yeah, her age gives her an easy confidence and comfort in her own body that I've never encountered in women my age... But that *still* doesn't mean I like her.

"Are you certain you can endure another feeding ritual?" Julia asks. She pauses at a headstone, bending to brush her fingers over the worn inscription.

My face heats up. "Yes."

"If you insist. Just remember this was not my idea." She continues walking, her cloak billowing behind her.

A train rumbles in the distance, unseen beyond the veil of fog and darkness. Its whistle splits the air, and I flinch, stepping closer to Julia again.

Does she see through my confident answer to the turmoil inside me? Does she know that the way she touches me leaves me confused and burning with guilt? That these feelings caused by the binding spell or the feeding or...whatever is going on...are battling for the same space as my feelings for Riley?

I push down those thoughts.

"I wish I left you in that book," I grumble.

"And deprive yourself of all this charm?" Julia says lightly.

I shoot her a glare she doesn't see.

Abruptly, she stops, staring at a headstone. The train continues rumbling in the distance, the noise piercing the night.

I use my phone to illuminate the marble, which has gone gray with age and is streaked with dark veins. The inscription shifts and dances in the light.

Florence Kwan
1847-1952
Beloved Mother, Sister, Friend
"Her wisdom guides us still"

"Someone you know?" I ask gently.

She crouches to run her fingers over the marble, tracing the name. Her hair falls forward so I can't see her face. When she finally answers, her voice is quiet. "My coven's high priestess. An elemental witch. This is what the tracking spell was guiding us to."

A chill runs down my spine, and not just because we're in a graveyard. If this witch is dead, then... "What does this mean?"

Julia stands and clears her throat, gesturing to the headstone. "If Florence became a mother, then she has descendants. We can find them."

I nod, grateful we have options. "Should we look up ancestry records or something?"

She hesitates. "There is a spell I can do."

"Okay." I sweep my arm, eager to get out of the graveyard. "Go for it."

Her fingers stroke the air, and then she balls them into fists, unmistakable frustration on her face. "I need more power."

I bite my lip. "So, you need..."

The hungry gleam in her eyes makes my stomach flip. "If you can handle it."

I ignore her taunt and straighten my posture. I won't let her be right about me. Better me than an innocent bystander.

Drawing a steadying breath, I step closer, my legs like noodles. I'm not afraid of what she'll do to me as much as I'm afraid of how it makes me feel.

The rumbling train fades, and then we're standing in the dead quiet again, just the two of us and the creaking tree branches under the moonlight.

"Good girl," she murmurs.

"Don't 'good girl' me. I'm not your pet."

She casts me that wicked smile of hers. "Mm, you're something far more interesting."

Before I can interpret what this means, she steps in to meet me, moving with such grace that she brings to mind a predator ready to pounce, right down to the way she controls her hips and shoulders.

My breath hitches. I catch her warm, apple-cinnamon scent, and my body melts under her despite every rational thought warning me to be cautious.

There's a tiny curve in her lips as she looks down at me, like she knows exactly what effect she has on me. "You're trembling."

"It's cold out."

"Of course," she says like she doesn't believe me. "Now, don't move until I'm done."

I dip my chin, my heart hammering.

God, she's standing close.

Her hands lift to my hair, and my scalp tingles as she gathers it and pushes it back behind my shoulders. The gesture is so surprisingly intimate that I almost lean into her touch.

Her fingers brush the back of my neck, and...

Oh no. Oh *God*.

The feel of this woman's fingers on my neck sends an embarrassing lick of heat through me, making me want to step back before I make it obvious how this is affecting me.

Then her fingers knot in my hair, and her touch becomes demanding. She pulls my head back, forcing me to tilt my face up toward hers.

"Good," she breathes, her other hand closing around my throat firmly enough that I feel my pulse hammering against her palm. "You need to learn to open up for me if we want this to work."

Something in her tone weakens my knees. I try to nod, but her grip won't let me.

Her fingers tighten in my hair. "Mine until we break this spell. Just like this. Understand?"

"Yes," I whisper.

I should be terrified by how good this feels. How much I like the way she claims me.

She begins the incantation, her grip never loosening. A strange pull builds inside me as the Latin words flow from her lips. It shivers across my skin and breaks like a wave on a rock, cold and sudden. Pleasure pulses through me from where her hands are touching my scalp and throat. Then the wave becomes a riptide, overwhelming, dangerous, and impossible to fight. My insides tumble. My chest flutters. It's wrong how good this feels, how I'm arching into her touch like I'm starving for it.

She pulls me closer. Our bodies are pressed together, her warmth seeping through my hoodie and chasing away the chill that's been gnawing at my bones. Every point of contact burns. I can feel the softness of her breasts against mine, the curve of her fitted bodice, the firm line of her hips. It's too much and not nearly enough. My body has apparently forgotten who she is. It only knows how perfectly we fit together.

She continues the incantation, letting go and running her hands down my neck, over my shoulders, and down my arms. She grips my wrists, brushing her thumbs over the tendons, the veins, the sensitive skin of my forearm. Her cool breath skims my cheek, my jawline, my throat.

It's like she's touching me everywhere at once, making my core clench in anticipation, making me want to beg her to keep going even though black spots are bursting at the edges of my vision. A small sound escapes me, half gasp, half moan. I bite my lip, but she must have heard it because her eyes find mine.

Our gazes lock. She's standing so close that her breath grazes my lips. Her pupils are dilated. Her breathing is unsteady.

God, she's intoxicating. Her round, icy eyes pierce straight through me. Her lips are full as she recites the incantation. Her thick, dark hair falls in waves around her face. For an absurd moment, I get the urge to ask her to touch me in a different way. In any other scenario, I would swear we were about to...

No. That's not what this is.

The sensible part of my brain fights for control—the part of me that still loves Riley and hates this murderous woman I'm stuck with.

I swallow hard and drop my gaze, but I only end up staring at the tantalizing line of her clavicle.

Dammit. My body is confused by the intimacy of this ritual—all the touching and closeness.

"So eager to sacrifice yourself for strangers." Julia combs her fingers through my hair again, gentle enough to make me shiver. "Are you sure you aren't enjoying this?"

Heat rushes into my cheeks. "I hate everything about you."

Her lips curve. "Curious. Your body seems to disagree."

Before I can form a retort, she releases me, stepping back with a satisfied sigh. Magic crackles around her fingers like black lightning, and I can see the renewed power in the way she holds herself. She's somehow become even more beautiful.

"Better," she purrs, examining her darkened fingers. Even through the nightfall, the same chilling darkness is visible around her eyes. Her chest heaves, deep and shuddering, like she's restraining herself from something.

As she turns back to the grave, I stay rooted, touching my throat where her grip bruised me. There's a pang in my temple, and my mouth is dry. It's like a hangover, but instead of alcohol withdrawal, it's...Julia withdrawal.

Fuck. I can't think of her like that. Like an addiction my body craves.

But having her hands on me, being pressed against her, and seeing that hunger in her eyes? There's no questioning what the primal part of my brain wants.

Is this who I am now? Have I always craved this and never knew it, or is this magic rewiring my brain?

"Now, let's find out where dear Florence's descendants are hiding," Julia says, bending over Florence Kwan's grave while I catch my breath. My body aches where she grabbed me—and likely marked me.

I run a shaky hand through my tangled hair, blinking back to reality.

I hate that I wish the ritual didn't have to end.

I hate even more that I want her to mark me up again.

9

JULIA

IS THE BINDING SPELL making Hannah more delicious and addictive? Or am I just now realizing how hard it is to have restraint?

She's quiet as she shivers behind me, unaware of what I'm about to do. Fog clings to the surrounding trees, their gnarled branches dark splotches against the cloudy sky.

She was so pliant beneath my hands, responding like Charlotte did in the beginning. This sweet, innocent young woman has no idea what she's inviting in. Perhaps I should feel guilty about the pleasure I take in watching her discover these desires. But a sanguine witch shouldn't feel guilty about ruining what she touches, just like ivy doesn't grieve for the tree it strangles.

The fresh power settles into my bones, warm and satisfying. It's still pitiful compared to a full feeding, but it's enough for some basic earth magic and a complex spell or two.

I crouch before Florence's headstone, brushing my palm over the cold, wet grass. The faint remnants of her magic rise through the earth, still there after all these years.

"What are you doing?" Hannah asks in a high voice, shuffling her feet. I'm too aware of her after that feeding—her shivering body, her hands tucked into her sleeves, the breath misting from her lips.

I extend a hand toward the headstone, and with a sharp *crack*, a jagged piece breaks off. "Necromancy."

Hannah gasps. "Absolutely not."

I look back at her, exasperated. "Your moral compass is exhausting."

"Your lack of one is terrifying!"

I sigh and pick up the broken piece of marble. "How would you have me ask the dead about my coven, then? Perhaps send a formal invitation to commune? This is our only lead, and we need to follow it."

"There has to be another way besides raising a dead body!"

I laugh, the sound carrying into the trees. "I'm not about to raise a corpse. This is a simple bone reading."

"Oh." Hannah crosses her arms. "But that's not much better. You're still desecrating a grave like some kind of—"

"Monster?" I finish, fixing her with a glare that silences her. "We've established what I am, pet. Either accept it or walk away." I pause, letting the words settle. "Ah, but you can't, can you?"

Hannah stiffens. "Don't call me *pet*."

"Would you prefer *darling*? *Sweetheart*?"

She looks away, and even the darkness can't hide her flush. "How about *Hannah*?"

"Where's the fun in that?"

She snarls. "I hate you."

"No you don't. But you want to."

Before she can protest again, I raise the marble and draw it sharply across my palm. Crimson wells up in the shallow cut.

The sting of the blade is strangely comforting—a sensation I can control, unlike everything else spiraling around me.

Hannah is frozen behind me. "But what if someone sees?"

"I'll make haste," I snap. "Now be quiet."

She covers her mouth, hands still inside her sleeves. Her rapid breaths become muffled.

Satisfied, I return my attention to the grave and let my blood drip onto the ground, the dark drops sinking into the earth.

The air shifts, becoming thicker, charged with a power that makes my hair stand on end.

"*Ossa surgant, spiritus loquatur.*" I press both hands to the cold grass. "*Kwan, surge et responde.*"

The incantation tears through me, consuming the magic I just gained. Necromancy is a ravenous art.

The grave trembles. Hannah must be backing away because the binding spell tightens its hold on my ribs, distracting me. How irritating that her proximity comforts me. Normally, being close to someone is anything but comforting.

The earth splits apart with a deep rumble, releasing the putrid scent of decay.

Hannah lets out a squeak, and the grass shuffles as she steps back further.

Pale particles rise from the jagged crack—bone dust. It swirls around us, catching the moonlight, and I breathe it in, letting Florence's essence fill my lungs.

"Ohmygod," Hannah says into her hands. "Is that— You're really— This is the worst day of my life."

"*Memorias revela,*" I command, my voice growing stronger as the necromantic energy builds. "Show me your bloodline."

The bone dust settles on my skin like snow, and the world around me dissolves.

I'm standing in a dimly lit space filled with sultry music. Cigarette smoke curls through amber light, and the stuffy air tastes like whiskey and perfume. The floorboards beneath my feet are sticky with spilled drinks. Behind a mahogany bar, a woman moves gracefully, her black hair long and shiny, wearing a red dress that hugs her curves. When she turns, it's Florence's eyes staring back at me, the same warm brown I looked at across coven circles for decades.

The vision shimmers and shifts, and the interior changes. The smoke clears, and the brass instruments fade. Piano music fills the room instead, and behind the bar, a different woman is serving drinks. She has the same smile, the same eyes. It shifts again, moving through time, through Florence's descendants. Above the bar, painted in red letters, are the words *The Crimson Moon*.

Finally, a location. A thread to follow.

But the image is already crumbling at the edges, turning to ash before it can show me what the place looks like now.

"Show me more," I whisper. I push harder, drawing on what little power remains, trying to anchor the vision. I need a street, a face, a name. Where is this establishment? What is the name of the person I'm looking for?

But the vision continues to fragment, leaving me grasping at the faint outline of red letters.

"Damn it all."

Darkness pushes through, and in my next breath, the shattered pieces dissipate like mist. I'm back in the dark cemetery, cold air biting my skin. Dampness seeps through my trousers where I'm kneeling on the wet grass. The bone dust falls to the earth, leaving a gritty residue on my tongue. I turn my head and spit away from the grave, then wipe my brow, where sweat beads along my hairline.

"Hurry and fix it before someone sees," Hannah whispers.

I'm vibrating, my heart pounding hard. Necromancy always takes its toll, but this felt more draining. I'm surviving on insufficient power, and my body knows it.

Pressing my cut palm against my cloak to stanch the bleeding, I sweep my other hand over the earth, settling it back to what it was.

Hannah lets out a breath, glancing around. "What did you see?"

I labor to my feet, drained. "Florence's descendants. I don't know how many she has or who we're looking for, but we need to find a saloon called The Crimson Moon."

"A saloon? You mean like a bar?"

I wave a hand. How should I know what people call them these days?

"Let me see..." Hannah pulls that rectangular device from her pocket, the one she used earlier for light. Her thumbs move across its surface, and it glows to life.

I step closer to peer over her shoulder. "What is this?"

"Phone." As she taps it, symbols and images appear on the glowing surface as if by magic. "The Crimson Moon... Yeah, here it is. It's a short bus ride away."

"What? How do you know?"

She casts me a small smile. "It's called the internet. It's like...a network of information."

I squint suspiciously at it, which makes Hannah laugh. It's a pleasant sound, especially in the gloom of the graveyard.

As we walk back to the road, she says, "Phones have come a long way since your time. It can show me maps of anywhere in the world, take pictures, play music, and you can share status updates with all your friends..."

"More powerful than most grimoires," I say.

She smiles again, and my own cheeks tug in response.

Back on the bus, I steal glances at her profile in the passing lights, taking in the way she worries at her lip, the way her hair shines in the street lamps, the delicacy of her nose and jawline, her even skin. There's something simple and lovely about her.

I shift in my seat, trying to ignore the building heat as I remember the press of her body against mine and the rapid flutter of her pulse under my fingers. The little sounds she made, breathy and desperate... It's like she was discovering something about herself she'd never known before.

And given what Charlotte always told me, that's probably exactly what's happening. I've shown Hannah how good it feels to be fed on.

Charlotte was never shy about telling me how much she liked it. The games we made of the feeding rituals were better than anything in the world. I used to push her limits, testing what sounds I could draw from her and how much I could make her lose control. I can see her clearly in my mind's eye, spread naked beneath me, her pale skin flushed, her blonde curls spilling across my pillow, that beautiful mouth begging me for more. I recall sliding my fingers beneath her skirts, and her legs wrapping around my waist, pulling me closer as I took what I needed while giving her everything she craved.

But now it's Hannah I see—those blue eyes darkening with desire, her warm-gold hair tangling across the pillow, her pale skin flushed pink. She's clutching me as I show her pleasure she never dreamed possible, her lips parted as she begs for more instead of fighting not to make a sound. I can almost feel her soft skin against mine, almost taste her essence. I'm drinking her in, draining her, tasting whether her skin is as sweet as her life force, until...

I dig my nails into my palm, using the sharp pain to push those thoughts away. I can't let Hannah's feedings end like Charlotte's did. My own life depends on my ability to have restraint with her.

This girl is a temporary inconvenience. I've lived my whole life without needing anyone, and I'm not about to start caring for some fragile non-witch who will be gone from my life by sunrise.

Besides, Hannah is nothing like Charlotte. She would probably faint if I touched her that way. And I have no business imagining it in the first place.

She made her feelings about my nature clear back in her kitchen, looking at me with such disgust when I wanted to feed on her neighbors.

She might be attracted to the ritual, but that doesn't mean she wants anything to do with the witch performing it. She is only letting me feed because she has to.

And why would someone like her—young, bright, virtuous—ever want to be tangled up with a sanguine witch? I've killed more people than I can count. I've done things that would horrify her sweet moral sensibilities. Even if she did want our feedings to become more, the way I want to pin her beneath me and make her mine would terrify her innocent heart. From what I can glean, she's not like that.

No, we'll be done with each other the moment this binding spell is broken, and then she can go find someone who can pleasure her without the constant threat of draining her life away.

I force my gaze away from her and down at my palm, which tingles where I cut it. It's slowly stitching itself back together with threads of magic that feel like spider silk.

Yes, it's better to appreciate her beauty from a distance and keep my darker desires locked away where they belong.

Hannah and I stop in front of a narrow door wedged between two shops, looking up at the glowing words *The Crimson Moon*. A full moon rises behind the letters, more scarlet than crimson.

I wrinkle my nose at the litter and grime around the door. "Charming."

Of everything that's changed in the last century, the filth of the city remains constant. This is why I prefer the woods.

A group of young women walk past wearing clothing that would have scandalized a brothel back in my time—skirts that reveal their entire legs, shoes that defy gravity, shoulders completely exposed, breasts all but hanging loose. It's...well, I'm no better than a man, because it's hard to peel my eyes away from them.

Hannah clears her throat. "Shall we?"

We follow the women inside, stepping away from the foul-smelling outside world and into a stuffy establishment with dim red lighting. It's so loud I can barely think, a deep beat reverberating in my chest. Is this supposed to be *music*? The air carries the scent of whiskey and something else—herbs, maybe sage, burned recently as if to ward off evil.

Too bad sage doesn't work on sanguine witches.

As I blink the room into focus, I stop in my tracks, wondering what we've walked in on. Bodies press together, writhing, sweaty, hands groping. Fingers roam up bare legs and down plunging necklines. Hips sway, lips devour, tongues plunge into mouths. Like watching animals in a mating game. No waltz, no pattern, no decorum, just desire on display.

When did such intimacy become acceptable outside closed doors? I can't decide whether to be scandalized or to envy their freedom.

Heat rises in my body, but when I feel Hannah's gaze on me, I look away from the crowd, remembering what we're here for.

At the perimeter, every seat and table is occupied, but none of the faces are familiar.

Behind the bar, a very tall, broad man with pale skin and red hair stands serving drinks. And beside him...

My heart leaps.

Florence.

Or rather, Florence's descendant.

She has the same piercing eyes, the same sleek black hair and light skin, even carries herself with the same elegance. She's in her forties, perhaps, and wearing simple black garments.

I lean closer to Hannah and point. "There."

Our shoulders brush, and maybe it's the atmosphere setting me on edge, but the contact sends a swell of heat through my middle.

As we stride up to the bar, I can make out the gold tag reading "Maya" pinned to the woman's shirt.

When she looks up from pouring a drink, those familiar eyes meet mine.

Her gaze flicks over my face, my hair, my cloak.

She freezes. Her jaw goes slack. The color drains from her face.

The glass slips from her fingers, shattering on the floor. While several people turn toward the commotion, she just backs away with her hands raised as if I might strike her down where she stands.

"Interesting," I say.

"Um," Hannah says.

Maya bolts.

Hannah and I take off after her, weaving between startled patrons who clutch their drinks.

She disappears through a door marked "Staff Only," and we follow her into a narrow hallway. Another door at the far end leads outside, already swinging shut on its hinges.

We thunder after her.

The alley is a maze of junk and pools of darkness deep enough to hide in. It reeks of rotting food and alcohol, and broken glass crunches under our feet. I can hear her rapid footsteps and panicked breaths heading toward the street, where she thinks she can disappear into the crowd.

The hunt awakens something primal in me. What little magic I have responds eagerly, practically purring as I track her movements through the shadows. This is what I was made for—the pursuit, the cornering, the moment when prey realizes there's nowhere left to run.

I lift my hand and hesitate, debating whether to use my small reserve of power this way. But I need to stop her. So I blast a bin in her path sideways, and it slams into her.

She cries out. The sound of her body striking the rough ground echoes off the alley walls.

"Please," she gasps, scrambling away until her back hits a brick wall. "I don't know anything. I'm not—I'm not one of you."

"We're not here to hurt you," Hannah says.

I laugh. "Well, *she's* not."

Hannah swats my shoulder. "Be nice!"

Maya looks between us, wide-eyed and breathing hard. Blood oozes from her scraped palms.

"Why did you run from me?" I ask.

She says nothing, her jaw tight.

I grab her arm and haul her to her feet. "You're descended from Florence Kwan, are you not?"

"I don't know who that is." The denial comes too quickly. Her gaze darts past me, as if calculating an escape route.

"Your ancestor was a powerful witch."

"My ancestors have owned this bar for generations. None of them were a—whatever you think they were."

I release Maya's arm and seize her throat, slamming her back against the brick wall. "Lying to me is a mistake."

"Julia!" Hannah rushes forward, her voice sharp. "Don't."

I ignore her, tightening my fingers enough to make breathing difficult. "I knew Florence before she had children. We worked together for decades. She made the most exquisite protection charms—little silver amulets shaped like crescent moons."

"I don't—know what—you're talking about." Maya's hands fly to my wrist, trying to pry me off.

Beneath my arm, at her collar, I catch a glint of silver.

Anger pulses through me at the sheer nerve of this woman for thinking she can keep me at bay like I'm some ghost or demon. I squeeze harder. "All this effort to protect yourself from evil, but none of these protections work against a coven sister, Maya Kwan."

"I'm not—who you think I am," she chokes out.

Pathetic. If she were a witch, she would have used her magic to defend herself by now.

"Even if the gift skipped you, that does not grant you an escape from who you are."

She meets my gaze for the briefest moment. The hesitation is all the confirmation I need. She's hiding something. And I'm too desperate to be gentle.

I press my palm against her clavicle. *One hex. I can afford it.*

I murmur an incantation—not to draw out her life force, but to make her talk. "Tell me what you know."

Maya's scream cuts through the alley. She convulses against the wall, her eyes rolling back. The veins in her face darken, her skin graying.

"Julia, stop it!" Hannah tries to pry my hand away, but I shove her back with my free arm.

"Not until she tells us something useful," I say before continuing the incantation.

Blood trickles from Maya's nose, dripping onto her collar. She shudders in pain, but her eyes stay sharp. She keeps her jaw clamped tight, giving no indication that she'll bend.

I grit my teeth, breathing hard. Sweat prickles across my back. I'm draining what power I have left, but I refuse to show it. As far as Maya is concerned, I could do this for hours.

"So stubborn," I mutter, pressing her harder.

"Maya." Hannah steps forward, her tone urgent. "Julia and I have been bound together by a spell, and if we can't find her old coven, we'll be stuck like this forever. Please help us."

Maya's eyes flick between us, her breathing ragged, sweat beading on her temples despite the cold. "Why should I care? Maybe the world will be safer if Julia Moreau is tethered to someone with a conscience."

Her use of my full name makes me pause. So she does know who I am. That's why she ran. Even if she's not a witch, does her blood still sing with recognition when she spots one? Should I be flattered that someone in her lineage feared me enough to warn her about me?

"I'm searching for Rebecca," I say, easing up a little. "And the others. A location is all we need."

Maya scoffs, looking venomous. "Why would I help a sanguine witch? My mom told me what that means. What you do to people. A warning about you has been passed down since Florence's time."

"A warning? About me?" I grin. Looks like I wasn't forgotten, after all.

"Just leave me alone, okay? I have no connection to that life. Don't make me call my bouncer out here."

I don't know what a "bouncer" is, but I'm willing to bet it won't hold up against a sanguine witch. Magic crackles between my fingers.

But Hannah grips my arm. "Julia, we can get what we need a different way," she whispers.

I curl my fingers, wanting to keep using force. But if Maya is even remotely as stubborn as Florence was, I'm not sure about my chances of getting information out of her.

Hannah's grip tightens, and she tries to pull me back. "Sorry to bother you. We'll be on our way."

I shoot her a glare that says, *We absolutely will not.*

Her returning glare says, *Let's talk about this.*

She had better have a plan.

Reluctantly, I release Maya and let her back away.

When the door slams shut behind her, I spin to face Hannah. She's taken a step back, putting space between us. We're alone in the shadows with only the distant hum of people and the putrid smell of the alley.

"She's lying," I snarl.

"Of course she is." Hannah's voice comes out shaky. She wipes sweat from her hairline with a trembling hand. "She knows exactly where the coven is. But that doesn't mean we have to torture her."

"Doesn't it?"

Hannah waves her hands in exasperation. "You can't throw people around with magic!"

"Why not? It's efficient."

"It's assault!"

I chuckle. "What a quaint modern sensibility. In my time, we called it justice."

"In your time, you called a lot of horrific things justice."

I straighten my cloak, ignoring this. "We'll have to wait for the establishment to close and follow Maya home. We'll restrain her while we turn her house upside down. She must have something in her possession that can lead us to them."

Maya Kwan thinks she can hide from her heritage, but she can't change that she is descended from one of the greatest witches ever to live.

Whether she likes it or not, she's about to help me find my way home. Even if Hannah won't approve of my methods when the time comes.

"Julia?"

My heart does something strange at the sound of my name on Hannah's lips.

I lift my chin and turn back to her.

She crosses her arms, a fiery look in her eyes. "If we want to get to her house, I have a better idea."

10

HANNAH

"I T'S CALLED A DRIVER'S license," I explain as we huddle around the corner from The Crimson Moon. "It'll have her address on it. We just need to get her bag."

It's a quicker solution than waiting for hours until the club closes and following her home, and a safer one. I'm not sure how I feel about tying her up and ransacking her house.

Guilt twists my stomach as I lay out my plan. What I'm suggesting isn't exactly legal, but then again, anything Julia comes up with will be much worse. Anyway, we won't be *stealing* Maya's wallet, just borrowing it. Once we've searched her place, we'll leave it on her kitchen table.

Julia looks at me in a way that could either be disgust or admiration. "So how do we get her bag?"

"One of us needs to occupy her and the bartender while the other searches." The cold air bites my cheeks, and my breath mists in the streetlights. I shuffle my feet to stay warm, jealous of Julia's long cloak. "It'll be in a staff room. Or maybe behind the bar."

Julia's eyes narrow with determination, and she flexes her fingers. "I'll distract them while you locate it."

I hesitate. Of course she wants that role. She probably thrives on the attention, the chaos, the chance to use her charm like a weapon. But a magical distraction is not the best way to be subtle about what we're doing. Besides, I can think of better uses for her magic. "No, if her bag is in a locker, we'll need you to break the lock. And if it's behind the bar, it'll be easier if you summon it instead of me trying to slip back there. Can you do that? Summon someone's bag?"

She snorts. "Don't insult me. Fine, if you think you can create a sufficient distraction..."

Nerves flutter inside me, but I nod. "I can handle it." I pull out my wallet and show it to her. "This is the sort of thing you're looking for, okay? It's full of little rectangular cards."

She studies it from all angles, pulling out a card to examine it. "Fascinating. What do they do?"

"That one...gives me points at the frozen yogurt shop..." I snatch it back. "Just give me a minute to start the distraction before following."

I pull my hood over my head, scanning her old-fashioned clothes. Yeah, it's better to send me in first. She stands out like...um, an ancient witch in a bar.

Julia reaches out to stop me, her fingers brushing my wrist. Her touch sends a pleasant ripple up my arm and a distracting rush of heat through my middle. "How will I know when you're ready?"

I flash a nervous smile. "You'll know."

I walk inside, and the stuffy air hits my face, thick with the scent of beer and sugary cocktails. People are still grinding on the dance floor, and clusters of people chat over their drinks, some already loud and tipsy. I duck behind the nearest group of people before Maya and the burly bartender can look up and notice me. My ribs constrict painfully as I get further from Julia, and I do my best to breathe through it. The separation will only be for a minute.

Heart pounding, I scan the room for options—drinks to spill, tables to flip, people to pick a fight with, dance floor...

There. A karaoke machine sits behind the dance floor, its screen cycling through advertisements for drink specials.

A nervous jitter rolls through me, but now is not the time for stage fright. Now is the time to make an absolute spectacle of myself in order to save my own life.

The karaoke machine's interface is blissfully simple. I scroll down the top hits of the year: "Single Ladies" by Beyoncé (too painful given my circumstances), "I Gotta Feeling" by the Black Eyed Peas (tonight is absolutely not gonna be a good night), "Poker Face," "Womanizer"...

I stop at "Gives You Hell" by the All-American Rejects. Perfect. Angry, loud, and it was only two months ago that Dean and I scream-sang this at his twentieth birthday while Riley laughed and filmed us. Back when I still believed we'd all be together forever.

I grab the mic before the memory can paralyze me.

You can do this. Pretend Dean is on backup vocals.

"Low" by Flo Rida stops abruptly, and my song's opening notes fill the bar. Dancing screeches to a halt and conversations die as people turn toward me.

No backing out now.

The lyrics appear on the screen, and I crank up the volume, throwing myself into the song with everything I have.

People stare at me in equal parts horror and fascination. The bartender and Maya gawk at me, and recognition dawns on their faces.

I smile and wave as I sing, climbing up on a chair to get higher.

Come on. Take the bait.

Their expressions cloud over. They lean in, exchanging words.

The man nods, and they both start toward me, going wide to come at me from two angles.

Yes.

My heart beats faster as I sing louder, belting out the lyrics like a drunk girl at a bachelorette party. My voice cracks on the high notes, but whatever. The worse this is, the better the distraction.

The uncomfortable tightness in my chest suddenly eases, which tells me Julia must be inside. Past Maya and the bartender, she darts toward the door behind the bar like a shadow.

I raise my fist and lean into the chorus, my voice growing hoarse.

"All right, sweetheart," the bartender says, barely audible beneath the music. "I think that's enough for tonight."

Shit, he and Maya are close enough to grab me.

I step onto the table, bumping the cluttered dishes. People scoot back as empty glasses crash to the floor.

"Hey! Get down!" the bartender shouts.

I dance out of his grasp, my voice bouncing as I keep singing.

The patrons are too busy laughing to help catch me, and I dodge him as I hop to the next table. My singing deteriorates as I concentrate on not falling.

Maya tries to grab my arm, and I leap away, landing in a booth between two college-aged girls. They giggle and lean away from me.

I'm running out of time. I pass the mic to the brunette on my left. "Take it away!"

She accepts it with a nervous glance at her friend, and I slide down under the table and onto the ground. I crawl between everyone's legs and out the other side, adrenaline making me speedy. I scramble to my feet—and come nose-to-chest with the bartender, whose face is the color of the bar's logo.

Run.

I bolt in the other direction.

His fingers graze my arm, but I pull away, sprinting toward the exit. Julia had better be done, because time's up.

I'm nearly at the door when Maya appears in my periphery. She sticks her leg out, and I'm too slow to dodge it. My foot slams into hers, and the rest of me is still on a forward trajectory.

I scrunch my face as the floor rushes up to meet me.

I land hard, the impact shooting up my arms as I catch myself with the heels of my hands. I skid across the sticky floor, pain exploding in my hands and knees, my sweater getting wet from spilled drinks. Gross.

A grunt of pain escapes, and I scramble forward, trying to get to the exit.

A rough hand grabs the back of my sweater and hauls me to my feet, practically lifting me through the doorway. "I'll escort her out, Maya."

"I'm going!" I cry. "You don't have to escort me. I'm leaving."

The bartender ignores me, continuing to drag me outside with one hand.

My heart pounds hard. Is he going to beat me up? Does that actually happen in real life?

Outside, he holds me by the scruff with two hands. "Who the hell are you, and what do you want with Maya?"

"N-no one. Nothing," I stammer, my breaths coming fast and panicky. "It was—a joke—"

He shakes me. "She told me you and that other woman threatened her."

Pain shoots through my neck. "This has nothing to do with you."

His face is even redder, and the veins in his arms bulge as he lifts me onto my toes. My legs shake as I try to keep my feet on the ground.

Abruptly, he flies backward like he's been hit by a cannon ball, letting out a deep grunt. As the grip on my collar vanishes, I lose my balance and fall to my knees. My ears ring with the sound of him slamming into the brick wall and crumpling to the ground.

I brace my hands against the rough pavement and look up, catching my breath.

Julia stands in the doorway, silhouetted against the warm light from inside. The door swings shut behind her with a bang. Her face is absolutely feral, her eyes blazing with fury and her lips curling into a snarl. Black magic crackles between her fingers and writhes up her arms, making the air around her hands shimmer with heat.

For a second, I can only stare, frozen in fear.

But then she growls, her voice so low and deadly it makes my skin prickle. "*Don't—touch—her.*"

Warm, sweet relief crashes through me.

The bartender scrambles backward, unsteady as he tries to get to his feet. "I'll have both of you arrested."

Julia cocks an eyebrow, stalking toward him. The icy wind lifts her hair and pushes her cloak back from her waist, revealing her taut, strong body poised for a fight. "Is that all?"

He finally manages to stand, and whatever retort he planned to say dies on his tongue as she raises her hands, letting him see the magic crackling there. His eyes widen, and he steps back, his mouth open in horror.

"*No one* touches what's mine without paying for it," she growls. "Understand?"

"Julia," I whisper, though I'm not sure if I'm asking her to stop or keep going.

Her attention is fixed on the bartender as she keeps stalking closer. "Go back inside before I make you beg for death."

He stares her down, apparently refusing to be intimidated. "I want you both out of here. Never show your faces here again."

Julia raises a finger to her chest. "Cross my heart."

He hesitates, then shakes his head and backs toward the door, keeping his eyes on Julia.

Only once he's gone does she turn to me, and the fury in her expression dissolves. She's breathing hard and her face is pale, like whatever magic she did came at a cost.

Her eyes rake over me and pause at my collar, where he grabbed me. Her jaw clenches. "Did he hurt you?"

"I'm fine," I manage, though my voice comes out breathy.

My insides are swooping out of control. Nobody's ever defended me the way she has tonight.

A sick part of me actually wanted the guy to resist so I could see what Julia would do. It's a little intoxicating, watching her use magic. Watching her fingers darken and her expression intensify.

I draw a shaky breath and tug my sweater straight, tamping down that reckless and shameful thought. The way Julia is, she would've had no problem hurting or even killing him. In fact, she probably restrained herself for my sake. "Thanks for..." My sweater is sticky and smells like beer, and I cringe as it gets on my palms. This had better be worth it. "Did you get it?"

She takes me by the elbow and speed-walks away from the bar. "Yes. Quickly."

My heart jumps in victory, and maybe a little from her firm touch.

I lead us to the nearest bus stop, praying one comes within the next half a second. There, we duck behind the small crowd of waiting people, and Julia passes me the leather wallet. I pull out the driver's license and punch the address into my phone.

"That was fast," I say. "Sorry I couldn't distract them for any longer."

"It was long enough. And you did well."

I look up at her, checking that the compliment really did come out of her mouth.

She's eyeing the passing traffic and the other people waiting for the bus as if it's all plotting against us, her fists clenched.

I smile to myself. "Looks like it'll take twenty minutes to get to her place."

She nods firmly.

The bus rolls up, and everyone shuffles closer to the curb as the doors hiss open.

I pull out my wallet, grimacing as I shake back my damp sleeves. "My poor hoodie. And kneecaps."

Julia's gaze rakes up and down my body.

I wish I knew what she was thinking when she looks at me that way. Is she judging me or...something else? Is it bad that I want her to keep looking?

"Are all modern women so unrestrained?" she finally asks.

I can't help the little smile tugging my cheeks. "What do you mean?"

The warm, stale air from the bus wafts out as the people ahead of us file on.

"That song and dance was..." Julia waves a hand. "And your trousers. They're scandalously tight."

I open my mouth, trying to decide how I feel about this. Am I flattered? Offended?

Then she adds in a murmur so low I almost miss it, "I think you would have made a good witch. There was a time when men would have wanted to burn you at the stake."

I grin. "Thank you."

We take seats near the front this time, since a group of noisy teenagers is taking up the back of the bus, playing music from a small speaker.

Julia sighs. "Today's music is strange. But I suppose it matches your performance in the saloon."

I whip my head toward her. "Excuse me?"

"The singing." She waves a dismissive hand. "Enthusiastic, certainly. Tuneful? That's generous."

My mouth falls open. "I was creating a distraction, not auditioning for a musical."

"And what a distraction it was. I'm surprised they didn't pay you to stop."

"You know what? You're welcome. Since my *performance* bought you the time you needed."

"I could have managed without the amateur theatrics."

"Right, because you're managing so well tonight. You can't even use a phone."

She smirks. "I've spent my whole life free of your modern trinkets."

"Yeah, well, you wouldn't have survived the last few hours on your own."

The smirk falters. Ten points to me.

Julia turns to look out the window.

"What sort of music did you listen to in the 1800s?" I ask.

"Not this assault on the senses, I assure you." She wrinkles her nose and glances back at the teenagers.

"Classical snob."

"I prefer music that doesn't make me long to be put back into a cursed sleep."

I shouldn't smile at that, but my lips curve anyway. The adrenaline and small victory make me feel lighter than I have all day. It almost feels like we're normal. Like I have no reason to be afraid of her.

11

HANNAH

WHEN WE GET OFF the bus, we speed-walk around the corner to Maya's apartment building, Julia's cloak billowing and my sweater just...soggily flapping. Ugh, she's so much cooler than me.

We get to the glass doors, and before I've finished saying, "It'll be locked," the lock clicks, and it swings open for us.

"Right," I say. "Great."

We take the stairs to the fourth floor, where Julia blasts Maya's door open and strides in without hesitation. Fortunately, nobody else is here.

I wince, trotting in after her and locking the door behind us. "The neighbors, Julia! You have to at least be a *little bit* subtle."

"No time for that." She inhales deeply and flexes her fingers as if taking in the room's vibe or something. "Tell me if you find anything unusual."

I flip on the light and scan the small apartment. One bedroom, one bathroom, patio at the back, plants on the windowsill. Normal enough at first glance...but heavy curtains block every window, the place smells strongly like burnt sage, and the door has *three* deadbolts—top, middle, bottom.

The decor is also a little unusual. A strangely shaped, padded red sculpture in the corner might be an armchair. Light fixtures made from twisted metal and bone hang from the ceiling. Paintings cover the walls, too abstract to discern what they are—but when I study the strange shapes and dark colors, a heavy feeling settles over me. It's like they're depicting something forbidden that the artist was trying to empty from their brain. The paint-splattered easel and brushes tell me they might be painted by Maya herself.

Julia is already rummaging through a stack of mail on the kitchen counter, where a cluster of dark red candles sits half melted, the hardened wax pooling on the countertop. I head for the laptop on the desk and bend over it.

"What is that?" Julia asks.

"A laptop. Gives you access to the internet and emails and stuff."

"None of those words made sense."

"I'll explain later."

It boots up to the desktop, no password required. I guess her paranoia doesn't extend to cybersecurity. I breathe a sigh of relief and start opening files.

My spine prickles at the stillness of the apartment and the frantic sounds of us both working. The smell of old beer from my hoodie and the chilly dampness is getting unbearable, so I take it off and drop it onto the floor. It's a little cold to be in a camisole, but I'd rather be in this than an alcohol-soaked sweater.

I feel Julia's gaze on me like a flame against my bare shoulders, but I don't turn. A secret and confusing part of me likes that she's looking.

"Who else was in your coven?" I ask as I scour the laptop, needing a clue as to what names I should be looking for.

"The only one we're concerned with is Rebecca." Julia moves to the bookshelf, and the soft scrape of books tickles my ears.

I click through Maya's emails, scanning subject lines for anything witchy. "Were you friends with everyone in your coven, other than Rebecca?"

Not a pertinent question, but I'm curious about the life of Julia Moreau.

"Some I liked more than others," she says vaguely.

There's nothing weird in her emails, so I try her browser history. *Recipes... Art... Online shopping...* "What about your family?"

A pause. "A coven is a witch's family."

I don't want to anger her by prying, but I want to understand more about this woman who's suddenly become central to my world. "Parents?" I ask hesitantly.

She continues checking each book. At last, she says flatly, "My mother's identity was discovered by a group of weak, scared men. They burned her at the stake when I was a child. I had no father."

The words punch me in the gut. I stop scrolling through Maya's browser history.

"I'm sorry." The words feel inadequate, but they're all I have.

"Don't be. The men who killed her got what they deserved."

A chill rolls through me at the cold satisfaction in her voice. I don't ask her to elaborate.

I force myself to keep scrolling for clues. We need to get out of here as fast as possible.

"Did she love you?" The question spills out without my permission. I've always been interested in the relationships other people have with their parents. I loved going to Riley's house for brunch on weekends and seeing the way she and her mom interacted. Hugging, laughing, making references that only the two of them understood.

But my question is about more than that. I want to know who Julia was before the world turned her into this—or maybe she was born like this.

Julia stares at a novel in her hands, her fingers drumming its spine. A muscle in her jaw flexes.

"Yes. She did." She slides the book back onto the shelf without looking at me. "My mother was a sanguine witch too. She understood me better than anyone else ever has."

I swallow hard and return my attention to the laptop.

Maybe Julia wasn't born a monster. Maybe the world made her this way by forcing her to witness a cruelty that no child should have to endure.

"Why do you ask?" Julia says.

I lift a shoulder. The words rise in my throat, threatening to spill. We're supposed to be searching for the coven, not trading trauma stories.

But Julia's watching me, waiting.

My fingers pause on the keyboard. "My parents didn't love me. Not really. They moved out on me as soon as I turned eighteen. Left me behind to travel. I was always an inconvenience to them, like a dead weight stopping them from living the life they wanted." I open Maya's calendar to avoid Julia's gaze. "I think the few years you got with a mom who loved you is better than eighteen years with parents who didn't. I'm sorry you had to lose her. That isn't fair."

When I glance back, Julia is watching me with an expression I can't read. Her brow is pinched—not in pity, thank God, but more like she's recalculating me.

I turn back to the screen, heat creeping up my neck. Yup, I've spilled too much again.

Focus. Find the coven.

On the laptop, Maya's calendar sits open, appointments and peoples' names scattered throughout the month. "Hey, tell me if any of these names sound familiar. Maybe she's still in touch with witches."

Julia abandons the bookshelf to come closer. "Sure."

I rattle off some calendar entries, waiting for her to stop me. She peers over my shoulder, and my mouth goes dry as her cloak brushes me. The soft fabric against my bare skin sends a tingle through me that settles deep in my belly. The heat of her body radiates into me, and her warm scent has a dizzying effect.

"Um." My tongue suddenly doesn't work properly. "*Yoga with Addy*... That's every Thursday, so I don't think there's anything suspicious there... *Meet with Elizabeth*? Know any Elizabeths?"

"I did," she murmurs. "What's the surname?"

I click the entry, but there's no further information. "One sec..."

I return to her inbox and type 'Elizabeth' into the search. A few emails pop up. "Elizabeth Barnwell?"

Julia's fingers close over my shoulder, warm against my cool skin. "That's her. A green witch. She'll know where Rebecca and my other sisters are."

The skin-to-skin contact awakens that delicious connection between us, pleasure flowing into me like an IV drip.

Then her words register, and my heart leaps. I look up at her in disbelief. Did I seriously just find something useful?

"What else does it say? Is there a location?" she asks, her tone growing urgent.

"L-let's see." I scan the email subjects, looking for context, though it's really hard to focus. She's standing distractingly close, her warm, apple-cinnamon scent making me drunk. And the fact I'm face-level with her cleavage is not helping. Her skin looks so soft and smooth, and her bodice is pushing her breasts up. My fingers itch to trace along that exposed curve.

As if suddenly aware of what's happening, Julia lets go, leaving a cool draft where her hand was.

"It's okay," I say. "You can—I mean, I don't mind if you—" I cut myself off, unsure what I'm getting at. *Touch me,* my annoying inner voice finishes.

She looks down at me, and my pulse quickens. When she licks her lips, my gaze catches on her tongue for long enough that it's obvious I'm staring at her mouth.

Dammit. I absolutely cannot be attracted to her. I'm not even convinced this is just the binding spell at work—she's objectively stunning. She's confident and gorgeous, and she has the most piercing eyes. But putting aside the fact that she's a sanguine witch and a literal murderer, she's also got to be twenty years older than me. Or like, a century older, depending on whether you count the cursed sleep.

And anyway, I already decided I'm done letting myself have feelings for anyone, so this fluttering can fuck right off.

I turn back to the laptop, my breaths shallow and my face hot. "I'll see if I can find an address."

"Good," she murmurs.

The way she says that single word of praise makes me tighten between my legs.

Stop it. Focus on getting info about Elizabeth.

Before I can move, my scalp tingles pleasantly, as if...

Oh God. She's playing with my hair. Combing her fingers gently through the strands.

My eyelids flutter, and I stay perfectly still. Each stroke sends ripples through me.

But *why* is she playing with my hair? Is she doing this absently because I happen to be in front of her? Or maybe this is how she treats everyone she feeds off of, buttering them up before she consumes them. Or...

Or she could be flirting with me. Seducing me.

My heart beats faster. Blood rushes to my face, making my lips numb.

I have to remember who I'm dealing with. I can't be attracted to her. I can't trust her.

And I can't trust the feelings I have when she touches me.

I blink the screen back into focus, scanning the emails from Elizabeth. There are six, and the first was received January 7, 2004. I open it with clumsy fingers.

A jolt of victory shoots through my chest. "Elizabeth asked Maya to come pick up family heirlooms."

Julia goes still, and her fingers stop toying with my hair.

I scroll down, scanning for an address. "Crap... Maya said she's not interested in joining any covens, given what happened to the other witches in her lineage...whatever that means..." I get to Elizabeth's final reply, and my breath catches. "Wait. *If you change your mind, here's where to find me.* Julia, it's her address!"

"Perfect," Julia says, a rare note of elation in her voice.

I grab a notepad and pen, scribbling the address with a trembling hand. "Do we need anything else?"

Before she can answer, the lock on the apartment door clicks.

We both freeze, eyes widening.

Maya is home.

12

JULIA

T HE APARTMENT DOOR RATTLES as Maya tries to enter, only to be
stopped by the three bolts.

We've run out of time—but Elizabeth's address might be enough to lead
us to Rebecca.

"What should we—" Hannah begins.

Shunk. The top bolt slides open on its own.

We look at each other, eyes wide.

Shunk. The middle one slides open.

Not a witch, Maya? I think, my skin tingling as her magic hits me like
fog rolling in.

Damn it all. I should have known she was lying. Should have smelled the
way she expertly suppressed it. She has the power of the Kwan family in her
blood, and I'm willing to bet that magic has never skipped a generation.

I raise my palms for a fight, but the gesture is laughable. Even blasting
open the door was an effort, and I doubt I could fight so much as a rat right
now.

Hannah's eyes dart around the room. She grabs my arm and pulls me
toward a door. "Balcony."

Hm, yes, fleeing is wiser.

Shunk. The third bolt slides open, and I hurtle after Hannah into the cool night air.

Hannah quietly shuts the door behind us just as the front door's hinges creak, the sound filling the small space.

"Who's here?" Maya calls out from beyond the closed door, her voice rough and menacing, not at all like the scared victim we cornered in the alley.

"Shit," Hannah whispers, leaning over the railing. "How do we get down?"

We're overlooking a courtyard far below, where hard stone pathways wind between grass and gardens. No one is around, though lights glow in square windows on all four sides. Across the way, a path leads back to the road. Now if we could just get there.

The temperature drops suddenly, and frost spreads across the glass with an ominous crackling sound. The crystals form a pattern until the meaning is clear: Maya is casting protection runes. I step back from it, feeling its sting without touching it.

"Oh fuck, oh fuck," Hannah whispers. She shivers and crosses her arms. Then she gasps, her face going white in the moonlight. "My sweater! I left it beside the computer."

I bite the inside of my cheek, holding back my annoyance at her foolishness. But Maya probably knows who her intruders are, anyway.

I return my attention to the drop. It's too high to jump without using magic to cushion us.

"Show your face, cowards!" Maya barks. A blast of magic lifts strands of our hair, and the glass door cracks, spider-webbing from the impact.

A charged hum fills the air, seeping through the walls—the crackling energy that builds with a witch's rage. Something crashes inside as her anger escalates.

Whatever she said about not wanting to be part of the coven, she's still a witch, and Florence's power pulses through her veins. And if she's inherited even half of Florence's abilities, she will incinerate us both when she finds us cornered out here.

I turn to Hannah, gripping her shoulders hard. "I need magic to get us out of here. Now."

Hannah nods, stepping closer without hesitation. "Take it."

Her breaths are shallow, her lips parted like she's ready to breathe her life into me.

God, she's lovely.

I shove her against the railing and press my body to hers, cupping her face. Her skin is silky and cool beneath my palms. I murmur the incantation, running my hands down her neck, bare shoulders, and arms. My whole body tingles as my magic begins to feed, drawing her sweet taste into me.

I settle my hands in the strip of bare skin at her hips, holding her to me. It helps that she's shed that bulky garment she called a hoodie, leaving less between us and more skin I can access. The lacy thing she's wearing is nothing short of scandalous, all delicate straps and sheer material that does nothing to hide the curves beneath. I can even see her nipples peaking the fabric.

I have to focus, to draw just enough to get us to safety. But *oh*, she tastes divine. The rush is intoxicating as power floods into me, and she shivers under my touch.

Maya's footsteps thump closer.

My pulse pounds. I need to hurry.

"Open your mouth," I whisper.

Hannah's breath catches. "What?"

"I need your essence. Your breath."

Her lips move wordlessly, like she's trying to process what I'm asking. But we don't have time for that.

I push two fingers into her mouth, parting her plush lips. The moment her hot tongue touches my fingers, my insides burn with desire. I try to focus on drawing power, but there's a split second where her tongue flicks over my fingertips, and I have to bite back a groan.

I pull my fingers out and slide my hands around the back of her head, tangling them in her soft hair that smells like peaches. I lean in so close that our lips are nearly touching and inhale deeply, drinking in her life force.

We're not kissing, but God, her lips are so close. They're a hair's width away, plush and open. The urge to cross that small distance and take her lips in mine is overwhelming, but I hold back. *Not like this.*

I tighten my fingers in her hair, tipping her head back so I can drink in more of her. She's so pliant under my touch, yielding to my every movement. What I wouldn't give to have more time.

Focus. Draw deeper. I'm wasting seconds we don't have, distracted by wanting her.

Hannah's hands come up to grip my cloak, but she doesn't push away. Just holds onto me as I keep taking. Power floods through me, and she trembles in my arms.

The door handle rattles as Maya grabs it from the other side.

I fling my hand out behind me to stop her, slamming the door before she can open it all the way. The wood groans under the pressure.

She roars in frustration, and it rattles so hard that a cloud of dust rises. My hair stands on end as she fights against my magic.

Power surges through my veins as Hannah's energy mixes with my own. It's more than enough to get us out of here.

"Hold onto me," I tell her, wrapping my arms around her waist.

Her eyes widen as she realizes what I'm planning. "Julia, no—"

But I'm already pulling her over the railing with me, and her protest gets lost in the wind. When will she learn that she's safe under my protection?

She screams as we plummet through the air toward the grassy courtyard.

I focus all my newfound power downward, calling to the earth. Chunks of soil tear free from the grass and garden beds, rising to meet us in a spiral. We hit them in stages—a pillow of soil, a mound of grass, an entire bush, until we land on the stone walkway with a thud that knocks the air from my lungs.

Hannah gasps, and as I try to disentangle my limbs, it becomes clear that she's landed on top of me.

"Are—you hurt?" I ask between breaths.

"I d-don't think so," she stammers, her breath tickling my lips.

She shifts, and one of her thighs slips between mine, pressing against my center.

She's staring at me, frozen, her face an inch away. Her scent envelops me, sweet and inviting.

For a moment, we stay there, the intimacy of the feeding still hanging between us.

Past her, high above, Maya's silhouette appears at the railing. Power crackles around her hands like white lightning. "You should have left me alone, Julia Moreau!"

Normally, words like that would make me pause to show her what a mistake she made by threatening me. But given my reduced power and my need to keep Hannah alive...

I push Hannah off me. "Run."

She scrambles to her feet, and we make it two steps when the earth erupts beside us. We fall to our knees, coughing and throwing our arms up in the wave of dirt and rocks.

Another blast hits even closer, and without thinking about it, I grab Hannah and pull her down, covering her body with mine as debris rains around us. She gasps in pain beneath me, but better bruised than dead. She's under my protection, and I will not let Maya's tantrum end what's mine.

"Wait," I snarl in her ear, using my magic to shield us.

I spin and send the uprooted bush toward Maya. She deflects it, and the pause is long enough for us to get up and keep running.

"If I ever see you again, I'll kill you both!" Maya shouts.

I gather my power from Hannah's sweet energy still flowing through my body. With a grunt, I hurl another wave of dirt and rocks toward Maya. As she raises her hands to shield herself, I take Hannah's hand and pull her back to her feet.

We race away through the darkness, following the stone path out of the courtyard and back to the busy street. Hannah coughs and wipes her face, dark streaks of blood dotting her pale skin.

A jolt of concern lances through me before I can suppress it. *Ridiculous.* I've watched hundreds of people suffer far worse without batting an eye. Why should these little cuts on Hannah be any different?

But somehow, seeing Hannah get hurt by Maya makes me want to turn around and burn down Maya's entire home. The entire *town.*

An explosion of earth erupts behind us, but nothing hits, and soon, Maya's furious shrieks fade into the distance.

My heart pounds hard, and it's from more than just the escape.

I can still feel Hannah's breath on my lips, taste her as she fills my soul, and hear her soft, hitched breaths as I fed. My fingers ache where her silky hair ran between them when I couldn't help but touch her.

I cannot deny it: my attraction to her has become impossible to ignore. I want to feed on her again and again, but it's more than that. I haven't felt like this since Charlotte.

And that's exactly the problem. Charlotte looked at me with breathless wonder once, and look how that ended.

Every bruise, scrape, and mark on Hannah's body is because of me. She's lied and stolen in the hours since we've met. I'm witnessing her corruption already—these small compromises, hour by hour, proving that the innocent woman from the beginning of the night will soon be gone, and it will be my fault.

But what am I meant to do? We're stuck together. I cannot simply send her home.

And even if I wanted to...

Well, even knowing what I'm doing to her, I don't wish to stop. I want to keep feeding on her, touching her, tasting her, ruining her.

And if I'm reading the way she looks at me correctly, she wants to be ruined.

13

HANNAH

I GRIP THE BUS seat with white knuckles as we wind through the dark roads toward Elizabeth's house. It's eleven and the moon is reaching its peak, which means our time is nearly half up. My palms are sweating from our escape, from almost getting blown to pieces by Maya, from the four-story drop that should have killed us both...and from Julia pressing against me on that balcony, her fingers in my hair and in my mouth.

When she tipped my head back, cold adrenaline flooded my veins, and yet my traitorous body leaned in. Even now, my skin dances everywhere she touched me, and I can't tell if I'm trembling from fear or anticipation of where this might go if I let it.

She shifts beside me, and my breath hitches, like I'm expecting her to grab me again and wrap her hand around my throat.

"Are you afraid of me?" she asks, her voice low.

She must sense my tension. "Should I be?"

"That's not an answer."

I swallow hard. "I've just never met a sanguine witch. Or knew witches existed."

In truth, I haven't forgotten for a second that hundreds of people have died at her hand, and several more would have been killed tonight if I hadn't stopped her. And now I'm alone with her on a very empty bus, heading deep into the darkness.

So yes, she scares me. But it's a different kind of fear than I've ever felt. It's not the fear that makes you run, but the kind that roots you in place and makes you wonder what it would feel like to let the danger consume you.

Besides, she's gone out of her way to protect me more than once, and that contradiction makes everything all the more confusing.

"I think I'm more worried about whoever we're about to meet," I say. "I mean, if Maya was a *descendant* of your coven and nearly killed us... Should I be afraid?"

"My coven was full of powerful witches. Elizabeth wrote some of the darker spells in the grimoire in her younger days. But as long as we don't anger them the way we angered Maya, we should be safe."

This doesn't bode well. But what choice do we have but to keep going? This is our only link to Rebecca.

At last, we step off the bus on a narrow road lined with ancient oaks, their branches forming a shadowy tunnel. The world is silent this far out of the city, only the churring insects and rustling leaves filling the air. We walk for ten minutes, our breaths misting and our feet crunching on the gravel shoulder, before we reach the iron gates guarding Elizabeth's house—no, her *estate*. A Victorian mansion is set back among the trees, its Gothic windows glowing amber against the night sky. Dark shapes that must be gargoyles perch along the roofline. The whole place radiates old money and older magic.

"Welcoming," I mutter, shivering in the cold.

Julia peers through the gate at the mansion. "Elizabeth always did enjoy her theatrics."

I stare at the intercom, a black box jutting out of the ground on an elegant iron post. But I don't push the button yet.

"Do you feel like you have enough power to handle them?" I ask, my stomach twisting.

Julia flexes her fingers, studying her hands. Magic flickers between her knuckles like lightning, but we both know it's not enough. "More than before, I suppose."

An idea takes form, tentative and tempting. If skin-to-skin contact gives Julia power...and if my breath gives her power...then what if...?

I recall the way her magic surged when she had her fingers in my mouth versus when she just grabbed my hands, and the way she seemed almost drunk on it when we were pressed together on Maya's balcony. More contact, more intimacy, more power? If she can't drain someone to death, does intimacy fill that gap?

My heart pounds harder in anticipation of what I want to say. What I want to do.

I study the sharp line of her jaw and high cheekbones in the moonlight. She's beautiful and menacing and totally unreadable. For all I know, she's planning how she's going to dispose of me the second we break the binding spell.

But my body doesn't seem to care about that, nor about the world of differences between us. In fact, I kind of want to let my brain stop caring too. Really, aren't her age and experience a comfort? Wasn't Dean saying earlier that people our age change too much? It's clear Julia already has herself figured out. She's seen more and done more than anyone else I know.

"Would kissing you help?" I blurt.

She goes completely still.

Slowly, she turns to face me, and a strange expression crosses her face. "What do you mean, *help*?"

I could just crawl into a hole, but I make myself continue. "When feeding. Would you be able to drink in more power if we... Like, if our lips and tongues were touching, too?"

My face is absolutely on fire.

She stares at me. Her hands clench and unclench at her sides.

In the silence, I try desperately to read what she's thinking. Why is she not answering? Is she disgusted by the suggestion? Amused?

Finally, she says, "That's a dangerous question."

I bristle. "I'm trying to help us handle whatever we're about to face."

"Is that so?" Julia steps in, her eyes glinting in the moonlight. "Or are you looking for an excuse?"

Heat floods my cheeks. "How dare you."

She tilts her head. "How dare I suggest you've been wondering what it would be like since I first touched you?"

I cross my arms and scowl. "You're insufferable. Sorry for suggesting it."

She chuckles and takes a slow step closer. "It is likely to prove helpful, yes."

My heart skips a beat. "Then why didn't you just say that?"

"I like to watch you squirm."

I realize I am, in fact, squirming, and I force myself to stay still. "So you're saying we should try it, then."

She searches my face with those piercing eyes, and I feel naked under her gaze, like she can see every confused feeling writhing inside me.

"I just think we need every advantage we can get," I say firmly. "If this gives you more power and keeps us both alive, it's worth it, and then we know for the future that..." I'm babbling. Trying to justify why I suggested it. Trying to convince myself this is about survival and not because I *want* to kiss her. To feel her lips on mine. To run my tongue over more than just her fingertips.

Finally, she takes another step closer, looking down at me with so much smooth confidence that it pisses me off. "You should know that the more intimate the feeding, the more it will affect you."

I raise my eyebrows. "Does this mean you've fed on someone without killing them before?"

"I fail to see how that's relevant."

I sigh. "What do you mean by 'affect me?'"

She's close enough that I can feel her body heat, and I suppress the urge to lean in and make her wrap her arms and cloak around me to keep me warm.

"Sanguine magic feeds on life force, yes, but not all life force is equal. Unwilling victims barely sustain me, which is why I have to drain them dry. But desire..." Her piercing blue eyes meet mine. "A willing participant gives me more power than I could steal from a dozen strangers. But you should know that you will come to crave the sensation. It will become difficult to tell whether you're feeling the incantation's effects or...other desires. Is that what you want?"

My breath catches. Is she warning me or tempting me? Does she realize the line between feeding and other desires has already been swept away like the wind over a strip of sand?

"Well, I've already got the binding spell muddying my feelings," I say, trying to sound nonchalant. "I think I can handle it."

Julia tilts her head, a curious look in her eyes. "The binding spell forces proximity, not desire. I have known bound witches who despised each other until death."

I stare at her, everything I thought I'd figured out coming to a screeching halt. "Wh-what? But you said..."

"Not once have I told you that the binding spell creates feelings, Hannah."

Oh my God. She's right.

So all this fluttering in my chest and the pleasure rocketing through me whenever she touches me…? "But the spell *wants* us to be close, right?"

"Pleasant physical sensations are not the same as desire. The binding spell does not control your emotions."

I keep staring at her, my heart beating fast. God, what *am* I feeling? Do I genuinely want her?

"Still think you can handle an intimate feeding?" She watches me closely, maybe seeing my panic as my world frantically reshapes itself.

I swallow hard, unsure how to answer. If I'm already this confused about how I feel, adding an intimate feeding ritual is not going to help.

But every inch of me is betraying me, leaning closer. I desperately want her hands on me again even though I know what those hands have done. Even though I can no longer blame the binding spell for making me want this.

"Whatever it takes to survive," I whisper.

"Liar." The word is so soft I almost miss it. "You want more than survival."

Before I can summon any semblance of self-control, her fingers slide into my hair as they have several times tonight, gripping hard.

I let my eyelids flutter closed as her lips hover over mine, achingly close but not touching.

For a few heartbeats, we stay like that, our breath misting between us in the charged silence. I can taste her exhale, feel the warmth radiating from her skin.

"Final chance to reconsider," she murmurs.

I *should* be reconsidering. How many people has this woman killed? But as the feeding lingers between us, right within reach, fear is the furthest thing from my mind.

I tip my chin forward, barely a centimeter, and our lips touch. Fire shoots through me, blazing hot and all consuming.

Julia hisses. She leans closer, her lips capturing mine, and I open for her with a whimper I can't suppress.

Her hips and breasts press against me. Her tongue traces my lips. Dips into my mouth. She makes a sound that's half moan, half growl.

She murmurs the incantation into my mouth, her breath hot and her lips tantalizingly soft.

Power crackles between her fingers as she grabs my arm, my shoulder, my throat, raking her hands over every accessible bit of my skin. Wild shadows dance in the air around us as she feeds. And it's not just on my breath this time, but something much deeper. She's reaching into my soul, drawing involuntary gasps and whimpers from my mouth.

She kisses me like she wants to devour me. Her teeth catch my bottom lip, and I moan into her mouth, my hands fisting in her cloak. The sensation is an overwhelming mix of pleasure and the terrifying awareness that she could drain me completely if she wanted to.

And somehow the danger only makes me want her more.

As my life force rises through my core and out through my mouth, fueling her magic, unbearable pleasure climbs higher in its wake. It's like my body is hurtling toward a climax, ready for a release like nothing I've ever experienced.

Yes. Yes.

I *need* this, and not just because a spell demands it. I'm desperate for it. I need her fingers inside me and her mouth on my breasts. I want her to strip me naked, to make me writhe and beg and scream.

A strange darkness hovers at the edge of my vision, threatening to overwhelm me.

This is how I die, I think, my inner voice growing distant. *Willingly feeding myself to a monster.*

Dimly, I think I feel her palms on my face, her thumbs stroking my cheeks. Something in my chest hums, warm and pleasant, like the place where the binding spell has settled is purring. But then her hands are on my throat again, and I must have imagined that moment that felt almost like tenderness.

She pulls back with a gasp, breathing hard, her pupils dilated and her eyes dark around the edges. Her fingers are black, magic crackling wildly between them.

I gulp down air as feeling flows back into my limbs. The tiredness ebbs, and in its place, I'm trembling with need. That can't be it. She has to keep going, to keep taking from me until we're both satisfied.

The air has thickened so it feels like we're inside a thundercloud, like touching something might get me electrocuted.

"Did it work?" I ask shakily, forcing myself to step back.

She blinks as if coming out of a reverie, then looks down at her fingers, where those dark tendrils of magic are bright and alive.

Her lips curve. "Yes."

That smile is the same one I saw when she cornered Nick, and the stranger in Fort Langley, and Maya. I'm getting in line behind them, and the worst part is that I'm walking into her web with my eyes wide open.

"God, this feels good," she moans, tipping her head back and closing her eyes.

I can feel it in the air and see it on her face: this is the most power she's held in over a century.

And I'm the one who gave it to her. My willingness, my desire, has fed her magic in a way that a violent feeding never could.

Should I be relieved or afraid that the infamous Julia Moreau has been restored to power?

That shameful, dark part of me is thrilled and fascinated by it. I want to see what she can do. I want to watch the rest of the world fear this powerful woman.

"Let's not keep Elizabeth waiting," she purrs, smoothing her hair and straightening her cloak.

As I reach for the intercom with trembling fingers, I lick my lips. I can still taste her. I can feel the ghost of her power in my veins, marking me as hers. Most confusingly of all, I'm tight between my legs, my body clearly wanting more.

Is this really happening? Am I becoming irresistibly attracted to her, and not because of a binding spell? The craving is so real, fueled by the way she looks at me and the confidence in her touch.

This is dangerous—both for my safety and my heart. This wasn't supposed to happen. I wasn't supposed to have feelings for anyone, least of all a woman who's killed hundreds without remorse, who would likely take pleasure in crushing my heart to a pulp. She can destroy me in every possible way, and she probably will.

When this is over and the binding breaks, I think desperately, *I won't have to worry about my feelings anymore because I'll never see her again.*

But it's hard to imagine going back to normal. Everything Julia warned me about has already settled into my soul, making me crave her. Making me want her at full power so I can see what she's capable of. Making me want to keep feeding her until I find out how deep the ritual can go, until there's no part of me she hasn't touched, until I'm so far gone I can't remember who I was before her.

14

JULIA

THE IRON GATES SWING open with a groan, and we follow the winding cobblestones toward Elizabeth's mansion.

The full moon taunts us overhead. Already midnight. Time is bleeding away like a wound that will not clot.

I clench my fists, ready for whatever awaits. My renewed power pulses hot beneath my skin, and Hannah's kiss is still on my lips, tasting like cake and white wine.

Of the hundreds of people I've fed on, none have made me want to linger in the aftermath like this, to savor rather than simply take and move on. What's so different about her?

I want to believe this hunger for her is just my nature as a sanguine witch, nothing more. But some deep part of me wants to know her intimately. To do more than kiss her, and not just for the purpose of feeding.

The autumn air bites at my cheeks, clearing some of the haze. I drag my attention from Hannah's warmth beside me to the path ahead, where the house looms against the night sky. It boasts a century and a half of accumulated wealth that renders the cottages in my memory pitiful in comparison. Light glows through the large windows, spilling onto the stone steps carved with protection runes. They don't burn bright at my approach, which bodes well.

The oak doors swing open before we knock, and Hannah freezes at the threshold, as if instinct is warning her not to enter.

I press my hand to the small of her back and guide her into the foyer, where a staircase curves around a crystal chandelier. Marble cats sit glaring at us along the perimeter.

"Come in," Elizabeth calls from deeper in the house.

My relief at finally hearing a coven sister extinguishes quickly as a ripple travels down my spine. I have to stay cautious. It's possible Rebecca wasn't working alone and I'm leading us into a trap.

I curl my fingers, ready to fight if that's what it comes to.

We follow Elizabeth's voice into a parlor, where shadows dance across overstuffed furniture, an enormous Persian rug, ornate sconces on the walls, and a large bookcase beside the fireplace. The decor is more reminiscent of my time, easing my mind after spending all evening in an unfamiliar world.

Two figures sit in wingback chairs facing the flames, bone china teacups steaming beside them on end tables.

My heart stutters as they turn.

Elizabeth's black coils are now silver, and her deep brown skin is wrinkled and age-spotted. Her bright green eyes are even sharper and more knowing than I remember. She wears a flowing green gown that shimmers like a pond, and her magic is as strong as ever, making my skin prickle. She smiles, but I can't smile back because the woman seated next to her has turned my blood to ice.

"How—*dare* you," I snarl, stepping forward. Everything I want to shout gathers in my throat at once, choking me.

Rebecca is still devastating after all these years. Those dark eyes that looked at me with desire before she cursed me now glitter coldly. Her blonde hair is streaked with gray, and age has carved lines into her face that only make her more beautifully severe. Her black dress clings to curves I remember too well, and when she smiles, the wickedness of it makes me wonder how I never saw her deceit coming.

"Julia," she purrs, crossing her legs. "You look radiant. Though I suppose a century of beauty sleep will do that."

My magic coils like a serpent ready to strike. "And I have you to thank for that?"

Rebecca's answering sneer makes molten rage bubble inside me. *I'll kill her.*

The fireplace crackles, sending sparks up the chimney. The heat should be comforting after the cold night air, but instead it reminds me of another fire, another house, the night she must have whispered a curse against my skin while I was too drunk on pleasure to notice.

"Tell me how to break it," I say, flexing my fingers.

Rebecca hums, pretending to consider.

I wonder what the best way to force her to talk is. Which method of torture would be most effective on Rebecca Cooper...

"It's nice to see you after so long, Julia," Elizabeth interjects, lifting her teacup to her lips. "How did you find us?"

"Necromancy. One of Florence's descendants."

Elizabeth and Rebecca exchange a knowing look. "Maya," Elizabeth says. "She's been a difficult one to recruit. More powerful than she pretends to be."

I scan the otherwise empty room, concerned with more pressing matters than Maya. "Are you all that's left?"

"The other sisters have gone home for the night." Elizabeth takes a sip and places her cup back on the end table. "Nina moved to Portugal, and we lost Florence and Patricia to some nasty business, but the rest have stuck around."

Do I risk asking what happened to them? Witch deaths are rarely simple, and the details are often gruesome. I open my mouth but stop myself, because Rebecca's gaze has landed on Hannah like a snake spotting a mouse.

"You must be Julia's new pet." Rebecca arches an eyebrow playfully. "She's quite lovely, Julia. Lucky you."

Something white-hot roars inside me, but before I can respond, Hannah snaps, "I'm standing right here. And I'm not anyone's pet."

Rebecca's eyebrows rise. "Oh, she has claws!" She turns to address Hannah. "Julia must *love* how feisty you are. How many times has she fed on you?"

"Enough, Rebecca." I step toward her, magic sparking between my fingers.

Rebecca jumps to her feet and lifts her hands in defense, all playfulness gone.

"Not in my house," Elizabeth warns, standing too.

I stop. We stare at each other, a standoff, the room humming with magic like lightning gathering to strike. Rebecca's chin is up, her nostrils flaring.

"Still the same witch who threw a bowl at Florence on her first day in the coven, I see," Elizabeth says, regarding me over her nose.

I drop my hands, balling my fists.

It's disorienting to see my sisters aged by a century while I remain frozen at forty. My gaze catches on features that betray their years—a wrinkle here, an age spot there, a gauntness in their cheeks that were once round and full. Even the way they speak has changed, like the way Hannah speaks. They've lived through a century of seasons, love and loss, and thousands of sunsets. Time has carved lines into their faces and wisdom into their eyes while they've led rich, full lives. I, meanwhile, have had nothing.

"If I were you," I say to Rebecca, "I would've just killed me instead of wasting time sealing me inside a book."

Rebecca hums. "I've had a word with the witch responsible for said relic."

"Speaking of, we have gained a few new coven members since you left us," Elizabeth says as if I went on a little holiday. "Descendants blessed with the craft. I believe your pet knows one of them." She raises her voice and calls out, "Riley, darling, come say hello."

Riley? Was this not the name of...

Beside me, Hannah goes rigid. Her sharp inhale cuts through the room. As soft footsteps approach in the foyer, her eyes widen and her face pales.

A young woman enters wearing a crimson cloak with the hood swept back. Her power is tangible beneath my skin, hot and prickling—a formidable witch in the making.

At first, I see no relation to Rebecca. She's just a fawn, uncertain and wide-eyed, with dark curls, brown skin dusted with freckles, and a lean, strong frame. But the more I look, the more Rebecca's features peek through: striking cheekbones, straight nose, light brown eyes that calculate everything around her.

Elizabeth's teacup clinks against its saucer, the sound too loud in the silence. "The coven elected me as the new High Priestess, by the way. So she and Rebecca have been staying with me while she completes her apprenticeship. Last night was her first coven circle."

Hannah has eyes only for the girl who broke her heart. "You're really a witch," she says through clenched teeth, her eyes growing glossy.

Fire surges through me as this girl who Hannah once loved lands in our midst. Who Hannah probably *still* loves. My fingers curl into claws, but I say nothing, afraid of what comments I'll invite if I defend Hannah in front of Rebecca.

Riley's eyes become glossy too. "I'm sorry. I had to."

"Had to what?" Hannah swipes her damp cheeks with a trembling hand. "Pretend you loved me so you could plant a cursed journal on me?"

Riley shakes her head, her eyebrows pulling down with desperation. "Break up with you. I didn't know I was— That I would—" Her breaths quicken, and she looks to Rebecca as if seeking reassurance.

Rebecca strides over and places a hand on Riley's shoulder. "When Riley came into her magic, her mother passed the journal down with the intent that she keeps it guarded, as all the women in my lineage have done since I cursed you."

"I only just found out I'm a witch," Riley blurts.

Hannah glares, this explanation evidently not good enough.

Before these star-crossed lovers can lament their breakup any further, I huff, smoothing my cloak. "So you got your revenge by sealing me inside a book," I say to Rebecca. "You passed it down to keep it safe, but this girl gave it away to someone who accidentally set me free."

Riley shifts, casting a guilty glance at Rebecca before dropping her gaze to her feet. She twists her fingers together.

"Why not just kill me?" I snap.

Rebecca tilts her head. "And let you get away with what you did? No, I'd rather force you to understand how it feels to be dependent on someone. I want you to feel the terrifying intimacy of giving someone power over your very existence."

Her gaze flicks to Hannah, a satisfied smile curving her lips.

An icy sensation fills me. I should have known her curse had layers. It was carefully calculated revenge that took months to plan and execute.

"You all knew about this and didn't stop her?" I ask Elizabeth, hating how my voice wavers.

Elizabeth raises her hands. "I swear on Mother Earth, I had no idea. I thought you disappeared of your own volition again."

"This is between you and me," Rebecca says.

Hannah scoffs, gesturing at everyone in the room. "Maybe at one time. I think it's safe to say the shit hit the fan, lady."

My nails dig into my palms. Enough of this. "Spells can be broken. Tell me how."

Rebecca walks to the fireplace, gazing into it. The light catches the silver in her hair.

Elizabeth sinks back into her chair with a sigh. "Rebecca, surely after a century you've had time to cool off. At least give her a chance."

When Rebecca turns back to face us, the glimmer in her eyes sends a chill through me. "Total surrender."

Beside me, Hannah stiffens.

I narrow my eyes. "What do you mean?"

"A clever design, don't you think?" Rebecca looks like she can barely contain a smile. "After all, why would *anyone* willingly surrender to the infamous Julia Moreau? Your reputation precedes you—I made sure of it. You're a legend for being exactly who you are. That is to say, the type of person nobody would ever surrender to. So, I guess unless you've managed to corrupt this young lady, you might be...stuck forever." She lifts a shoulder, pushing her bottom lip out in mock sympathy.

My throat tightens as the full scope of her revenge becomes clear. This isn't just about punishment, but about forcing me to reap the consequences of who I am. I'm the predator who takes what I need and discards empty shells, who's never had to depend on anyone for survival. I've never had to show self-restraint or be vulnerable.

But there's something deeper lurking beneath Rebecca's satisfied expression.

I know what this is really about, even if she won't say it aloud.

Charlotte. Her sister. The woman I drained completely after she fell in love with me. The woman who trusted me to feed off her night after night, until... I don't know what happened. I lost control.

If I let myself remember, I can still feel the moment her pulse stopped. The way her fingers went slack in my hair. How her final breath tasted.

No wonder Rebecca is forcing me to make a bond with the girl I'm feeding from. After what I did to her sister, she wants me to feel the threat of loss, to feel what it's like to be fully vulnerable.

The binding spell ensures I can't just drain Hannah and move on. I have to live with the consequences of our intimacy. I have no choice but to protect her and keep her alive.

"So in the moments before you cursed me to sleep..." I say, recalling the fire in her eyes, the way my fingers slid into her, her hitched breaths as she clung to me with her thighs.

Rebecca's eyes narrow and her lip curls. She knows what I'm trying to ask. "I needed to make you vulnerable so I could place the spells on you. It's pathetic, really, how easily you fell for seduction."

"Minx," I snarl. Of course it wasn't real. I was a fool to think Rebecca would want me.

Hannah clears her throat beside me, pulling my attention back. "What do you mean by *surrender*?"

Rebecca waves her hand vaguely. "The word is what you make of it. Royals have used the spell to subjugate people, to force them into obedience. In the case of Julia..." She studies me, her mouth twisting as she considers. "Well, given her particular nature as a sanguine witch, perhaps the ultimate surrender would be offering one's life entirely. Allowing her to drain you."

"No." The word tears from my throat.

The room goes silent except for the crackling fire. All eyes turn to me, but I only see Rebecca's raised eyebrow, the surprise and satisfaction flickering across her features.

"The great Julia Moreau, refusing the perfect feeding opportunity?"

"If I drain her, we'll both die," I snap. "That's how a binding spell works."

"True." Rebecca shrugs. "Well, this isn't for me to figure out. I don't care if and how you break it. But you wanted to know how, and I've just told you. Complete surrender is your only path to freedom."

My jaw clenches. What does this mean? Am I to reduce Hannah to a hollow shell? Hope she allows me to drain her to near death?

"And if I refuse to surrender?" Hannah asks.

"Then you'll spend the rest of your short life as Julia's pet," Rebecca replies. "Bound by magic you can't escape. She'll keep feeding from you to sustain her power, and you'll grow weaker and more dependent with each feeding."

A slow death. A torturous end that could take years to reach its conclusion, depending on how much control I have. I imagine her growing pale and listless, her body weakening, her hair falling out as she clings to life while still begging me to keep feeding on her.

How often would I need to feed on her? Every few days? Each time, she will weaken. Each time, I will have to choose between my survival and hers. And Rebecca knows exactly what choice I've always made before.

"I still think you could have gotten your revenge without dragging some poor victim into this," Elizabeth says, sounding about as tired as someone who has been hearing about Rebecca's grudge for an entire century.

Rebecca shoots her a glare before returning her attention to Hannah. "You could always ask Julia to end it quickly when the suffering becomes unbearable. I'm sure she'd accommodate you. She has *much* experience with murder."

Hannah flinches, and rage boils in my veins. Rebecca is trying to make her fear me even more than she already does.

And it's working. I can see the growing horror in Hannah's eyes as she realizes exactly what kind of trap she's in.

"Enough," Elizabeth says, barely audible. "You've made your point. No need to terrorize the girl further."

Rebecca opens her mouth, but I cut her off before she can bring up Charlotte and do more damage. Good Lord, I *cannot* let Hannah find out what happened to Charlotte. "If that's all the information you have, we'll be off."

I have no idea where we'll go, but I need to get away from here and think. My insides feel like a raging fire, the smoke muddling my thoughts.

Rebecca checks the grandfather clock in the corner. "I should turn in. Thank you for hosting such a lovely circle tonight, Elizabeth. The evening turned out better than I ever dreamed."

She flashes me one more cold smile on her way past, and what I wouldn't give to blast it right off her face. But I must be patient. I'll have my opportunity to get revenge once I'm free from her spell.

Before leaving the parlor, she turns back, stone-faced. "Try not to drain this one dry before morning, Julia."

I flex my fingers and say nothing, unwilling to open that box by responding.

Her perfume lingers in the air after she's gone. Jasmine. It makes me nauseous.

I turn away to find Riley and Hannah staring at each other, a silent conversation passing between them. It adds to my annoyance. This is not the time or place for juvenile love stories.

Rebecca's slow footsteps retreat up the curved staircase. *Creak, creak, creak.*

Only once the sound has faded does Elizabeth say quietly, "I don't wish to get in the middle of whatever business you and Rebecca have with each other, Julia. You're both my coven sisters, and I open my doors to both of you. Stay. I'll consult the grimoire and do what I can to help."

Relief trickles through me. Any help by a coven sister is welcome in this desperate situation.

Hannah and I make eye contact, fleeting and tentative.

In that brief glance, I see as much confusion as I feel raging inside me. Somehow, she's going to have to offer me everything...and trust me not to take it all.

15

HANNAH

*T*OTAL SURRENDER?

I can't do this. I can't make myself that vulnerable for someone, least of all Julia.

Panic claws up my throat, suffocating me.

What did she do to make Rebecca exact such complicated revenge? Am I teetering on the edge of death with every second I spend with her?

"I—I need to think," I stammer.

I bolt for the door, my feet carrying me into the cold October night before my brain catches up. The wind bites my bare arms and shoulders as I stumble down Elizabeth's stone steps and into the darkness beyond the manicured gardens.

I want to run to the road and hitchhike somewhere, anywhere, and pretend none of this happened. But the binding spell tugs hard at my chest—this magic leash that won't let me stray too far from my personal monster.

I grit my teeth to keep from grunting in pain. Fighting the pull with every step, I reach a dense forest beside Elizabeth's property. Evergreens scrape my arms and legs as if trying to help the spell drag me back, but I keep going.

When the pain becomes blinding, I lean against a tree, clutching my chest. Every cell in my body is screaming for me to go back to the house to ease this agony. I wheeze each breath, refusing to give in.

Julia hasn't followed. Why would she? She knows I can't escape. I'm trapped in her orbit like a satellite, destined to either burn up on reentry or slowly freeze in the darkness.

My heart stumbles, like it's struggling to stay beating.

"Dammit," I hiss.

I take three careful steps closer to Elizabeth's mansion, which is just a faint glow peeking through gaps in the trees. My heart beats a little easier, so I stop, breathing through the agony.

Branches creak. Dying leaves rustle. Somewhere, a critter chirps, making me flinch.

Sweat prickles my hairline, but the night is biting. I shiver, still in my freaking camisole and leggings.

An oak tree sprawls beside me, its branches stretching out to offer a place to sit. I brace against it, feeling the rough bark and soft moss under my clammy palms as I ease down onto a thick branch.

Knowing Julia must be experiencing the same pain makes it easier to stay put. She deserves this. I don't know why Rebecca did this to her, but in this moment, I hate her as much as Rebecca does for putting me through this torture.

"Hannah!"

Riley's voice.

Her silhouette appears through the trunks, chasing after me, her dark curls wild in the wind. Part of me wants to stand and keep running, but my traitorous heart still skips a beat at the sight of her.

She stops a stride away, out of breath. The moonlight catches the tears on her cheeks, making them look like silver scars.

"I need you to understand," she says between breaths.

"Understand what? How you lied to me for two years? How you gave me a *curse* and then abandoned me to deal with the consequences?"

"I only found out I was a witch three weeks ago." Her voice is strong. "One day, I was normal, and the next, I was setting things on fire. Hurting myself. I nearly burned the whole house down in my sleep."

That explains the marks on her arms.

I can feel the unnatural heat radiating from her, and when I look into her eyes, there's a tinge that wasn't there before. Red-gold, like a phoenix.

"Magic doesn't always manifest," Riley continues. "My mom isn't a witch, and neither was my grandma. I'm the first since Rebecca to have power, and she showed up at my door like she'd been waiting for it. She took me to Elizabeth's to teach me how to control it before I—" Her voice breaks, and she draws a shaky breath. "Before I hurt the people I love."

I swallow hard. "You could have told me."

She steps closer, and her familiar lilac scent envelops me. At least that hasn't changed. "And say what, Han? Turns out I'm a witch and I have to leave you to join a coven and learn how to control my powers?"

I scowl at the sarcasm. "Why did you give me that journal?"

In the faint moonlight, her expression crumbles. She comes to sit beside me on the big oak branch, close enough that I can feel her body heat. "I didn't understand what it was. I just knew it was an heirloom I was supposed to keep safe, and I wanted you to have something meaningful. I thought it was romantic to give you poems written in a book that had been in my family for over a century."

I blow out a breath, my anger deflating. "And I burned it."

"That's my fault. I hurt you."

I grimace, remembering the bonfire and the bitter satisfaction of watching our memories turn to ash. "And I...might have acted melodramatically."

She cracks a small smile, which I can't help returning. For a moment, we're just us again—two girls who fell in love over a hot summer, who spent our mornings tangled in bedsheets, who planned a future that will never exist.

But reality crashes back as tears spill down her cheeks. "Now you're caught in a war between ancient witches, and it's my fault. I never meant for this to happen. If I hadn't given you that journal—"

"You didn't know it was cursed," I say automatically. It sounds like forgiveness, but I don't know why I said it. I don't forgive her.

Riley reaches over and places her hand on my knee. Her touch is warm and gentle. "I've missed you like crazy. I've wanted to call you and explain everything."

"But you didn't."

"I couldn't. This is bigger than us, bigger than what I wanted. Rebecca made that very clear."

"So you chose them over me."

"I chose keeping you safe over being with you. I can't be with someone who isn't a witch." Her hand closes over mine, and I let her take it despite my anger. "I still love you, Hannah."

The words I've been desperate to hear feel hollow. "Love doesn't matter when we can't be together."

"I know." She leans closer, her free hand coming up to cup my cheek. "But I want you to know how I feel."

I meet her eyes. She's so beautiful it hurts. Her presence is so comforting and familiar that it's like putting on my favorite pajamas after an excruciatingly long day. But there's a deep pain behind my ribs, like she took my whole heart with her when she left, and now she's here trying to stuff it back into place.

"Riley," I whisper, not sure what to say or how I even feel.

She makes a small, soft noise.

I bite my lip, studying the familiar features of her perfect face. Her eyes, her nose, her lips.

She leans in.

I don't pull away.

I've missed her too much to say no. And I need the comfort of her lips on mine right now.

So I lean in to meet her.

Her lips taste like peppermint tea and simpler times. I sigh into her mouth and melt into her, wishing we could go back to normal. Her soft hands brush over my bruises and scrapes, gently and reverently. It's the sort of caress Julia has never offered—healing instead of bruising.

Can I pretend Julia never happened? Can I forget her taste, her magic, the way it feels when she touches my skin?

Something twists in my chest. Her dark eyes and predatory smile flash across my mind's eye. And suddenly Riley's kiss feels too soft, too sweet—nothing compared to the way Julia kissed me like she wanted to devour my soul.

Why do I want that? Shouldn't I *want* Riley's gentleness instead? I'm not supposed to want the monster over the sweet girl who's here making sure I'm okay.

But Julia is all I can picture. Her hands and mouth are all I want. As terrifying as that is, it's the truth.

I pull away and stand up, breathless and dizzy. "I can't do this."

Riley stands too, stepping in to cup my cheeks tenderly. "I don't expect you to forgive me right away—"

"This isn't about forgiveness." I step back, wrapping my arms around myself. "There's a literal magic spell connecting me to someone else."

"That spell isn't love, Hannah. It's supernatural dependency." Her tone is surprisingly sharp.

"And what we had?" I snap back. "Was that real, or were you playing a part?"

"It was real. It still is."

"Then why does it feel like I never knew you at all?"

Riley's face falls. "Because I was trying to protect you from this world. From witches like—" She stops herself, but I know what she was going to say.

"Witches like Julia?"

"She's dangerous, Han. Whatever you think you feel for her, it's not real. Sanguine witches feed on more than just life force. They feed on desire. She's probably already started changing you, making you want things you wouldn't normally want."

The truth of it hits like cold water. Have I been corrupted? Is my attraction to Julia just another symptom of her influence?

It's possible. Probable, even. What else would explain how much I want her to mark me up, to claim me and feed on me until I'm gasping for breath?

Riley's warnings should terrify me. Logically, I know that.

But Julia is the most powerful person I've ever met, and when she looks at me like I belong to her, I've never felt more alive. I want to know more about who she is, and I want to do more than kiss her.

"I need time to figure this out," I say. "This is all a lot to process."

Riley nods, though disappointment is written across her features. "Be careful with her, Hannah."

I nod firmly and say nothing more. She hesitates, then takes her cue, leaving me alone with her warning lingering in the air.

But even knowing how dangerous Julia is, even with terror coursing through my veins, I can't help my attraction to her. Watching her exert power over other people, making men and other witches fear her, is more exhilarating than anything.

Moments after Riley's footsteps disappear beneath the rustling leaves, the binding spell eases its grip suddenly, loosening in my chest.

My breath catches. Julia must be coming closer.

I should back away. Keep this distance between us. *Anything* but stand here waiting for her like prey that's already accepted its fate.

But I'm tired of protecting myself behind walls that only leave me more alone. I was determined never to be vulnerable again after Riley left, and where did that get me? Bound to an ancient witch by magic I don't understand, caught between a woman who lied to protect me and one who might kill me.

I have to surrender.

There are probably several ways to interpret the word, but only one keeps circling my mind like a moth to flame.

If that's what it takes to be free, then I'll do it. It's the only way I can be free of magic, free from Julia, free to return to my safe, ordinary world where monsters don't exist and ancient witches don't kiss you like they're trying to steal your soul.

That's what I tell myself, anyway.

But the truth pulses hot beneath the lie: I want this. I want her hands on me, her mouth claiming mine, the intimacy of giving her everything under the full moon. Freedom is the excuse I'm using to justify doing what I've wanted since she first touched me. Maybe I'm surrendering to break the spell, or maybe I'm surrendering because some reckless part of me wants to be hers, even if it's just for tonight.

When Julia emerges from the shadows between trees, moving with that effortless grace that makes my pulse skip, I don't back away or tell her to leave. I've been running from the truth all night. The binding spell might have brought us together, but this ache low in my belly and the way my heart races when she looks at me is all me.

So, I'll surrender. This is how I take control over an uncontrollable situation, and if I stop lying to myself, this is what I want more than anything.

16

JULIA

I COULD HAVE STAYED in the house and let Hannah have a moment with the girl who broke her heart. But the thought of her out here without me, hurting, choosing someone else, is unbearable. She's mine to protect, mine to hurt, mine to heal until this spell breaks. And I do not share.

I stalk through the dark forest, following the pull of the binding spell toward Hannah. The October wind moans through the skeletal branches above, carrying the scent of decay and damp earth as winter approaches.

Rebecca thinks she's won. The smug satisfaction radiating from her in the parlor, not to mention the way she savored every detail of my helplessness, all confirms what I already knew: she believes her binding spell has defanged me.

She's going to learn a hard lesson in how wrong she is.

As soon as I figure out how to break this pathetic leash, she will find out what happens to those who try to cage me. A century of planning, and she made one fatal miscalculation: she assumed I would grow soft in my imprisonment. She thought guilt over Charlotte would dim my capacity for vengeance.

If anything, this injustice has honed my edges to razor sharpness.

Riley stalks toward me in the other direction. I flex my fingers, rage boiling in my veins. What does she think she's doing? Hannah isn't hers anymore.

I grab her arm as we pass, and she shoots me a glare, her breath catching.

"Did you touch her?"

She goes rigid. "That's none of your—"

"*Did—you—touch—her?*" I ask again, each word sharp.

Riley lifts her chin. "What if I did?"

"You don't deserve her," I growl. "And if you *ever* hurt her again, you'll learn why your ancestor trapped me for a century."

She rips her arm away. "Of the two of us, I'm not the one Hannah has to worry about."

My skin prickles as she walks back to the house. I should have come out here sooner.

I keep going and find Hannah standing in front of the silhouette of an ancient oak tree, barely visible in its shadow. The full moon has cast everything in silver and black. Her bright hair is loose around her shoulders, and the whites of her eyes gleam. Her breath mists, and she's shivering, her tight clothes offering no warmth at all. She looks like a woodland sprite, beautiful and fragile and utterly out of place.

"I didn't come all the way to Elizabeth's for you to freeze to death," I say as I walk closer. "Come inside and we can figure this out."

"Figure out *what*? We know what we need to do. Rebecca told us."

"Elizabeth is consulting the grimoire." My voice is flat and defeated. A heaviness settles over me, as if being alone in the woods with her has finally given me permission to feel how hopeless this all is.

Hannah lets out a one-note laugh. "You expect her to find a loophole?"

I don't, but I refuse to admit it. The truth is, Rebecca is a skilled witch, and she crafts every spell with precision.

"What were you doing out here with Riley?" I ask, the question spilling from my lips.

She huffs, like she finds it amusing. "Did you really come here to ask me about Riley?"

I grind my teeth, watching her fidget with the hem of her tiny chemise. Her hands are trembling.

"Why do you care what she and I were doing?" she asks.

Heat floods my cheeks. "I don't want anyone interfering with what needs to be done to break the binding spell."

A pause. "I see."

She's still playing with her chemise, giving me glimpses of the smooth, pale skin at her hips.

"I just want this to be over, Julia," she says, barely audible.

I watch, frozen in place, as she pulls the delicate fabric over her head and lets it fall to the forest floor. There's nothing underneath. Just her perfect, round breasts, her nipples hard peaks in the wintry air. Her chest rises and falls, each breath a puff of white mist.

The sight of her bare skin steals the breath from my lungs. She's luminous in the moonlight, a goddess standing in the harsh darkness.

The wind picks up, sending dead leaves skittering across the forest floor. The ancient trees seem to lean closer, as if drawn to witness this. The old magic in this place ripples beneath my skin, responding to my hunger, the earth itself recognizing me. Perhaps it's trying to warn Hannah against this.

"Don't." The word comes out rough. "Do you have any idea what you're doing?"

"I'm surrendering." Her hands move to her bottoms, and I'm helpless to look away as she slides them down her long legs, revealing her pale skin inch by inch.

In the next beat of my heart, she's standing confidently before me, completely bare and vulnerable. The sight of her naked body ignites a flame inside me that threatens to consume everything. I follow the line of her throat down to her round breasts, down her belly to the soft curves of her hips, and between her legs.

"If breaking the spell requires me to submit to you, then here I am," she says. "Yours."

My heart beats faster. To hear this beautiful woman speak those words awakens a deep, ravenous hunger that's been building inside me since the moment I first touched her.

But underneath the desire, something else grips my chest. I've felt this hunger before. The last time, it ended with Charlotte's lifeless body beneath me. This is how it started with her—this intoxicating willingness, this beautiful surrender. And I destroyed her.

Hands at her sides, Hannah stretches out her fingers as if opening herself to me. She's shivering, goosebumps rising all over her perfect skin.

"Hannah, it's freezing out."

She steps closer. "So warm me up."

I step closer too. "We can find another way to—"

"I want this, Julia." Her eyes are dark, her pupils dilated.

The temperature drops. My breath mists between us, mingling with hers. Around us, the forest has gone silent. No rustling leaves, no distant owl calls. Even nature knows to hold its breath.

My feet will not move. Do I want to ruin her the way I ruined Charlotte? She's too good, too perfect, too innocent for what I am.

But the hunger in her eyes mirrors my own, and it's clear she wants this as much as I do.

We passed the point of no return long ago, whether I admit it or not. "Hannah..."

Before I know what I'm doing, I'm grabbing her and pulling her flush against me, kissing her hard.

She kisses me back hungrily, sliding her hands under my cloak and gripping my bodice. Power flares beneath my skin like fire. The trees creak and groan as if bending in an invisible wind.

Her heartbeat pounds against my chest, rapid and strong—at least for now. *How quickly that can change.* Already she is trembling in my arms, fragile in the harsh night air.

But I silence my doubts, letting any sense of what I should or shouldn't do dissolve.

I walk her backward until she bumps into the oak tree. She whimpers at the contact with the rough bark, and I press closer, trapping her against it.

I pull back enough to elicit a little gasp, savoring the fullness in her lips and the hunger in her eyes. My head is foggy, desire guiding my actions.

I grab her hips and spin her around. "Hands on the tree. Arch your back for me."

She braces her hands against the bark, breathing hard. The moonlight paints silver streaks across her back, highlighting every curve and hollow.

Her perfect obedience makes me throb between my legs.

I slide my hands around her front and squeeze her breasts, feeling her nipples under my palms. She lets out a sweet, needy exhale.

Finally. How long have I wanted to touch her this way? Since I first set eyes on her?

The flame inside me grows as I drag my palms down her waist and around her hips. Her skin is cold and pebbled with goosebumps. I trail my fingers down her spine, watching her shiver.

With one hand on her hip, I trace the other up her arm, over her shoulder, and around her throat, squeezing enough to make her tense. "Do you know what you're doing? I could drain you."

"But you won't," she says, breathless.

"How do you know?" I tighten my grip, feeling her pulse flutter beneath my fingers.

A pause. "I'm trusting you."

Foolish girl.

I kiss and nip her neck. She tastes heavenly, like everything I've been craving. I begin murmuring the incantation against her skin, letting the Latin words vibrate through her body. With each syllable, the air around us thickens and becomes charged with static.

Her breath hitches. She trembles harder. With a moan, she leans back against me, her head tilted to expose more of her neck.

I'm aching between my legs as I kiss her neck and shoulder, my body and my power responding to her submission with equal hunger.

Slowly, I move the hand at her hip inward, trailing my fingers over the soft skin of her thigh.

"I want your fingers inside me, Julia," she begs, gripping my wrist and guiding my hand between her legs.

Her desire coats my fingers. She's soaking wet, her body betraying how much she truly wants this.

"So ready for me," I purr into her ear. "Such a good pet."

She moans as I slide two fingers into her folds, the sound rising into the still forest.

"Yes," she breathes. "That's so good..."

She releases my wrist to reach up and slide her hand around the back of my head, leaning back into me as I rub slow circles between her legs.

My power drinks hungrily as I murmur the incantation against her skin. My head grows cloudy. My magic recognizes how willingly she's offered herself, and it's purring inside me. It's been so long since I've fed from someone this intimately, so long since I've drunk my fill that any sense of restraint dissipates on the cold wind. The thought should frighten me, but Hannah's essence is making me forget why I should care.

Time to bring her to total surrender. I'm going to take what I need and enjoy every second of it.

I withdraw my hand from between her legs, ignoring her whimper of protest, and wrap my fingers around the back of her neck. I push her forward so she's bent over the large branch sweeping out from the trunk, her breasts pressed against the bark.

"Spread your legs for me. Show me how much you want this."

She gasps, grabbing the branch for support. Her hair falls forward, already tangled from my touch. The position leaves her completely exposed, vulnerable, *mine*.

"Beautiful..." I run my free hand down her spine. "You have no idea how irresistible you look like this."

The rough bark has left red scrapes on her tender skin, which I want to lick.

With my foot, I nudge her legs further apart. She lets me, spreading her stance and leaving the most intimate parts of her ready for me.

"Stay like this. Don't move until I tell you to."

"Y-yes."

I'm growing wet, throbbing with need as anticipation burns inside me like molten metal. The scent of her arousal meets my nose, making my head spin.

I thrust two fingers into her from behind. She's so wet and ready for me that I slide in easily, and she welcomes me with a soft, desperate cry.

The feeling of being inside her makes the flame within me grow into a blazing fire, roaring out of control.

The forest floor beneath us pulses. Bare branches overhead shift and sway, creating shadows that dance across Hannah's skin. Dark tendrils curl from my hands and arms. They grip her hips and wrap around her waist, holding her to me.

A little whimper escapes her, as if she's trying to suppress the sounds of her pleasure.

"Don't hold back," I say. "I want to hear you scream."

As I curl my fingers and stroke her inner walls, she obeys, crying out into the night. The noise sends a wave of pleasure through me. The dark tendrils tighten around her, leaving pink marks.

"That's it. Take my fingers. You were made to be claimed by me."

I stroke her inner walls again and again, drinking in her moans, making her whole body shake with the rhythm. She's tight around my fingers, each movement drawing fresh sounds from her lips.

The ache between my legs grows unbearable.

I pull my fingers out and glide them over that sensitive pearl, which is swollen with desire. She shivers and cries out, her knees buckling. Only my grip on her waist keeps her on her feet.

"Julia—oh God—" She can barely form words, her voice broken.

I lean down to kiss and bite her back as I fuck her, my teeth finding spots that make her whimper. She tastes mouth-wateringly good. I can feel her ecstasy feeding me, her pleasure radiating through the woods.

She's making incomprehensible sounds, a string of curses and moans flooding from her lips. Her knees weaken further, her whole body trembling as she sinks lower.

I spank her, a sharp slap that echoes through the forest. "I told you to stay until I'm finished with you, pet."

"Y-yes," she stammers, straightening her legs. The submission in her voice, the way she immediately obeys despite her body's protests, sends another spike of hunger through me.

I reward her by thrusting my fingers back inside. I pull out to toy with her, then push back inside, finding a rhythm that makes her moan my name.

"I'm going to come," she gasps between ragged breaths. "Julia—"

I pull my fingers out, denying her the release. "Good girl. Turn around."

I spin her to face me, and she's a vision of desperate need, her face flushed and sweaty, her hair wild, her lips swollen. I push her down onto the carpet of leaves, following her to cover her body with mine.

The cold ground makes her gasp and arch beneath me, pressing against my still-clothed body.

I straddle her hips, looking down at the beautiful creature who's somehow become mine tonight. Her eyes are dark, her pupils wide, and there's something almost worshipful in the way she looks up at me.

I need to make sure this is going to work. That she's fully submitting to me.

"You're mine, and mine alone," I tell her, my voice rough with desire. "Say it."

"I'm yours," she whispers.

I grab her face, holding her gaze. "Mine to touch. Mine to fuck. Mine to consume until you're shaking and spent."

"Completely yours," she gasps.

The tingle beneath my skin comes alive like a rushing river. My power is ravenous, and it's time to finish the best meal it's ever had.

This is going to work. With the way she's given herself to me, it *has* to work.

I push her thighs apart. The moonlight catches on the moisture between her legs, making her glisten. She's so radiant, so perfectly offered, that for a moment I can only stare.

"Beg me for it," I say.

Her chest is heaving. She's shivering in the cold. "Please. I can't take it anymore."

I lean down over her, resting my hand over her center, teasing her.

"Please," she says more insistently, writhing beneath me. "I've been so good for you."

I slide my hand, now soaked with her desire, back between her legs. This time, I don't hold back, sweeping my index finger relentlessly over her most sensitive part.

"Tell me you don't belong to anyone else."

"I d-don't belong to anyone else." Her voice is strained and desperate.

"Tell me you exist for my pleasure."

"I exist for your pleasure."

"Good girl. Now let yourself go. Don't suppress anything. I want all of it."

I lean down and capture her mouth with mine, drinking in her hitched breaths and whimpers. The leaves beneath Hannah curl and wither, crumbling to dry dust, as if my magic is accelerating their decay.

The incantation flows from my lips between kisses. I work my fingers quickly over her center, faster, faster, pausing to thrust inside before tracing another circle.

She arches beneath me, her hands fisting on my cloak, pulling me closer. The forest floor is cold and damp, but it doesn't matter.

A shiver rolls through her.

"Yes—yes—" she gasps, the words smothered as I crush my lips against hers.

I feel the moment she breaks apart, convulsing with pleasure.

Dark tendrils of magic snap toward her like greedy fingers, pulling her life force into me. They swirl and twist in the air, wrapping around her and holding her close. The temperature plummets. Ice crystallizes on the dead leaves beneath Hannah, spreading outward in patterns.

I drink in her climax, feeding voraciously as her ecstasy flows into me. Never have I tasted anything so good. Never have I felt such an all-consuming energy surge into my body, flooding every cell like fire.

I moan, pleasure coursing through me. I keep drinking, sucking, taking everything she has to offer. Her essence is utterly intoxicating.

And fuck, it's good. *She's* good—the best I've ever had in decades of feeding.

It's addictive, this pure connection. I can feel her flowing into me, warm and willing.

It's even better than Charlotte used to feel.

The thought jolts through me like a warning bell. This is how it happened before—this moment where I knew I should stop and chose not to. Where pleasure eclipsed conscience. Where hunger won over everything else.

I should pull back. I *need* to pull back.

I don't. I can't.

Not yet.

Not when she tastes this good, not when her essence fills the empty spaces in my soul.

As her orgasm subsides, I keep drinking. She's gasping into my mouth, writhing beneath me, her thighs clamped around my hips like she's trying to keep me as close as possible. Her nails rake down my back through my cloak, leaving trails of fire in their wake.

More. I need more. My power demands it, singing with greed as it tastes something it's been denied for a century. Hannah's energy is like sunlight after endless darkness, and I'm drowning in it.

And then something shifts in Hannah's breathing—less pleasure, more desperation. The dark tendrils between us shudder. Branches creak as if trying to reach for me. Her fingers dig into my shoulders, not with passion, but with something that might be panic. The change is subtle, but I've felt it before.

Stop. It's time to stop.

A voice in the back of my mind, small and desperate, fighting to be heard.

Through the haze of power and pleasure, it keeps whispering, begging me to pull back. This is exactly what Rebecca wanted—for me to prove I'm still the monster who killed Charlotte. For me to drain another innocent woman who offered herself to me and confirm that I haven't learned a thing.

But the voice is too quiet, and Hannah's essence is too sweet, and the power flowing into me feels too good to stop. I'm starving, and I have been starving for over a hundred years, and she's offering herself so completely...

Hannah's movements grow weaker, her gasps turning shallow. The warm flow of energy falters.

She goes limp beneath me.

The sudden stillness breaks through my frenzy like a splash of ice water.

"Fuck." I jerk back, gasping, and the tendrils of darkness snap with a deep, sharp echo that reverberates through the forest.

The magic cuts off like a door slamming. The silence is deafening—no wind, no pulse of power. Just the sound of my ragged breathing. Frost has spread outward, climbed every tree, and encased every branch and leaf.

Her face is ghostly in the moonlight. Her eyes are closed. Her head lolls to the side, her arms falling slack on the decayed leaves.

My hands shake as I press my fingers to her throat in search of a pulse—the same ones that are still wet with her desire. Veins of darkness form webs under my skin.

Monster, snarls a voice in my head.

But her pulse is there, steady but weak, beating against my fingertips. Her chest rises and falls in shallow breaths, but she's unconscious.

"Hannah?" I brush her hair back from her face.

No response. Her skin is pale, almost translucent, and there are dark circles under her eyes that weren't there before.

The frost begins to melt, the ground around us crackling, water running off the trees in rivulets.

I sit back, breathing hard. I'm uncomfortably aware of how soaked my undergarments are. In other circumstances, this would not be over, and it would not have ended in one of us losing consciousness.

But this isn't other circumstances.

I clutch my chest, searching for a sign of the binding spell. Did Hannah's surrender break it? How can I tell?

I study my blackened fingers. Magic crackles between them, and I feel it stirring properly for the first time since I awoke. It's strong—perhaps stronger than ever.

Have I done it? Am I free to leave this girl, this place, this century of imprisonment? Free to find Rebecca and show her what real power looks like?

A laugh bubbles up inside me, erupting from my lips. It fills the forest, making crows rise in a flurry from a nearby tree, cawing.

God, this power feels good.

Standing on unsteady legs, I straighten out my clothes. Hannah remains motionless on the ground, her breathing the only sign of life. She'll recover. I somehow stopped in time and didn't drain her completely.

I take one step, then pause.

I might not have drained her, but what a waste of restraint it would be to have her die from the cold after all that.

So, I take off my cloak and lay it on the forest floor. I move her onto it, wrapping it around her for warmth.

With my new power, I light a fire beside her for good measure.

How sweet it is to have my magic so responsive.

I turn away from her still form, my heart beating stronger than it has in over a century.

Rebecca is somewhere in that big house, smug in her victory, unaware that her perfect trap has snapped open.

It's finally time to get revenge.

17

HANNAH

WARMTH. SMOKE.

I float in the space between sleep and waking, like I'm swimming up from the depths of a dark ocean. My body is heavy and disconnected, making even opening my eyes feel impossible.

A crackling sound reaches me. Orange light bleeds through my closed eyelids.

Something is wrapped around me. Fabric that smells like woodsmoke and apple cinnamon.

Slowly, sensation returns. My fingers and toes are no longer numb. The forest floor beneath me is damp and cold, but whatever covers me has trapped enough warmth to stop me from shivering.

How long have I been out?

My skin tingles everywhere, and I'm throbbing between my legs. My lips are swollen from Julia's kisses. Heat floods my cheeks as I remember how desperately I begged for her, how good it felt to come apart and let her take control, and how shamelessly I spread myself beneath her.

I've never experienced anything that intense before. Her power seemed to flow between us, consuming me, connecting us on a level I didn't know was possible. Like she was inside my skin and my mind.

I keep my eyes closed for a long moment, reliving every detail. Her body pinning me down. The way I arched into her, giving her everything, letting her take and take until...

My eyelids fly open.

I sit up with a gasp, and whatever is covering me slides off my shoulders.

I'm completely naked.

A fire is crackling beside me.

"Julia?"

My voice carries into the darkness, swallowed by the trees. No answer. Just the pop and hiss of burning wood and the whisper of wind through bare branches.

I look down at what was covering me. Black fabric pools around my hips. Her cloak.

Something twists behind my ribs. She left her cloak to keep me warm. Built me a fire. That was...thoughtful.

But where *is* she?

I grab the fabric and pull it around my shoulders, suddenly desperate for the illusion of safety it provides. My fingers tremble as I clutch it closed over my breasts.

My chest tightens. Each shallow breath comes faster than the last. I press my palm to my sternum, trying to feel past the thunder of my heartbeat to the binding spell beneath.

Is it still there? Did we break it?

I can't tell if this crushing sensation is magic or panic.

Aching everywhere, thirsty, and groggy from passing out, I scan the small clearing for my clothes. They're discarded right where I shed them when I stripped down for Julia.

So she built a fire, left her cloak, but couldn't be bothered to gather my clothes while I was unconscious? Or freaking *stay* with me?

I bite my lip to keep from screaming.

She *left*.

The minute she drank her fill of my essence and the spell presumably broke, she abandoned me, unconscious, naked, still wet between my thighs.

Hot fury roils inside me. Not just at Julia, but at myself for being so desperate. For feeling powerful in my surrender, for feeling chosen, for confusing magic with desire. For spending even half a second thinking what happened was meaningful, even though I *knew* we only did it to break a spell.

My cheeks burn with humiliation. I've never felt so used. Whatever that sex meant or didn't mean, I deserve better than to be left on the forest floor.

My hands shake as I pull on my clothes, fury building with each jerky movement. The fabric is rough against my oversensitive skin. Every muscle and every inch of skin aches from what we did, from how thoroughly she claimed me.

I leave her cloak on the ground and storm through the trees toward Elizabeth's house. Branches catch my hair and claw at my skin, and I welcome the pain because at least it's real and mine, not tangled up in her magic or her touch. My body is still singing with the aftershocks of what we did, and I hate it. I hate how good it felt.

The trees blur past me. My feet pound harder against the frosty ground. My breaths rasp so loudly I can't hear anything else. I want to find her to scream at her, to make her look at what she did and see me as something more than a convenient body to feed from. I want her to feel even the tiniest shred of remorse, if she's even fucking capable of that.

At last, I burst through the front door, my pulse pounding in my neck. I pause, listening.

A thump comes from upstairs. Then, a choking sound.

I race up the stairs two at a time.

Julia's voice prickles my ears, but I can't make out what she's saying. I follow the sound through an open door into a dimly lit guest room.

Julia stands between the four-poster bed and the ensuite, a stride away from Rebecca, her outstretched hand crackling with magic. The invisible force pins Rebecca against the bookshelf without a touch. Rebecca's feet dangle, her eyes bulging as she claws at the unseen noose suspending her. She's dressed in nothing but a long blue T-shirt, clearly hauled straight from bed.

"Final chance to help me," Julia snarls.

Seeing her hair neat and her body clothed while I was lying naked on the ground a moment ago makes my face burn even hotter.

"Julia!" I shout, my voice hoarse with anger.

She spins. Her expression is wild, her eyes dark around the edges. Her magic flares when she sees me, darkening her fingers before she controls it. Then she casts me that wicked smile I'm beginning to hate.

"You're awake." Her tone is maddeningly casual, as if she didn't leave me for dead in the woods.

"Next time you want to abandon someone after fucking them unconscious," I snarl, "know that wrapping them in your cloak doesn't make you less of a monster."

Something unreadable flickers in her eyes before her expression hardens. She releases her magical hold on Rebecca, who crumples to the floor with a gasping cough.

As Rebecca wheezes and clutches her throat, Julia scans me up and down, her nostrils flaring. Her gaze lingers on my neck, bitten and bruised, and then my hair, tangled with leaves and twigs, before settling on my eyes. "I needed to confirm that the binding spell had been severed."

"By *leaving*?" My fists are clenched so tight that my nails bite into my palms. "By seeing how far away from me you could get?"

Her gaze turns frosty. "What did you expect? That we would embrace tenderly after the spell broke?"

Shame washes over me so fiercely that my eyes prickle. I offered her my body, my life force, my submission, and she took it all before abandoning me the second she thought she was free.

It's not that I wanted to wake up in her arms. Not really. But I didn't expect to be abandoned.

My throat is too tight to say any of this, so I just stare at her, blinking back the hot prickling in my eyes. I refuse to cry and let her see how deeply this cuts.

She drops her gaze and turns back to Rebecca's crumpled form. "Anyway, it didn't work. We're still bound."

The words take a moment to sink in. A heavy sensation settles in my chest, and I step back. "That can't be. I—I submitted like I was supposed to. Gave you everything."

"It wasn't enough."

On the floor, Rebecca lifts a hand toward Julia, magic crackling. But Julia is too quick, sweeping Rebecca's hand away without even touching her. Rebecca grunts and hits the bookshelf again, blood trickling from her nose.

My stomach drops. That feeding has clearly made Julia stronger. Too strong.

Footsteps thunder closer in the hall. Elizabeth and Riley burst through the doorway, out of breath. Elizabeth is wearing a black nightgown edged with lace, with a black satin robe flowing open. Riley is still in jeans and a white top under that crimson cloak, like she was nowhere near ready to sleep despite the late hour.

"Enough!" Elizabeth roars. With a sweep of her arms, she forces Julia and Rebecca apart, sending them flying to opposite walls. The whole room shudders, and books fall from the shelves.

"Hannah." Riley's voice breaks on my name, no more than a whisper.

I turn.

She's staring at me like I'm something ruined. Her hand covers her mouth, and her wide, watery eyes trace over every visible mark Julia left. The bruises from her fingers and teeth. The scratches from the tree bark. The leaves tangled in my hair from when I lay spread beneath her.

My face burns hotter.

Julia gets to her feet, breathing hard as she fixes her hair. Rebecca is slower to stand, wiping blood from her nose. The three of them face each other in a triangle, the magic in the room so taut that it feels like the air is statically charged.

The grandfather clock downstairs chimes, and we all go still. Three in the morning. About four hours until the moon sets and I'm stuck as Julia's pet forever. The binding spell tightens like a vise around my ribs, like it knows time is running out.

I catch Julia's eye, seeing my own frantic questions reflected back at me.

What did we do wrong? Did I not submit enough? Was I holding back?

"Everybody *out*," Elizabeth commands. She points to Julia with her fingers curled into claws. "Except you."

Rebecca squares her shoulders and shoots Julia a deadly glare before obeying. She grabs a blue silk robe off the back of the door, then guides Riley out ahead of her.

As I turn my back on Julia, her voice stops me. "Stay close, pet."

I scoff and keep walking, my spine rigid with barely contained fury.

I can't tell if it was a threat or a joke. With Julia, nothing is sincere.

The moment we're downstairs, where the front door is still open from when I burst through it, Riley whirls to face me with watery eyes.

"You surrendered to her." It's an accusation, not a question. Her voice is so broken, so hurt, that a flash of unexpected guilt shoots through me.

Rebecca ties a knot in her robe with jerky motions. She swipes her hand, and the front door slams so hard that the chandelier rattles. She paces the foyer, clenching and unclenching her fists as if itching to blast something with magic.

I look past Riley, where an oval mirror hangs behind one of the cat statues. The woman staring back at me is almost unrecognizable.

My hair is a wild tangle, leaves and twigs caught in the strands like I've been dragged through the forest. Dark bruises bloom across my neck in the clear shape of Julia's fingers. Scratches rake down my collarbone and arms. My lips are swollen.

I look *ravaged*. Like someone who begged a monster to devour her.

Humiliation burns through me so intensely that I have to look away.

But I tamp down those feelings, refusing to be embarrassed that everyone in this house knows what we did. It's not my fucking fault I've been bound to a sanguine witch. "Don't look at me like that, Riley. You broke up with me. And it's not even like that. I did what I had to in order to get my freedom back."

"Did it work?" she asks, her tone telling me she already knows the answer.

My jaw tightens.

The silence that follows is suffocating. My rage is still there, coiled tightly, but it's bumping up against the reality that I'm running out of time and options. The fury doesn't change the fact that I'm still bound to Julia. Still trapped.

Riley takes my hands. "Hannah, please don't try it again. There must be a way to break the bond that doesn't involve her feeding on you. Right, auntie?"

Rebecca glances at her. "Surrender is the only way."

"But—"

I pull away from Riley. "This doesn't concern you."

I can't stand the pity in her eyes. It's the last thing I need right now.

"It does," Riley insists. "I love you, and I won't watch you become another Charlotte."

I furrow my brow. "Another who?"

Rebecca stops pacing. Riley goes very still. Even through my anger and exhaustion, I can feel the shift. A creeping dread settles in my stomach like ice.

"She didn't tell you," Rebecca says, almost inaudible.

My heart stumbles. "Tell me what?"

"What she did to my sister."

Between her dark tone and the knowing glance they exchange, I'm not sure whether I want to hear this.

She moves closer, and I fight the impulse to step back. Having Riley beside me is a small comfort.

"Auntie, don't scare her," Riley says, but Rebecca slices her hand through the air to silence her.

"She deserves to know." Rebecca's eyes bore into mine. "*Charlotte* deserves to have people know."

Riley bites her lip.

Rebecca moves even closer, her hands glowing with pale light. The room swims around me, and I sway.

"What's happening?" I ask, my voice wobbling.

"Auntie..." Riley says, sounding far away.

A sliver of another room ripples into my vision, like peering through blinds. Ornate picture frames and bone china on the walls. Bright yellow wallpaper.

I want to back away and refuse whatever Rebecca is about to show me. But I can't move. I need to know who Julia really is.

So I let Rebecca come closer. I stand still and squeeze my eyes shut as she presses her glowing palms against my temples.

The world dissolves.

18

HANNAH

I'M SEEING THROUGH REBECCA'S eyes, much younger, watching my sister through our bedroom doorway.

Charlotte sits at her vanity, brushing her long blonde hair with slow strokes. The lamplight catches the strands, turning them to spun gold. Eighteen years old and grown into her womanhood, she's the kind of beautiful that makes men stop in the street, that makes our parents keep the curtains drawn and insist she never walk anywhere alone.

But right now, she's not looking at her reflection. She's looking at my grimoire, which lies open on her bed.

"Becca?" she calls softly. "When you cast spells, what does it feel like?"

I lean against the doorframe, the floorboards creaking beneath me. In truth, it's like I lived my whole life underwater, and coming into my power gave me the first real breath of air I've ever taken. It's like being the storm instead of the sea, the flame instead of the moth. Everything responds to me, bending to my will, and every day I awake excited to learn what else I am capable of.

But I don't want my sister to feel worse than she already does, so I search for more mundane words. "It is like the world is an instrument and I am learning to play it."

This was, evidently, still the wrong thing to say. Her face crumples, but she smooths it away quickly. "That must be wonderful."

"Charlotte..."

"I am happy for you." She sets down her brush and closes the grimoire reverently. "Truly."

But I can see it in her eyes—the hunger for something beyond these walls, beyond being decorative and protected and powerless. She wants to be feared instead of desired. She wants magic in her veins.

Charlotte is hunched over my grimoire in the kitchen, surrounded by herbs and candles. The house sleeps around us, silent except for the ticking parlor clock and Father's distant snoring. I should stop her, but something makes me wait in the shadows, watching. Wanting to see what happens.

She lights the candles with trembling fingers. Wax drips onto the scarred wooden table where Mother kneads bread each morning. Carefully, she arranges the rosemary and sage in a circle, then recites the words for a simple charm to extinguish a flame, her voice barely a whisper.

Nothing happens.

She tries again, louder this time, and I can hear the desperate plea in her tone. My heart cracks a little.

The candles flicker. For one brilliant second, I think it might work.

But it's no more than a draft from the window, and the flames keep burning bright.

Charlotte's shoulders shake. She presses her hands over her mouth to muffle her sobs, and I slip away before she knows I saw.

Charlotte is retching into a chamber pot, her whole body convulsing. The acrid smell of vomit mixes with the lavender sachets Mother keeps in our linens.

Mother holds her hair back, shooting me an accusatory look. "What did she drink, Rebecca?"

I examine the empty vial on Charlotte's nightstand, my shoulders slumping. "A courage potion. Poorly made."

"I only wanted—" Charlotte gasps between heaves, "—to feel brave—"

"You might have killed yourself," I say, trying to sound angry instead of terrified.

"What is the point of living if I can never truly live?" she whispers.

Mother shakes her head, her jaw tight. "Stop speaking nonsense."

That night, I hide my grimoire beneath a loose floorboard in the corner. But it doesn't stop her from peeking through the window whenever I leave for coven circles, her face pressed against the glass like a child watching adults at a ball she cannot attend.

I'm Charlotte now, following Rebecca through dark streets. My heart pounds with rebellion and excitement. I shouldn't be here, but I cannot stay in the suffocating safety of the house one more night.

Ahead, Rebecca slips through a gate into a walled garden. I creep closer, peering through the iron bars.

Nine women stand around a fire. The garden is wild and untamed, nothing like the plots our neighbors tend. Their voices rise and fall in a language I do not understand, and the flames dance in impossible shades of green, purple, and silver. Power crackles in the air.

And then I see her.

She is older than Rebecca, in her thirties, with thick dark hair that falls past her shoulders and winter-blue eyes that seem to see through everything. She moves with a confidence I have never witnessed, as if the world bends around her instead of her bending to fit it. She wears trousers and a blouse instead of a dress, unconstrained by corsets or bloomers.

I must know her name. I must know more about her.

She laughs at something another witch says, and the sound makes my chest ache with longing. She is powerful, free, and beautiful in a way men fear instead of in a way they think they can control.

The gathering ends. I should run home before Rebecca catches me.

But I cannot stop watching that woman as she says her goodbyes and leaves for home.

Before I can think about what I'm doing, I follow her.

I'm Julia, walking home from the coven circle. The street is empty, fog rolling in from the river and clinging to the cobblestones. Gas lamps cast pools of weak yellow light that barely penetrate the mist.

A young woman appears beside me like a ghost, and I stop in my tracks. She is breathtaking, her blonde hair catching the moonlight, a thin shawl draped loose over her curves, her green eyes wide. Her dress is mud-splattered at the hem, as if she has been sneaking through the forest.

"I—" Her voice shakes. "I saw you. At the gathering. I'm Charlotte. Rebecca's sister."

I should keep walking. Rebecca would be furious if she knew I was talking to her little sister. But there is something in the way she looks at me—like she's starving for something and I'm the only one who can offer it to her.

"Does Rebecca know you're out here?" I ask, eyeing her up and down. "Or are you in the habit of following strange women in the dark?"

She flushes but holds my stare. "Only the ones worth following. What is your name?"

"Julia Moreau. And you ought not to be out here alone."

She lifts her chin. "I'm not alone. I'm with you."

She's bold.

I chuckle. "You think *I* shall keep you safe?"

"My parents think I require a husband for that, but men are vile and fragile creatures who have never interested me."

Fascinating. I'm beginning to like this woman.

"What do you want, Miss Cooper?"

"I want..." She swallows hard. "I want to know what it feels like. The power. Being free. Being you."

I step closer until we're nearly touching, curious what she'll do. Her breath hitches. She shivers, but she doesn't back away.

"And what makes you think I would show you?"

"I don't know." Her eyes meet mine, and there's such desperate hunger there. "But I hope you can find it in your heart to help a woman who is tired of being small and decorative and safe."

She's right. The thought of this beautiful woman wasting away as the wife of some brutish man makes my jaw clench.

"I saw how the other witches look at you," she whispers. "With respect, not pity. No one has ever looked at me that way."

I reach out and trace my fingers along her jawline. Her pulse jumps beneath my touch. "If you want to feel power, I can show you. But sanguine magic comes at a price."

"I'll pay it," she breathes.

I shouldn't. But her willingness is intoxicating, and it's been years since I've had someone offer themselves freely.

I smile, holding out my hand for her to take it. "Come."

In my cottage, I light the fire with a wave of my hand, letting its heat flood the small space. The flames catch eagerly in the hearth, illuminating shelves lined with bottles and herbs.

"Sit," I command.

Charlotte obeys, choosing my bed instead of a chair. She's trembling in anticipation, looking up at me through her lashes.

I move to stand in front of her, and she has to tilt her head back to meet my eyes.

"This might frighten you," I warn.

"I am not afraid of witches or magic."

Foolish girl.

I sit beside her and angle toward her, close enough that our knees touch.

Outside, an owl calls, and the wind rattles the windowpanes.

I place my fingers on her temples and begin feeding slowly. Her skin is feverishly warm. The incantation flows from my lips, and her eyes widen as she feels the first pull of her essence.

"Oh—" She gasps. Her back arches, pressing closer to me. "That's—it's—"

"Good?" I murmur.

Her hand comes to rest on my waist, gripping my bodice. "Yes," she moans. The sound goes straight through me, and I have to force myself to maintain control and take only what I intended.

But the feeding is as good for me as it is for her, and I let my eyes flutter closed as I drink in her sweet, pure essence.

"Julia," she whimpers, and hearing my name on her lips like that nearly undoes me.

I drink in just a taste—enough to make her dizzy, but not enough to hurt her. When I pull back, she makes a sound of protest, her fingers tightening on my waist to keep me close.

"Finished," I say, extracting myself.

She groans and lets herself flop back onto my bed, boneless, her lips parted as she catches her breath. She looks at me with stars in her eyes.

"That was divine," she whispers. "Can we continue?"

And there it is: that dangerous question that should make me refuse.

Instead, I smile down at her, this beautiful woman who's splayed on my bed with a dazed look on her face. "Tomorrow night."

I'm Rebecca again, confronting Charlotte in our bedroom.

"You have been slipping out every night for a fortnight." I grab her wrist as she tries to leave. "Where do you go?"

Her wrist is so thin beneath my fingers that I pause, studying it. Her bones are protruding, and her skin is so pale I can see blue veins.

Charlotte notices my gaze and wrenches free. "That doesn't concern you."

"You are my sister. It is very much my concern. Charlotte, you look ill—"

"I am perfectly well." But dark circles have formed under her eyes, which are wide and feverish.

"Please. Whatever this is, it's harming you."

"You don't understand." She clenches her fists. "For the first time in my life, I feel truly alive. I feel powerful. I feel—"

"Drained," I finish. And then the pieces click together—her nightly absences, her weakening state, the way she smells faintly of cinnamon and... "Oh God. Sanguine magic."

Her silence is answer enough. The truth hits me like a slap, forcing me back a step. Then fury hits me, hot and ferocious.

Julia. How dare she.

"Charlotte, no. Sanguine witches feed on life force. You are not experiencing magic, you are giving Julia your life—"

"I know what I'm doing!"

"Do you? Look at yourself!" I drag her to the mirror. "You're wasting away. You can scarcely stand—"

"I don't care." She meets my eyes in the reflection, defiant. "Being with her is worth it."

"She's killing you."

"She loves me."

"She is *using* you—"

Charlotte spins around and strikes me across the face. The crack echoes in our small room.

"You're jealous," she hisses. "You possess magic, and still you would deny me this. But I won't let you." She pushes past me toward the door. "I would sooner die than give her up."

I cup my stinging cheek and watch her go, helpless to stop her.

I'm Charlotte, sitting at the supper table while my parents loom over me. The dining room is suffocating. Heavy velvet curtains block out the evening light, and the air is thick with the smell of roasted meat I cannot bring myself to eat.

"We have spoken to the doctor," Mother says, her voice tight with fear. "He warned us that if you don't eat properly—"

"I am fine."

Father slams his hand on the table, making the dishes rattle. "You are not fine! You're skin and bones. You won't tell us where you go at night. You look half-dead—"

"My life is not your concern!" I shove back from the table, and the effort makes me dizzy. I grip the edge to stay upright.

Tears spill down Mother's cheeks. "Please, Charlotte. Tell us what's wrong. We can help you."

"You cannot help me. You have never helped me." My voice breaks. "You have only kept me locked up like a doll in a box, too precious to touch, too delicate to live. I'm done being your perfect, protected daughter. I'm done being powerless."

I storm out, ignoring their pleas.

That night, I spread my legs beneath Julia, taking her hand firmly and guiding her fingers where I want them. This is *my* choice, my body, my pleasure. *She* is who I want, not some husband chosen by Father who will force me to be obedient and dutiful.

Julia obeys, her eyes darkening with hunger. I see in her eyes that she needs me as much as I need her.

"Inside me," I whisper.

As she slides her fingers into me, my breath hitches, and I rock my hips against her hand.

"Yes. Just like that." I arch into her touch, fisting my hands in her dark hair, pulling her closer and claiming her lips.

She makes a small sound of pleasure, kissing me harder.

The room spins as her body presses against mine, her skin hot through the thin fabric of our chemises. Her breath caresses my lips as she whispers the incantation.

She feeds from me for longer than ever. The temperature in the cottage drops, but even as I shiver on her bed, sweat beads along my hairline.

This is the only time I have had control over my life. I am choosing this pleasure, this purpose, and I will not let anyone take it from me.

I'm Julia, watching Charlotte crawl into my bed. She's so thin I can see every rib and vertebra. The lamplight casts shadows in the hollows of her collarbones, and her skin is pale as milk. Her beautiful blonde hair comes out in clumps on my pillow.

I ought to send her away and tell her not to come back until she's recovered. "You should not be here tonight. You need to—"

But she's already kissing me, pressing against me, and my hunger rises to meet her desperation.

"I need *you*." Her skeletal fingers fumble with the buttons on my blouse. "Please, Julia. I need to feel it again. I cannot bear another night without it."

"Charlotte…"

"Do you not want me anymore?" Her eyes fill with tears. "Am I too unsightly now?"

"No." I cup her hollow cheek. "You're still beautiful."

"Then feed on me." She pulls me down and kisses me desperately. "Make love to me. I can't sleep without it. Can't breathe without you. Please."

I should refuse. I should send her home before…

But she's begging so sweetly, and I'm so hungry, and her essence still calls to me like nothing else in this world.

She takes my hand, guiding it to her breasts.

"Just a little," I whisper, smiling against her lips.

I tug at her skirts, sliding the cotton up her thighs. She parts her legs for me eagerly, moaning in relief.

When I slide my fingers between her legs, she's already wet. She clutches my neck as I start to feed, my magic and touch working together to pleasure her in every way possible.

"Yes, yes..." she gasps, arching beneath me with a broken cry.

I work her with practiced fingers, knowing how she likes to be touched after all these weeks. Her thighs tremble, and I drink deeper as her pleasure builds, the two sensations intertwining until she cannot tell where one ends and the other begins.

"Julia..." She whimpers my name over and over, begging me to keep going.

Her body tenses, tightening around my fingers, and when she comes undone, it's with a strangled cry that she buries against my shoulder. The rush of her climax floods through our connection, her life force pouring into me in a torrent of pure bliss.

Just a little, I tell myself.

But it's never just a little. Her essence is too sweet and intoxicating. She is weakening beneath me, her heartbeat becoming erratic, and some distant part of me knows I should stop.

Just a bit more. She is still breathing. Still conscious.

I take and take until she goes limp in my arms, until her breathing becomes shallow and her heartbeat flutters like a dying bird.

When she collapses in ecstasy, I prop myself up on my elbow at her side, stroking her hair and kissing her softly, until her eyes flutter open again.

She turns her head and smiles drunkenly at me. "You are the best thing that's ever happened to me, Julia Moreau."

I'm Rebecca, storming toward Julia's cottage with fear gripping my chest.

Something is wrong.

Charlotte never came home last night, and Julia missed this evening's coven circle.

I push through the trees, and her cottage comes into view, overgrown with thorny vines and dark flowers. The door is standing open.

That's odd. Julia never leaves her door open, not even in high summer.

The night air is cold against my face, carrying the scent of woodsmoke and something else that makes my stomach clench with dread.

I push the door wider, peering into the darkness.

"Julia?"

No answer. The house is frigid, the fire long dead. Shadows crowd the corners, thick and menacing.

I step inside, and that's when I see her.

Charlotte lies on Julia's bed, her body limp and lifeless, her skirts rumpled. Her skin is the color of old parchment, waxy and translucent in the dim light. Her lips are blue. Her green eyes stare sightlessly at the ceiling.

"No." The word comes out as a whisper, then louder. "No, no, no!"

I rush over, pressing my fingers to Charlotte's throat even though I know it's useless. She is as cold as marble beneath my touch. She's been dead for hours. A whole day. My beautiful sister who only wanted freedom, who wanted a way out of the cage the world had built around her...

Dead. Because of Julia. Because I didn't stop this when I should have.

The truth winds me, and I fall to my knees, gripping the bed for support. I *saw* Charlotte wasting away. I saw the obsession in her eyes, the way she became thinner and paler and more desperate. I knew what Julia was doing to her, knew the feeding had gone too far.

And I didn't do enough to stop it.

I told myself it was Charlotte's choice. That she was willing. That Julia, my coven sister, would end the feedings before this happened.

But she didn't, and now my sister—my brave, foolish sister—is dead.

Rage rises in me like a red tide, hot and terrible and all-consuming. My hands shake with fury. The air around me crackles with heat as my magic responds to my emotion, wild and uncontrolled.

Julia did this. Julia, who I've known for decades, whose hands I've held during countless coven circles. Julia, who I trusted to know her limits, to control her hunger.

Julia, who ran like a coward and left Charlotte's corpse in her bed like discarded refuse.

I stand straight, my vision blurred. This cottage is filled with Julia's books, her jars and herbs, her clothes folded neatly in a trunk, her dishes on the shelves. Evidence of a life of comfort and power while Charlotte withered away for her pleasure.

My fingers ignite.

The flames are red-gold at first, then white-hot as my rage feeds them. They leap from my hands to the bedsheets, and I watch with savage satisfaction as they catch and spread. Charlotte's body will burn too, but at least she'll have a pyre. At least there will be nothing left for Julia to come back to.

"You took everything from her," I say to the empty room, my voice shaking. "So I'll take everything from you."

The fire spreads faster than natural flame could, racing up the walls and across the floor. It devours Julia's furniture, clothing, and every trace of the life she built. The intense heat drives me back toward the door. Smoke billows thick and black, carrying the smell of burning wood and cloth and fragrant dried herbs.

I step outside and watch it burn. The flames roar up through the thatched roof, sending sparks into the night sky like angry stars. The windows shatter from the heat, glass exploding outward in glittering shards.

I back away. I must disappear before anyone connects me to this.

But first, I press my still-burning hand to my chest, letting the pain sear through me and brand this moment into my memory. "I will make you pay for this, Julia," I whisper to the roaring flames. "I will not rest until you've suffered."

The fire answers me with a crackling roar, as if sealing my oath.

I will have vengeance for Charlotte, and for every life Julia will ever destroy.

I turn and leave Julia's cottage—now Charlotte's funeral pyre—blazing behind me.

The night swallows me whole, but the rage in my heart burns as bright as the flames.

I slam back into my own body with a gasp, stumbling backward. Riley catches me before I fall.

I can still feel Julia's hunger and taste Charlotte's essence. I can still feel the agony in my heart from when Rebecca found her corpse.

Worse, Charlotte's desperation is still there, dark and suffocating. Her hunger for magic, for freedom, for something beyond the cage she grew up in. Her willingness to die rather than go back to being powerless.

"I filled in the gaps with Charlotte's diary," Rebecca says, lowering her hands. The glow fades from her palms. "Now you know what Julia is."

I cover my mouth, fighting nausea.

The way Charlotte begged her for that moment of ecstasy was too familiar. Just like I begged in the forest. Just like I spread my legs and offered her everything, knowing the dangers.

"M-Maybe it was an accident," I say, my voice shaking.

"Maybe. But Charlotte died believing Julia loved her, and Julia ran. She disappeared for three years after that. Didn't even stay to close Charlotte's eyes. When she finally returned, she never mentioned Charlotte's name again. As if it hadn't happened."

My chest is tight. "Do you think she ever cared about Charlotte?"

"Does it matter? Whatever she felt, it wasn't enough to stop her from draining her."

My breaths come faster. The woman who touched me everywhere last night, who made me feel cherished and wanted, killed someone who loved her and walked away after.

Riley takes my hands. "We see the way you look at her, Hannah. If you don't step back soon, you're going to become another Charlotte."

"She'll do it to you too," Rebecca says. "Maybe not tonight. Maybe not tomorrow. But eventually, she won't be able to stop herself. It's her nature."

Shame burns through me. She's right. I offered myself to Julia completely last night, begged her to take what she needed, and she nearly killed me.

Upstairs, a door creaks open.

Riley and I flinch at the sound. Rebecca just keeps staring at me with those knowing, pitiless eyes as footsteps thump closer overhead.

My mouth is dry. I swallow hard. "I won't let that happen," I whisper.

I'd rather die than surrender to Julia again. I'd rather let this spell kill us both than become another one of her victims who wasted away believing a monster cared about her.

Satisfaction flashes across Rebecca's face. Riley slumps in relief, squeezing my hand.

But realization crashes over me like an icy wave. By showing me what happened to Charlotte, Rebecca has guaranteed I'll never surrender to Julia again. And without surrendering, we can't break the binding spell.

We're stuck. Julia is bound to someone who knows exactly what she's capable of, and I'm bound to a monster who will slowly drain me dry without remorse. Neither of us is going to give the other what she needs, but we can't escape each other either.

Rebecca has gotten her perfect revenge. Julia will be helpless, just like Rebecca was when she found Charlotte on the bed. And I'm the sacrifice caught in the middle, destined to waste away no matter what I choose.

The binding spell pulses behind my ribs, ticking closer to the moment I'm trapped forever.

Unless I can find another way out of this nightmare.

There has to be a way to break this spell that doesn't require me to trust a woman who kills the people who love her. I have four hours to figure it out, and I'm not giving up until I'm free—or dead.

19

JULIA

THE MOMENT THE DOOR to the guest room closes, Elizabeth's magic slams into me, buffeting the air from my lungs. My wrists snap together as if bound by invisible shackles, and I'm forced to my knees on the wood floor. My magic flares hot beneath my skin, searching for a weakness in her attack, but as powerful as that feeding made me, I'm no match for an ancient witch in her own domain.

"You dare attack a guest under my roof?" Elizabeth says, her voice low and dangerous.

I struggle against the restraints, but they only tighten. How humiliating, being on my knees like a chastised child. "She's the one who—"

"I don't care what Rebecca did to you." Elizabeth circles me like a predator, her fingers trailing green sparks. "There are laws older than your vendetta, Julia. Laws of hospitality that even you should respect."

"I need her to tell me how to break this spell." The words come out strangled. "I'm running out of time." *And kneeling on this damned floor isn't helping.*

"You think torture is the answer?" Elizabeth stops in front of me, her green eyes blazing. "You think making her bleed will somehow undo what she's done?"

"It's worth trying."

"No, it's desperation masquerading as strategy." She backs up to a padded armchair by the door and sinks into it. "You want to break this spell? Show some remorse. Apologize to Rebecca for what you did to Charlotte, and try to find some way in that black heart of yours to make it up to her. Maybe then she'll have mercy on you."

Remorse? As if feelings could solve this.

I glare up at her. "What happened between Charlotte and me is none of her business."

"It became her business when her little sister's life fell into your merciless hands," Elizabeth snarls. "Have some compassion, Julia."

I laugh bitterly. "If only that were possible for someone like me."

She furrows her brow, searching my face. "You really believe that about yourself?"

I lift an eyebrow. Is she honestly asking that? I've spent my life feeding on others, taking what I need to survive. I've watched bodies collapse at my feet and felt nothing but satisfaction as their life force filled the endless void inside me. "What else could I be?"

Elizabeth sighs, leaning back. She crosses her legs beneath her elegant black nightgown and bounces her slippered foot. "Julia, this binding spell is designed to force you to confront that question. You have to decide what you are."

"Sanguine witches don't get to decide that."

She stares at me, and I stare back, struggling against the invisible bonds. My magic pulses erratically, trying to help me escape, but her hex is too strong.

"You left Hannah the moment you thought you were free." Elizabeth tilts her head. "Why?"

Nausea rises, but I swallow it down. I will not feel guilty for choosing my freedom. "Because that's my nature. I take what I need and I leave."

"Is it? Or were you running from something else?" She stops bouncing her foot. "Perhaps from what you felt when she surrendered to you so completely?"

Heat rushes into my face at the memory of Hannah spread beneath me, begging for me, offering everything. The way she looked at me felt dangerously like trust. I open my mouth to defend myself, but what can I say? That I panicked? That seeing her so vulnerable, knowing I could have killed her, terrified me?

Instead, I say flatly, "I felt nothing."

"Really? Nothing at all when she offered you her life, her soul?" Elizabeth's voice is too knowing. "Surely, from what I gather about the nature of these feedings, you felt something when she came apart beneath you—"

My chest tightens. "Stop."

"You care for her."

I scoff. "It's not in a sanguine witch's nature to care. Anyway, Hannah won't surrender to a monster, which means breaking this binding spell is impossible unless we find a loophole."

Elizabeth's laugh is soft and pitying. "You truly don't understand your own power, do you?"

I flex my fingers, a spark of magic prickling between them. I don't have time for this. "I understand it perfectly. I drain life to survive."

"You think sanguine magic is only about taking?" Elizabeth leans forward. "Tell me, Julia. In all your years of feeding, when did you feel the most powerful?"

Tonight comes to mind, after I fed on Hannah. And there was Charlotte, of course. Those months when nothing could stop me.

Elizabeth seems to know what I'm thinking because she nods. "Why do you chase freely given power when you have the option to steal it?"

Because Hannah won't let me kill, I think, though I know there's more to it. Feeding on Hannah is more pleasurable in so many ways.

"Sanguine magic thrives on connection," Elizabeth continues. "On genuine intimacy. The willing surrender born of real feeling is more powerful than anything you could take by force."

"That's not—"

"Charlotte didn't just offer you her essence. She offered you her heart. And you felt something for her too, didn't you? That's why she was so intoxicating."

The memory threatens to choke me. Charlotte's beautiful face as she undressed for me one last time.

She was supposed to be different from everyone I'd fed on before her. She offered herself willingly, and so I wouldn't *need* to drain her dry. For a few precious months, I thought I could be something other than a parasite. Maybe I could give as much as I took.

"You're so certain that you're beyond redemption."

"Aren't I?" I try to laugh, but it comes out strangled. "I killed her, just like everyone said I would."

"Not everyone."

"Enough of them. Don't think I forgot their words. *A hungry ghost, forever feeding, never satisfied. A monster who destroys everything she touches.*"

"You were young with Charlotte. Inexperienced in matters of the heart and in your craft."

"That doesn't excuse what I did."

Elizabeth's eyebrows shoot up. "So you do feel remorse."

I say nothing, unwilling to put a name to this feeling.

Elizabeth waves her hand, releasing me from her magical bonds. I rub my throbbing wrists, though they bear no marks.

"Letting yourself feel these emotions will save you from this curse, Julia."

I sigh. "If you mean to convince me that I can overcome my nature, you're mistaken."

Elizabeth stands. "Then I suppose you're going to prove Rebecca right about you."

"Unless we find another way to break the spell," I challenge, standing too. "Surely you've found something in the grimoire?"

She studies me for a long moment, a slight drop in her shoulders, like she was hoping I would come to a different conclusion. "I remember when you first joined us, Julia. 1866. You were so young. So angry."

"The world gave me reason to be." I still recall the sensation of my magic guiding me to the coven after my mother died. Like my power was protecting me by taking me to the only women who could keep me safe.

"It gave all of us reason." Elizabeth's gaze goes distant. "I don't know what would have come of me if I hadn't met you all. Alone with my power, making plants sprout, being labeled a freak."

I scoff. "I know exactly what would've happened to you. You would've had the same fate as my mother."

"None of us ever regretted helping you exact revenge on those men, Julia. That's what sisters are for."

I almost smile at the memory. Their fear, their screams...the first hint that my life was about to change now that I'd found my sisters.

"The others have missed you," Elizabeth adds, watching me closely. "I know they'll love to see you again, if you'll stick around."

I know what she's doing, trying to get me to remember the early days of our sisterhood before this rift fell between Rebecca and me. Trying to get me to feel something. But that will not help me get out of this mess.

"Have you found any unbinding spells or not?" I ask shortly.

She studies me for another moment, then sighs. "I might have. Two potential paths, actually."

Her serious expression doesn't reveal how good or bad these options are.

My chest squeezes with desperate hope.

"Then why are we standing here?" I cannot keep the edge out of my voice.

"They're dangerous, and not the solutions I wanted to find. It's safer to break the spell the way Rebecca intended instead of trying to find a loophole, Julia."

"I tried to break the spell the way Rebecca intended, and it didn't work," I say through my teeth. "A loophole is all we have left."

She studies me, then rolls her shoulders and smooths her night-gown as if to compose herself. "Meet me in the parlor. I'll fetch the grimoire."

She opens the door and leaves the room, and for a moment, I stand there in the heavy silence.

The guest room feels hollow. My reflection stares back at me from the darkened window—a woman who hasn't aged in a century, per-manently unchanged.

I turn away.

Elizabeth's words echo in my head. *You care for her.*

Ridiculous. Even if I could care, I can't afford to. Not when I've proven what I'm capable of.

She thinks I was just young and inexperienced? Ha. I'd been feeding for long enough to know better. I just couldn't stop. In that moment, with Charlotte surrendering everything to me, I felt powerful enough to transcend my nature.

And then she was gone, and I was exactly what everyone always said I was. Exactly what I've always known I am.

I square my shoulders and sweep out of the room, following the hum of voices toward the foyer.

I descend the curved staircase, where the others are huddled togeth-er like conspirators. Hannah's back is to me, tension in her posture. Riley has a protective hand on her arm.

The urge to rip them away from each other is so strong that my fingers twitch. Hannah isn't hers anymore. Hannah has fed me, surrendered to me, opened herself for me, and what has Riley done? Broken her heart?

As I approach, glistening streaks become visible on Rebecca's cheeks. Tears. My stomach gives a nauseating lurch.

"Having a pleasant chat?" I ask.

Hannah whirls around, and the look in her eyes—fear, disgust, betrayal—punches the air from my lungs.

I've seen that look on countless faces. It's never mattered, and it shouldn't matter now.

But it does. She knows what I did.

Of course she knows. Rebecca would never miss an opportunity to turn Hannah against me. To ensure that Hannah will never trust me enough to break this spell.

The twisted thing is, Rebecca isn't wrong. Hannah should fear me. She should hate me.

But now that she sees the truth, I can't bear to meet her eye.

"Hannah, follow me," I say, my voice coming out flat and emotionless despite the storm raging inside me.

Riley steps protectively in front of her. "I am *not* leaving you alone with her so you can drain her dry."

I ignore the twist in my gut and sigh. Past them, through the open parlor doors, the grandfather clock shows past three. We're running out of time.

"Riley," Hannah says quietly. "She won't kill me. We're bound."

"That doesn't mean she won't hurt you," Riley snarls.

The nerve of her, acting protective after she shattered Hannah's heart.

"I'm not here to hurt her," I say through my teeth. "Now step aside and stop wasting our time."

Riley clenches her fists, refusing to budge.

"I'll be with them, dear," Elizabeth says from above, and we all turn to see her walking down the stairs with a large, leather-bound grimoire propped against her hip. "Rebecca, Riley, give us space."

Riley stands taller. "But—"

Rebecca touches her shoulder, and they exchange a wordless conversation full of hard stares and raised eyebrows. Riley looks desperate, her eyes growing watery.

Elizabeth walks through our midst, forcing us all back a step, and into the parlor. I shoot Rebecca and Riley one last glare before following.

Hisses break out behind me, and a moment later, Hannah hurries along, leaving the other two.

I sweep my hand to slam the doors, closing me in the parlor with Hannah and Elizabeth.

Frustration coils inside me. I don't know what Elizabeth thought she was doing, trying to convince me I'm not a monster. The fact isn't debatable. I know it, she knows it, and Hannah knows it, and as long as that's true, Hannah is never going to surrender to me as fully as the spell requires. We need a plan that doesn't involve asking anyone to trust me.

Time to find out what an ancient grimoire has to say about breaking curses.

20

HANNAH

I STAND BY THE parlor door, my arms wrapped around myself, unable to look at Julia. The binding spell pulls at my chest, demanding I move closer, but I stay back.

The grandfather clock ticks on, and the dying fire pops, its warmth fading.

Elizabeth sits in a wingback chair, and the room is so silent that the groan of material beneath her is loud. She opens the grimoire, its ancient pages crackling. "I've found two potential solutions to your predicament that don't involve total surrender."

My heart beats faster. "Really?"

"The first is a separation ritual." She drags her finger down the page. "We would take Hannah as far away as possible while performing protective spells on both of you to help withstand the binding's resistance. If you can endure the pain long enough, the tether will eventually snap from the strain."

An icy sensation washes over me. "Oh. That sounds..."

I glance at Julia, remembering the agony of being separated from her when I went into the forest. The thought of deliberately subjecting ourselves to that torture—and *worse*—makes my stomach clench.

"How long would we need to stay apart?" Julia asks.

"Forever." Elizabeth's tone suggests she's not optimistic about this option either. "You'll need support from the side effects for several weeks, so you'll both need witches to live with you until the pain subsides."

"We'd be in pain for *weeks*?" I ask, my voice squeaky.

"Like I said..." She looks sternly at Julia. "These solutions are more complicated than—"

She snaps her gaze toward the parlor door, her nostrils flaring. Julia looks too, her brow pinched.

I look over my shoulder at it, seeing nothing.

Elizabeth sweeps her hand, and the door flies open to reveal Riley standing there, eyes wide, looking distinctly like someone who's been caught eavesdropping.

She glances over her shoulder before darting inside, shutting the door behind her. "If you try the separation ritual, I'll stay with Hannah to keep her safe," she says shamelessly.

I don't miss the way Julia goes rigid. She clenches her fists, and tendrils of dark magic snake from her fingers. "That's not necessary," she says through gritted teeth.

Riley lifts her chin defiantly. "Hannah shouldn't have to go through that alone."

"She won't be alone. She'll have the coven's protection."

My gaze darts between them like a tennis match. This is getting more heated by the second. Does Julia not like the idea of Riley protecting and comforting me, or...?

"I don't want to do that, anyway." I cross my arms and avert my gaze to the dying fire. "It sounds..."

"Excruciating," Julia finishes.

There's a pause. Now it's Riley's turn to look between us like a tennis match.

Riley steps closer to me. "But if it means you'll be free from *her*..." She shoots Julia a nasty glare. "You have to try it, right?"

Julia's fingers stroke the air like she's ready to blast Riley across the room.

"There is another option," Elizabeth interjects before this can escalate. Her knowing look suggests she's well aware of the tension crackling between us. "More complex, but less painful."

"What is it?" I ask.

"A redirection ritual. Spells follow the Rule of Three—they can be strengthened or weakened by forming a magical triangle." Elizabeth traces a triangle in the air with her finger. "If we can temporarily bind the two of you with a third person, the original binding becomes unstable. Think of it like distributing the magical load across multiple connection points until the stress causes all the bindings to snap."

Julia's eyes widen. "Of course," she whispers.

"The ritual would require someone close to Hannah," Elizabeth explains. "And this person would need to surrender themselves to Julia the same way Hannah did."

I step back. "They have to *what*?"

Julia stares at Elizabeth in stunned silence.

Another feeding. Another person splayed under Julia, offering their essence while I sit back. My stomach lurches as I imagine what might happen if Julia can't bring herself to stop feeding.

I mouth wordlessly for a moment before I manage to speak. "When you say *the same way*, do you mean—"

"I'll do it," Riley says, and she's already stepping forward.

"Riley, no," I grab her wrist. "You don't understand what you're agreeing to."

Her skin is fever-warm, and I swear I can feel her magic humming beneath it.

She sets her jaw, looking as strong and fierce as ever. This is the Riley who never backs down from a challenge, the Riley on the soccer field who takes the shot and isn't afraid to get hurt. "If it means saving you from being bound to a sanguine witch forever, it's worth it."

I shake my head fiercely. I absolutely cannot let Riley become one of Julia's victims.

"I'm willing to try it if she is," Julia says casually, sliding her hands into the pockets of her trousers.

I look sharply at her.

There's a hungry look in her eyes that I don't like. Is she looking forward to feeding on another victim, or is this about the potential to feed on Rebecca's descendant?

"Julia, if you hurt her—" I snarl.

"Hurting her won't help," Elizabeth says. "You need her alive if you want the ritual to work."

There's a heavy pause. My breaths quicken as my chest tightens with panic.

"Are—are you sure about this?" I ask Riley. "We can find someone else. It doesn't have to be you."

Riley's gaze traces over my neck and shoulders, no doubt cataloging every mark Julia has left on me tonight. The red-gold fire in her eyes blazes brighter than ever. "We don't have time to get someone else. Anyway, I can handle it. I broke your heart because of what I am, so let me do this one brave thing for you, Hannah."

I walk a small circle, rubbing my face like I can smother myself and make this all go away.

What else are we supposed to do? Surrendering didn't work, the torture of separation will probably kill us...and we have a willing volunteer right here, ready to try a redirection ritual.

Elizabeth rises from her chair. "Into the sanctum."

Before I can protest, she flicks her hand, and the bookcase rumbles. Slowly, it slides aside, revealing an arched stone passageway. She steps through it and descends, disappearing from sight. Riley beckons for me to go ahead, shooting Julia a glare. I obey, placing a hand on the cold stone wall and stepping down into a dank chamber that smells like burning sage. She and Julia follow.

The ceiling is domed like a cave, gleaming with green veins. Symbols are etched into the walls at eye level around the perimeter, and the far end is full of wooden shelves covered in black candles, gemstones, leather-bound books, and jars of natural ingredients like bones and herbs. I rub my arms, my skin prickling in a static charge.

The bookcase rumbles across the exit, sealing us inside. The dim light from the flickering black candles and green veins casts us all into an eerie glow.

"Riley, fetch the candles," Elizabeth says, laying the grimoire on a wooden table. "Julia, help me draw the pentagram."

I watch with my pulse pounding as the witches prepare the space, drawing a pentagram on the stone floor with some kind of sand or ash, and setting candles at three points. Their flames dance brighter, casting writhing shadows on the walls.

At Elizabeth's direction, I stand at one candle, Riley at another, and Julia at the third, all of us at arm's length. My palms are sweating.

So I'm going to have to watch the woman who broke my heart offer herself to the witch who's introduced me to the most intimate moments of my life. And somehow, I have to be okay with it, even though I know what that witch is capable of.

"Each of you must do exactly as I instruct." Elizabeth consults the grimoire. "Hannah, you need to remain perfectly still to anchor your existing bonds with Julia and Riley. Julia...you'll need to feed from Riley while maintaining your link to Hannah. The triangle will amplify your power, but you must be careful not to take too much."

Julia dips her chin, a wicked gleam in her eyes.

Fuck, *amplified power?*

Riley meets my gaze across the triangle. "It's going to be okay. I can handle this."

Maybe, I think, *but I'm not sure if I can.*

First, I'm not convinced Julia won't drain her dry. Riley is Rebecca's descendant, and we all know how she feels about Rebecca. The question is: does she hate Rebecca enough to sabotage this ritual in order to get revenge? Or will she obey Elizabeth's orders and stop feeding before she kills Riley?

And then there's the other thing: as I stand here watching Julia prepare to touch Riley the way she touched me, hot fury surges through me.

My jaw clenches as I watch Julia's gaze rake over Riley's body. Those are the same eyes that looked at me with desire in the forest, and now they're fixed on Riley like I don't even exist.

And Riley... The skin I've kissed all over is about to be claimed by someone else. Someone else is about to touch her, undress her, make her feel pleasure.

Riley stands taller, glaring at Julia. "My safe word is venom."

"Safe word?" Julia asks.

"Yes. You hear the word, and you fucking stop. Got it?"

Julia chuckles. "You won't want me to stop, love."

"I say venom, you stop," Riley repeats firmly.

"All right, then."

There's a pause.

"Any other terms?" Elizabeth asks.

Riley shakes her head.

"Are you ready to surrender?" Elizabeth asks.

Riley nods. She doesn't even hesitate.

"Julia, you're ready to feed?"

Julia's lip curls.

"You may begin," Elizabeth says. "Stay within the pentagram."

They step toward each other.

My stomach twists, and I have to lock my knees to keep from moving. The binding spell tugs at my chest, wanting to be closer.

Julia's gaze rakes over Riley's body—the same hungry assessment she gave me in the forest. Those piercing eyes trace Riley's collarbone, the curve of her neck, the rapid rise and fall of her chest.

I know exactly what Julia sees. I've kissed every inch of that skin in my bed, in her car, against my kitchen counter… I've tasted the spot where Riley's shoulder meets her throat and felt her pulse quicken under my lips.

And now Julia is going to put her mouth there and draw sounds that only I'm supposed to draw from her.

My fingernails dig into my palms. The candle beside me flares higher, maybe responding to my agitation.

"Hannah." Elizabeth's warning is soft but firm. "Stay still. Any disruption could destabilize the triangle."

I force myself to breathe. To watch.

Julia reaches out slowly—she's savoring this, the bitch—and cups Riley's face with both hands. Her fingers look pale and ghostly in the strange lighting.

Riley's breath catches, just like mine did.

"Look at me," Julia murmurs, and Riley's eyes lock onto hers.

I've heard that voice before, velvety and commanding. The voice that made me want to surrender everything.

Riley sways forward, drawn by Julia's magnetic pull.

Something hot and vicious unfurls in my chest.

Knowing what Julia did to Charlotte and having experienced what Riley is about to feel, I can't stand this.

But is it Julia I'm jealous of, or is it Riley? Whose place do I want to be in?

Julia holds Riley's face, just like she did with me. Riley's pupils dilate as Julia begins the incantation.

"Tua essentia mea fit..." The Latin words flow from her lips, deep and seductive.

Riley's back arches, her lips part, and a soft sound escapes her throat, like reluctant pleasure. It's the same sound I made when Julia first fed from me. I know precisely what Riley is feeling as Julia's first brush of power slides under her skin.

Heat floods my cheeks. This is how I looked, isn't it? Desperate and wanting, completely under Julia's spell.

Julia's fingers darken as she unbuttons Riley's hooded cloak, letting it fall to the ground. Underneath, Riley's sleeveless top shows the lean muscles of her shoulders and arms.

Arms I've held, shoulders I've kissed, skin I've licked.

I have to watch, motionless, as Julia's hands sweep up and down her bare skin, increasing the points of contact. Dark tendrils of magic trail behind her fingers in swirling, mesmerizing patterns, which I never noticed when I was lost in the sensations.

"Oh," Riley gasps. "That's so..."

Her head tips back. Her lips part. Her pupils dilate until her eyes are almost black.

This is the moment when Julia's magic stops feeling like an invasion and starts feeling like the only thing you've ever wanted.

My hands tremble. I want to be the one making Riley gasp like this. Or I want to be Riley, feeling what she's feeling. Or maybe I just want Julia to stop touching anyone who isn't me.

God, I'm losing my mind.

The candles flare brighter. The green veins in the ceiling throb. Power builds in the sanctum like a gathering storm. The part of me that's bound to Julia recognizes her magic, and it swells deep inside me.

My pulse quickens. Watching Julia feed shouldn't make my core clench with desire. It shouldn't make me remember how those hands felt on my body, and how her voice sounded as she purred in my ear.

Riley's chest heaves. She grips Julia's wrists, not to push her away but to pull her closer. Orange magic glows beneath her skin, like fire pulsing through her veins.

Julia's fingers and eyes darken, and Riley trembles under her touch.

All I want is to push Riley away and take her place.

The realization hits me like a punch in the gut, taking my breath away.

It's Riley I'm jealous of. It's Julia I want.

The way she looked at Riley? That's *my* look. Her fingers, her mouth, her tongue...they're all mine.

God, what's happening to me? Julia is turning me into someone I don't recognize. Someone who craves danger, who's addicted to the edge between pleasure and destruction. Is this what happened to Charlotte? Is my life doomed to end the same way?

Julia's hands find the hem of Riley's shirt next.

No. No, she can't—

She tugs it upward, and Riley raises her arms, letting Julia pull the shirt over her head and toss it aside.

My vision goes red at the edges. Nausea rises inside me.

Riley is wearing her lacy white bra—the same one I've caressed, unfastened, left in a heap on my bedroom floor.

She takes Julia's hands, guiding them over her bare midsection, her ribs, her chest. Like she *wants* this. Like she's daring Julia to keep going, to take more.

Julia hisses as the contact increases. She slides one hand around the back of Riley's head, leaning close as if to kiss her—but it's not a kiss, and I know that. She's taking her breath, just like we did on Maya's balcony. Riley's eyes flutter closed in something that looks far too much like bliss.

My chest burns. I clench my jaw so hard that pain shoots through my temples.

This isn't right. I'm the only one Julia should touch that way.

The triangle amplifies everything. I can feel Riley's pleasure low in my belly, even sense her life force flowing into Julia like a breeze passing over my skin. And underneath it all, Julia's hunger intensifies, a deep ache that refuses to be satisfied.

The room pulses, a ripple passing right through me. The candles gutter and flare wildly, and cracks appear in the pentagram at our feet.

Julia spins Riley around, pressing her chest against Riley's back. Her hands roam, one cupping Riley's breast through the lace, the other sliding down her midsection. Riley's head falls back on Julia's shoulder, her breaths shallow.

"Please," Riley whimpers, the same desperate plea I made in the forest.

Julia's mouth finds the curve of Riley's neck, and she grazes her lips up and down the sensitive flesh. "What would you like?" she whispers.

"Touch me. I want you inside me."

No. Absolutely not.

"Julia," I say, a warning.

But her grip on Riley tightens, and the incantation grows rough and desperate. The shadows on her fingers spread, creeping up her wrists and forearms like nightfall. The darkness around her eyes bleeds into the whites like spilled ink.

Something's wrong. I've never seen her like this. The pentagram, the redirection ritual—it's making the feeding too intense.

Riley grips Julia's wrist, guiding her hand down to her waistband. "Please, I need…"

My heart stops. This is how it started with Charlotte. The addiction, the desperate need to keep feeding even when it's going wrong. And Julia, drunk on power, can't stop herself from taking too much.

Julia's fingers slide into Riley's jeans, making her legs tremble.

"Oh, God…" Riley moans, her knees buckling a little.

"Julia, that's enough," I say loudly.

Riley's face goes ashen, the fire magic beneath her skin flickering. Her knees give out, but Julia holds her up, pressing their bodies together as she continues to feed. Riley's head falls back, and Julia's mouth hovers at her neck.

I look desperately at Elizabeth, who stands abruptly from her chair, her gaze fixed on the feeding. "Julia, stop."

This doesn't feel right. The magic is too chaotic, too hungry. Instead of weakening our bond, it's making Julia's power spiral out of control.

"Julia!" I shout.

She looks at me, and my breath catches. There's no recognition. Just the blank hunger of a predator that's found prey.

Riley goes limp in her arms, her skin gray and waxy. She's dying, and Julia can't stop.

"No!" The word rips out of me.

I rush forward, abandoning the plan, and the first step is enough to break something. The candle beside me explodes in a shower of wax and black flame.

Elizabeth shouts something I can't hear through the whooshing in my ears.

The spell screams in my chest, a spasm that nearly drops me to my knees. I push past it, launching myself across the pentagram.

Magic lashes at me as I burst through the drawn lines, like running through barbed wire. Hot streaks of pain make my skin burn and my bones ache.

I don't care. I can't watch Riley die, and I can't watch Julia lose herself to her hunger the way she did with Charlotte.

And between both those things hides the bitter truth: I can't watch Julia touch someone else this way.

She's mine.

The thought blazes through me with absolute certainty as I grab Julia's wrists and try to wrench her hands away.

The moment I touch her, her magic slams into me.

If I thought the feeding in the forest was rough, it had nothing on this. A tidal wave of power and hunger crashes through me, right into my core, flooding my system with dark, intoxicating energy.

My back arches. My vision distorts. Pleasure and pain become indistinguishable as Julia's magic pours into me, amplified by the broken ritual into something catastrophic.

I'm burning. Freezing. Falling apart.

"Hannah!" Elizabeth is shouting, her voice far away.

I convulse, sinking lower on my knees, but I refuse to let go of Julia.

Through the haze, Julia's eyes snap to mine. She's still holding onto Riley, but she's frozen, breathing hard. The shadows around her eyes are creeping further out like dark veins, as if the power is consuming her from the inside out.

"Julia," I whisper. "Please stop."

21

JULIA

As Hannah's fingers close around my wrists, Riley's essence dissolves in my veins. In its place rushes Hannah's familiar sweetness, flooding my system and filling the hollow spaces in my soul I didn't know existed until she carved them out. The difference makes me suck in a sharp breath.

My magic roars, changing focus, demanding that I keep taking what's mine until there's nothing left.

I gulp down her essence, desperate for it.

"Julia," she whispers, her voice distant and distorted through the haze. "Please stop."

The magic pouring through me is far from controlled. The pentagram has turned it into a torrent. Hannah's heartbeat stutters, her breath coming in short gasps, her life force draining much too fast.

A tiny, feeble thought forms at the back of my mind: *I'm killing her.*

With a gasp that feels like surfacing from drowning, I wrench backward to break contact from both her and Riley.

The loss is agonizing. My magic screams in protest, clawing at my insides, demanding I reach for her again. Dark tendrils creep up my arms, alive and writhing under my skin, and I clench my fists to smother it.

Riley crumples to the floor like a puppet with cut strings. The sound of her body hitting stone makes me flinch.

The pentagram scatters as if caught in a violent wind. The candles extinguish, plunging the sanctum back into the eerie green glow from the ceiling.

Someone is breathing in harsh, desperate gasps. It takes me a moment to realize it's me.

"Dammit," Elizabeth hisses, already at Riley's side. Her composure has cracked, and there's fear in her eyes as she drops to her knees and rolls Riley onto her back.

And through it all, the binding spell pulses as strong as ever. Still intact. Still unbreakable.

Another failed attempt.

Hannah scrambles across the floor to Riley, her hands shaking so badly she can barely check for a pulse. "Oh, God... Riley, can you hear me?"

My throat constricts. I turn away, sucking in deep breaths, trying to understand what I'm feeling.

I didn't expect Riley's taste to be so agonizingly familiar. I knew she was descended from Rebecca, but what I didn't anticipate was *Charlotte*.

The blood connection between them was more than I was prepared for.

For one horrible, perfect moment, I had Charlotte back. And the hunger that rose up in response was something I couldn't control, that inner monster who devours and never lets go.

I thought I could bring Riley to the brink of death to make Rebecca regret what her spell led us to, but I didn't expect Charlotte's taste to flood into my veins after all this time. I didn't expect her ghost to reach up and drag me under.

I straighten up and smooth my hair, composing myself.

But seeing Hannah's panic as she cups Riley's face makes hot shame wash over me.

What was I thinking? God, if Hannah hadn't…

My stomach churns.

I would have killed Riley to spite Rebecca, and I would have destroyed my only chance at freedom. Hannah would have watched me prove every terrible thing anyone has ever said about me, and I would be forever tethered to someone who despises me as much as Rebecca does.

If she doesn't already.

Foolish. I nearly sacrificed everything.

Hannah's fingers flit over Riley's face and throat, searching for signs of life with that undying compassion she hasn't stopped showing all night.

My chest squeezes.

She deserves so much better than to be bound to me.

"She's alive, but barely," Elizabeth says, her voice tight with anger. "Both of you stay here. I'll take her to Rebecca."

My heart skips a beat. "Rebecca?"

She shoots me a glare that could wither a tree. "She'll find out what you did here sooner or later, and it might as well be now, when Riley can still survive this."

As usual, the consequences of my actions occur to me far too late. The thought of Rebecca seeing what I did sends ice through my veins. This will certainly make her believe that a cursed sleep and a binding spell are merciful compared to what I deserve.

"So—so she *will* live?" Hannah asks from the floor, out of breath.

"She will. She's in good hands." Elizabeth murmurs an incantation, and Riley's form lifts onto an invisible stretcher. She guides Riley from the sanctum, but not before shooting me one last glare.

Distantly, the bookcase rumbles aside, and the parlor doors open and slam, leaving Hannah and me alone in the suffocating silence.

Hannah stands, her fists clenched and her chest heaving. The fury in her eyes is so blazing hot that it hurts to look at.

"What—was—that?" she asks through her teeth.

"I was trying to break the binding spell. It's not my fault the ritual involved me feeding on a Cooper."

"Yeah, you clearly have a weak spot for them," Hannah spits. The color rises in her cheeks, and she turns away, blinking fast.

I stare at her profile and her rigid shoulders. Is that what she thinks? That Riley meant something to me beyond the ritual? "Riley was *your* lover, last I checked."

Hannah lets out a wild laugh. "I dated a Cooper, Julia, but I didn't drain any of them dry. I didn't leave any of them dead. God, you really are…"

I step closer. "I'm *what*?"

Hannah shuts her mouth and steps back, suddenly quiet.

"A monster?" I supply. "An abomination? Whatever word you have, I assure you, I've heard it before."

"You left me unconscious in the woods," she growls.

"With my cloak for warmth."

She rolls her eyes. "Oh, well, that makes it fine then. A cloak. How thoughtful."

"I also built you a fire."

"Do you want a medal of honor for not murdering me?"

I ball my fists. "You know exactly who I am, Miss Schmidt. Don't act surprised."

"Do I?" Her voice is deadly quiet. "Tell me about Charlotte."

My throat tightens. I don't wish to relive that memory, especially not right now. "This isn't the time—"

"Tell me." Her hands curl into fists too. "I want to hear it from you."

I could lie. Spin some tale that makes me look less awful. But the ice in her eyes tells me she already knows every excruciating detail. And she deserves the truth, after what she's witnessed.

So, I step in, summoning my magic to let her see it for herself.

Drawing on the memory is physically painful. I grit my teeth against it, my eyes stinging and my throat tightening.

I have never shown anyone what happened. The moment has only lived in my nightmares.

Hannah's gaze drops to my glowing palms. Recognition flashes across her eyes, and she sets her jaw before stepping in to meet me.

I press my hands to her temples and show her.

22

HANNAH

I'M SEEING THROUGH JULIA'S eyes, a wildness in my heart, drunk on power I'm still learning to control. And beneath me, writhing on my bed, is my beautiful Charlotte.

It's been six months of feeding on her, and I know her essence like I know my own name. I know the honey-sweet taste of her skin, the pitch of her cries when I touch her just so, the way she trembles on the edge of release, the glimmer in her eyes when she looks at me like I'm divine instead of damned.

"Please," she gasps, arching into my touch. Her skirts are bunched around her waist, baring her pale thighs. My fingers are slick from pleasuring her, and she spreads wider for me with shameless need. Her thin blonde hair is matted with sweat, spread across the pillow like a halo.

But something is wrong with her skin today. It's far too pale, almost translucent, blue veins visible. Her hip bones jut sharply, and I can count each rib. The hollows of her eyes are too deep, shadowed like bruises. But to acknowledge it would mean stopping these blissful feedings.

Her pulse stutters beneath my lips as I kiss her throat. A warning whispers in the back of my mind. *Something is different today. Something is wrong.*

But her essence calls to me like a siren song, and I silence the doubt.

"I love you," she whispers, and her total devotion makes my magic surge with possessive hunger. "Take all of me. I am completely yours."

The words ignite something ravenous in me. *Mine. Yes. All mine.*

My fingers darken as I begin the incantation, my other hand still between her legs, my thumb circling that sensitive pearl while two fingers curl inside her. Her back arches, a moan escaping as her body grows weaker. She tangles her skeletal fingers in my hair, holding me close. "Yes! Oh God, Julia—"

More. I need more.

The magic and the pleasure build, feeding each other. I whisper the words against her lips, drinking her gasps, and my fingers move faster, deeper. She clenches around me, close to the edge, her essence rising like a tide.

"Give me everything you have," I command, my voice rough with desire.

Dark tendrils snake from my fingers, wrapping around her. She shivers beneath me, release crashing through her as I pull her life force from her mind and body. The sensations rip a cry from her throat.

Power floods into me. Every cell in my body ignites. My vision goes white-hot with it. It sings in my veins like nothing I've ever felt. I'm invincible. I'm whole. I'm—

I'm taking too much.

The thought surfaces dimly through the euphoria, but I cannot stop. Her essence is a torrent, pouring into me faster than I can control it. I freeze, my fingers still inside her, scrunching my face against the competing desires.

I try to pull back, but the dark tendrils snake tighter around her, holding me there.

She's still trembling, but it's convulsive and desperate.

Her nails dig into my shoulders, no longer from passion. Her mouth opens, but only a thin wheeze comes out.

I pull my fingers from her body, staring down at her.

"Charlotte?" My voice sounds far away, muffled by the roar in my ears.

I jolt back, trying to stop the feeding, but the magic has taken on a life of its own. It's devouring her in great gulping draughts, and I can't—I can't—

"Stop," I whisper, as if I can tell my magic what to do with such a simple word. "Stop!"

She goes rigid beneath me. Those beautiful green eyes stare up at me in confusion and fear and something that might still be love. Her lips form my name, but no breath carries it.

The sudden silence is deafening. The flow between us cuts off like a plug pushed into a drain, leaving me gasping. The room spins.

Realization hits like icy water. Bile rises in my throat as I stare down at her still form. Her eyes are open but empty, that adoring gaze frozen. Her lips are blue. Her chest doesn't rise.

"Charlotte!"

No response. No breath. No heartbeat.

I press my fingers to her throat, searching for a pulse I know I won't find. Her skin is already cooling beneath my touch. The warmth of our passion is fading, replaced by the cold truth of death.

"No, no, no..." I shake her, gentle at first, then harder. "Charlotte, wake up."

But her head lolls, her blonde hair sliding across the pillow.

I scramble off the bed, my hands shaking. My fingers are still wet from being inside her. The sheets are soaked with sweat and other evidence of our coupling. The room reeks of sex and magic and death. What have I done? How did I not realize? How did I—

But I did realize. Some part of me has always known I've been taking too much. I felt her weakening body, her faltering pulse, the desperation in her touch. And I kept going because it felt too good to stop.

That is what truly made me the monster. Not a single moment of violence, but a thousand small decisions to take a little more. Just one more taste. Just until I am satisfied...while deep down, I knew I would never be satisfied.

A sob rises up, and I cover my mouth, forcing it down.

I back toward the door, unable to look away from her corpse. She looks almost peaceful. Her skirts are still rucked up around her waist, exposing her in death as she was in life—vulnerable, trusting, mine.

What have I done?

I make myself step closer and pull her skirts back down, my hands shaking violently as I touch her lifeless form.

"I'm sorry," I whisper over and over, but the words are meaningless. She can't hear me anymore. She'll never hear anything again.

Then I run.

I gasp, the dark cabin fading and Elizabeth's sanctum returning in a dizzying rush.

Oh, God. Oh, Charlotte....

I sway. I'm shivering. Sweating. I can't get enough air into my lungs.

The worst part wasn't even the killing. It was how good it felt, and how utterly out of control my magic—*Julia's* magic—became as she drank in Charlotte's essence. It took over. It wouldn't let me stop feeding. The power had its own hunger, its own will, and Julia was the vessel it poured through.

Charlotte's pleasure amplified Julia's power, which in turn intensified Charlotte's ecstasy. Round and round until there was nothing left.

I meet Julia's eyes. They're glossy, wide, and vulnerable. I've never seen her look so ashamed and afraid.

My heart cracks. I try to speak, but my throat is too tight. I swallow hard and try again.

"Was it truly a mistake?"

23

JULIA

MY HEART SKIPS A beat as Hannah voices the question I've been unsure how to answer since it happened.

But as she looks at me with those devastating eyes, I know what I desperately want to believe. So I let myself nod. "I never meant for our feedings to...to end in her death."

Hannah dips her chin, studying me closely. "Did you love her?"

The question catches me off guard. I open my mouth, but nothing comes out.

Was what I felt for Charlotte love? Or was it lust and obsession?

I cared for her, certainly. I enjoyed her devotion and the way she made me feel needed, wanted, and less alone. But was I truly in love? Am I capable of such a thing?

"I thought I did," I admit. "But perhaps I loved what she gave me more than who she was."

Hannah flinches like I've struck her. "And am I another Charlotte to you?"

The question hits me like a stake through the ribs.

She is nothing like Charlotte. Charlotte was pliant and eager to give me everything I wanted. Hannah fights me at every turn and sees through every lie I tell. She threatens something far more dangerous than obsession.

But how can I possibly voice all this? Will it be enough?

I shake my head and step closer, but she steps back, keeping distance between us. And for once, watching her back away from me doesn't put a thrill in my chest, but something a little painful.

"You still don't trust me?" My voice comes out sharp and angry. "After I've spent all night keeping you alive?"

"Only because you have to. Our lives are bound by a spell. If it weren't for that, you would have killed me the moment you saw me. Because that's what you do best."

I clench my teeth. She's not wrong. Without the binding spell to constrain me, I would have drained her in her backyard and left her corpse among the ashes of her fire.

"Rebecca only told you about Charlotte to poison your mind against me," I say.

"She told me information I deserve to know. And it all fits. Did you not try to abandon me in the forest as soon as you thought you were free?"

I open my mouth to argue, then close it. I can't deny it.

I step closer again, backing Hannah into the shelves so she's forced to meet my eyes. "Rebecca told you all this because she is setting us up to be trapped forever. We're both her victims, and we cannot let her win."

"Whatever Rebecca is doing to us doesn't change what you did to Charlotte."

I flex my fingers, fighting a constricting sensation around my ribs. She's right, but I won't admit it.

Hannah leans against the shelves and closes her eyes. The green light from the veins in the ceiling shifts over her exhausted, pale face. The dark circles under her eyes are more pronounced, evidence of how long a night it's been and how much energy I took from her.

An awful certainty settles into my gut: if we don't break this spell, being bound to me is going to kill her.

"Hannah, I need you to trust me. If you don't, we're going to be stuck like this forever."

Her eyes snap open. "How am I supposed to trust you, Julia?"

I draw a breath, trying to think of some way to prove to her that I don't want to hurt her. "You have my word that what happened with Charlotte won't happen with you."

"But how can you promise that? You tried to leave me unconscious—"

"My thoughts were on the binding spell."

"And just now, with Riley—"

"I stopped feeding on her because of you!" The words tear out of me. "You're the only person who's been able to make me stop, Hannah."

Hannah stares at me, her lips parted, her eyes wide.

My words hang between us, and I realize what I've revealed. Not just that she affects me, but how much. In a lifetime of taking what I want, she's the first person who's made me want to stop.

If she didn't know before what she does to me, she knows now. She knows how much power she holds over me.

I shift my weight, desperate to take the words back. Dammit. I shouldn't have admitted that.

The binding spell that's been rooting behind my ribs all night throbs, tightening and loosening. I rub my chest as if that will calm it.

At last, she drops her gaze, swallowing hard. "But once the spell is broken, you'll be done with me, won't you? It won't matter what happens to me."

I've been so focused on how to break the bond that I haven't paused to consider what happens after. When we're no longer forced into each other's lives, will I simply disappear back into the shadows and find new prey like I did before?

The thought should appeal to me. Freedom, independence, no more binding spell to force me to care about another person's wellbeing.

So why does the idea make my chest hollow? Why does the idea of never seeing Hannah again, never touching her skin, and never tasting the particular sweetness that belongs only to her, feel less like freedom and more like loss?

I push the thought away. I'm confusing the bond with genuine feeling. Once we're free of each other, whatever this is will fade.

It has to.

"I don't know what will happen after the binding breaks," I say, and I'm disturbed by how much the uncertainty bothers me. "But we won't have to worry about that if we don't break the spell to begin with. Which looks more and more likely, with Rebecca's meddling."

Hannah studies my face, and for a moment, I think I see something soften in her expression. But then she looks away.

A long, unbearable silence stretches between us.

I've run out of ideas. How do you convince someone to trust a monster?

Even I have to admire Rebecca's brilliance. She has ensured that breaking the spell requires the one thing Hannah will never willingly give me.

Heaviness settles over me. Rebecca has won. By telling her about Charlotte, she's put the final nail in the coffin.

"I need to be alone right now," Hannah says, and before I can tell her to wait, she's fleeing the sanctum, racing up the stone steps toward the closed bookcase.

The binding spell tugs painfully at my chest, demanding I keep her close.

Mine to protect.

But the pull feels different now, like something else is buried beneath the magical compulsion. I want to stop her and call her back, and not just because of the tug in my chest that's throbbing so hard it hurts.

Instead, I wave my hand to open the bookcase and let her pass. I don't wish to trap her here with me. I suppose sometime between the forest and the sanctum, Hannah Schmidt has stopped being prey.

Her footsteps retreat through the parlor and across the foyer.

I wince as Elizabeth's front door slams shut, the sound echoing through the house.

I'm alone again, just as I've been for over a century.

Except now, for the first time, something is missing.

24

HANNAH

FROST CRYSTALLIZES ON THE lawn as I march back to the road, my ragged breaths forming clouds that dissolve into the darkness. The cold bites my skin, but I barely feel it past the burning in my chest—half pain from the binding spell, half something I refuse to name.

I get to the iron gates and loop my fingers through the icy bars, using the bite of freezing metal to distract me from the pull that demands I go back.

Do I believe Julia's promise to keep me safe, or is she just saying whatever she must to break the binding spell?

I want to believe her. I want to think I'm different from everyone else—that she secretly cares about me, and I'm the only person she can feed on without killing, and this irresistible spark between us is real.

But I'd be a fool to trust a sanguine witch.

Fuck, I need to talk to someone.

My hands shake as I pull out my phone, my fingers so cold I nearly drop it. The screen's brightness stings my eyes and makes me squint.

It's five in the morning. An ungodly hour to be calling. But Dean has talked me down from major life crises before, and if he managed to talk me through the day my parents moved away on me, he can talk me through anything.

My thumb hovers over his name for several breaths before I get up the nerve to tap it.

Dean answers on the third ring, his voice groggy from being woken up. "Han? You okay?"

"Yeah. I mean, not really." I know he can't do a thing to help me, and if I tell him what's happened since he left my yard, he's going to think I've lost my mind, but... "I just need your advice."

"Sure. What's up?" He sounds more awake now, maybe reading the distress in my tone.

"I've...spent all night with a woman," I say, hoping this is a good enough metaphor for being magically bound to her.

"Tonight?" A pause. He gives a muffled grunt, like he's rubbing his face. "Did you go clubbing after I left or something?"

I hesitate, my breath fogging in the pre-dawn air. It's the most plausible explanation that doesn't open an entire barrel of worms. "Yeah."

"Wow. I'm offended you didn't invite me, but go on."

"Sorry. Well, we hooked up, but it's hard for me to... Like, I'm having a hard time surrendering to her." I cringe as the words come out.

"Surrendering? That's a poetic way of putting it. Or a kinky way, maybe. I'm not sure which."

Despite everything, I huff out a laugh. "Trusting her, I mean."

"You *just* got your heart broken, Han. Give yourself time."

I tip my head back. The sky is still so dark and the stars so bright, belying how little time we have left. "Right. Yeah."

How do I explain that I don't *have* time? That I need to surrender in the next couple of hours if I don't want to be tethered to a sanguine witch for the rest of my life?

"What's she like?" Dean asks.

I turn around. Down the long driveway, Elizabeth's house sits like a Gothic shadow against the night sky. What's Julia doing right now? Is she hurting as much as I am?

Her face swims into my vision, with her wicked smile, wild hair, and piercing blue eyes that make me forget what life was like before she came along.

"Mysterious. Clever. Gorgeous. Older. More confident than anyone I've ever met. I just...can't figure out if she actually cares about me or is manipulating me to get what she wants."

Dean is quiet for a moment. "How much older?"

"Does it matter?"

"Depends. Are we talking cougar territory or predator territory?"

If he knew the truth, his head would explode. "She's experienced and knows who she is."

"But you're afraid she's going to abandon you," he says gently.

The word "abandon" makes me flinch. My throat is too tight to respond, so I say nothing.

In the silence, a bird calls from the forest, and the sound is so normal that I could almost convince myself that the last few hours were a nightmare.

"I still think you need to give yourself time to heal from having your heart broken," Dean says, "but I also think you're so scared of getting abandoned again that you're looking for reasons to push people away before they can hurt you."

"Can you blame me? My own parents couldn't wait to get rid of me the second I turned eighteen. And don't get me started on Riley." I shiver, my fingers, nose, and ears going numb.

"I know. You deserve better than all that shit."

"So how am I supposed to tell who's going to hurt me and who's here to stay?" My voice cracks. "What if I decide to trust her, and she disappears like everyone else in my life has?"

"Not everyone has disappeared."

"You're different."

Voicing this fear makes something twist in my chest. Why do I care if Julia is gone from my life? Do I actually want her to stay?

Of course you do, says a small voice in my head. *You like her, and not just because it feels good to be fed on.*

"I know it's hard, but try not to let Riley or your parents impact your relationships," Dean says. "They lost the right to have any sway over your life the moment they chose to leave it."

He's right. I've been letting old wounds dictate my choices, using their betrayals as a reason to never be vulnerable again.

"You're someone worth staying for," he adds, "and the fact that your parents and Riley couldn't see that is their loss. If this woman is as mature and confident as you say she is, then I bet she sees that too."

Tears burn my eyes. "And if she doesn't?"

"Then you'll survive it, just like you survived Riley, and just like you survived your parents. But Han, what if you *don't* try, and you spend the rest of your life running from anyone who might want to stay?"

A gust of wind rattles the gates, and I shiver harder. I shuffle my feet to try and warm up. I wish I could tell him this isn't just about whether or not I'll get my heart broken. Where Julia is involved, my actual life is at risk.

"Anyway, you're putting the burden of vulnerability all on yourself," Dean says. "What about her?"

I furrow my brow. "What do you mean?"

"Like, do you feel like she's being totally vulnerable and trusting with *you*? Trust is a two-way thing, Han. Or surrender, if that's what you want to call it."

"I—I guess she's got her own issues too." I bite my lip. What am I saying? She has a *lot* of her own issues. "She did almost leave me after we hooked up."

"Okay, see? You don't have to bear your soul without receiving vulnerability in return. The trust you're looking for will happen when you're both ready, if that's what you want."

"I doubt she'll..." I stop shuffling my feet, going still. *Wait.* Does he have a point about this going both ways?

Rebecca never said I had to be the only one to surrender. She just said total surrender was the way out.

What if I'm not the only one who needs to surrender to break the binding spell?

"Han? Still there?"

My heart beats faster. I clutch my chest, recalling the warm purr there when we kissed for the first time, and Julia brushed my cheeks with her thumbs in a fleeting moment of tenderness. Was that sensation the spell cracking? Was she already beginning to surrender her heart in that split second? And all those other moments when she looked at me with unexpected softness...the warmth behind my ribs, like the spell was squeezing and releasing...

Holy crap. This could be the answer. It makes terrible, perfect sense. Of course Rebecca would design a spell that requires Julia to—

My excitement crashes. "What if she's incapable of being vulnerable?" I ask, barely a whisper.

"That's not for you to fix." Dean's voice gets serious. "Anyway, if she's got her own baggage and already just about ditched you tonight, maybe it's for the best if you go home and chalk this up to a rebound one-night stand."

I bite back a hysterical laugh. If only it were that simple. If only I could go home, shower off the night, and never think about Julia Moreau again.

In any ordinary circumstance, I'd agree with him. But I don't have time to wait for Julia to go to therapy or do some soul searching, and I don't have time to process my breakup. We need to break this spell within the next couple of hours—and I might finally know how to do it.

"You can take a leap of faith with this woman if you want," Dean says into the silence. "But you can't be the only one jumping."

He's right.

I swallow hard. If breaking the binding spell requires both of us to be vulnerable, then I know what I have to do. I need to get her to surrender to me. To make her open her heart enough to let me in. If she can do that, not only will we break the spell, but then I'll know that this connection between us is real.

I drop my shoulders and let out a slow breath. "I love you, Dean. Thanks."

"I love you too. You sure you're okay? Want me to come get you?"

"I'm good. I've got this."

We say goodbye, and I start walking back across the lawn, my shoes crunching on the frost-stiff grass. The binding spell loosens with each step closer, like my body is sighing in relief.

In the forest, birds begin their dawn chorus, their songs cutting through the silence. The world is waking up, oblivious to the impossible task ahead of me.

One thing I've learned tonight is that a sanguine witch always takes what she wants. She doesn't ask. She doesn't yield. Now, somehow, I have to flip that. I have to convince Julia Moreau, a woman who believes she's a monster incapable of love, to surrender to me the same way I surrendered to her.

Somehow, I need her to let me take control.

25

JULIA

A LONE IN THE SANCTUM, I seize the grimoire Elizabeth left behind and drop to my knees, flipping feverishly through the pages. I'm willing to try anything at this point—blood magic, necromancy, nothing is off limits.

I've scanned a few pages when an explosion rattles the stairwell, and I gasp, leaping to my feet. Wood splinters and books tumble down the stone steps in a cloud of dust.

"You just couldn't *wait* to take another innocent life." Rebecca stalks into the chamber, her hands glowing with white-hot magic. "Is that all you know how to do? Take and take until there's nothing left?"

I raise my hands defensively. "She volunteered—"

Rebecca's hand cuts through the air, and an invisible force slams into my chest, the full weight of a century of grief behind it. I fly backward into the wooden shelves with a thud that rattles my bones. Wood cracks and jars shatter, raining glass across the floor.

Coughing, I push myself up, tasting blood where I've bitten my tongue. "She offered herself to break your damned spell," I grit out.

"Liar," Rebecca snarls. "Riley would never submit herself to a sanguine witch. She knows what you are."

I wipe blood from my lips, grinning through the pain. "You underestimated how far she would go to protect the love of her life. When you cursed me, I suppose you didn't consider how your curse would affect your own descendant."

In Rebecca's moment of shock, I lash out with my own power, sending the surrounding glass shards at her like bullets.

She raises her hands and deflects most of them, but hisses as red cuts open in her palms. "Just because someone offers themselves to you doesn't give you the right to kill them!"

My hair lifts as magic fills the sanctum, trapped and amplified by the stone walls and runes. The air crackles with our combined fury, stinging my skin like biting insects.

"Charlotte knew the risks—"

"Don't you dare speak her name!" Rebecca's voice breaks as she summons the sand from the scattered pentagram. "You don't get to justify what you did to her."

She hurls the sand at me. It stings my face and burns my eyes, filling my mouth until I cough and splutter.

"I should have killed you," Rebecca hisses, just a voice now. "I should've burned you to ash instead of trapping you in that journal."

I force my eyes open and send the wooden table at her, the memory of Charlotte throwing me off balance and making my attack clumsy. She swipes it aside, and it shatters against the wall.

Everything is blurry. My skin stings and my eyes are streaming. I can see enough to know that every flaming candle, jagged bone, and glass shard has lifted into the air at her command.

"But you didn't kill me," I say, my voice rough from sand and something else I will not acknowledge. I hold up one hand, not to retaliate, but as a plea for her to stop. "You gave me a chance. Let me prove to you that I deserve it."

There's a pause. Everything in the room hangs suspended.

"Bullshit," Rebecca snarls. "You proved what you are the night you killed Charlotte, and now you're going to do the same thing to Hannah."

The binding spell cinches around my chest in Hannah's absence, and suddenly it's hard to breathe. Rebecca's right. History is repeating itself, and I am letting it happen.

My vision blurs—from the sand or something else, I cannot say. "You think I don't know that? You think I didn't spend years grieving her, waking up in a sweat, seeing her every time I closed my eyes?"

Rebecca stands frozen, hands up, chest heaving. Everything around us trembles in the air, magic sparking between the debris like lightning.

I raise my hands, ready for the attack. God, this is going to hurt. But I deserve every cut and bruise coming my way.

"Stop!" Elizabeth's voice cuts through the chaos.

Green light explodes between us, forcing us apart with such violence that I slam into the wall. The impact knocks the wind from my lungs. Rebecca hits the opposite wall with equal force, and all her suspended weapons clatter to the floor.

"Enough!" Elizabeth stands on the last stone step, her silver hair wild, magic radiating from her in waves. "Rebecca, return to Riley's bedside, for fuck's sake. Julia, a word."

I labor to my feet, trying to steady my ragged breathing. My magic sparks erratically around me, uncontrolled.

Rebecca glares at me as she climbs the steps, and I return it, wiping blood from my nose.

Once she's gone, Elizabeth rounds on me, nostrils flaring. "Have you lost your mind?"

"She came after me!"

"After watching you nearly drain another person she cares about!" Elizabeth's eyes flash dangerously. "Is that your grand plan? Kill everyone Rebecca loves?"

I pace a small circle through the debris, my fingers crackling with unspent magic. "Nothing is working. We've tried everything, and the binding spell is ironclad. The moon will set soon, and then—" I swipe my hand, and a crystal slams into the wall, where it explodes in a shower of glittering purple fragments. "Then I'm trapped forever with someone who despises me."

"Hannah doesn't despise you."

I laugh bitterly. "Rebecca told her about Charlotte. Of course she does."

"I don't think it's that simple."

My throat is so tight it hurts. I grind my teeth, looking down at the shattered glass, wood shards, and herbs scattered around me.

Elizabeth sighs. "Julia, you're so determined to be the monster that you can't see what's right in front of you."

I clench my fists, and the debris trembles. "I killed Charlotte, I tried to kill Riley, and I would have killed Hannah long ago if not for this damned binding spell. That is my nature—I destroy everything I touch."

Elizabeth crosses her arms and taps her fingers. "You stopped feeding on Riley tonight."

"What of it?"

"Do you wish you hadn't stopped? Do you wish Hannah had let you drain her?"

I pause. How *did* I want that to end? Surely not with another dead woman, especially with Hannah watching. "No."

Elizabeth opens her hands. "There you go. Monsters don't feel grateful when their prey escapes."

I huff out a humorless laugh.

"You know I'm right," she says. "You didn't want to kill Riley, and you didn't want to kill Charlotte. There are two halves of you, Julia."

I blink away the burning in my eyes. "Every time I fed from Charlotte, part of me wanted to stop, but...the power was too intoxicating. It was in her final moment, when I killed a woman I cared about, that I realized killing is in my nature. That I have no choice."

"But tonight you had a choice, and you chose to let Riley live."

"I stopped out of self-preservation. If I'd killed Riley, Hannah would never..." I wave a hand, unsure how to finish that sentence.

"Never trust you? Never surrender to you?" Elizabeth steps closer, her voice softening. "Or never look at you again the way she does when your back is turned?"

Heat floods my face. "The way she looks at me is just intoxication. Feedings and the binding spell and—"

"Don't be a fool. You know as well as I do that the binding spell doesn't create affection, and feedings are no more than physical pleasure. No magic made her throw herself between you and Riley to save you both."

I scoff. When Hannah broke into the pentagram, she had eyes only for Riley, and I was nothing but the devil who hurt her. "She was saving Riley, not me."

"She was saving you from becoming the monster you're so convinced you are." Elizabeth sweeps her hand, and the fragments around the room begin to drift into a pile like a gust of wind is pushing them together. "That girl sees something in you worth saving, Julia. The question is whether you'll let her."

"There is nothing to see. I am what I am."

"Your nature is not your destiny."

"Words easily spoken by a green witch. Your magic doesn't require you to hurt people." My hands are shaking. I clench my fists, fighting the urge to sink to the floor and close my eyes. "You don't have to live each day knowing that someone has to suffer for you to survive until the next lunar cycle."

"No, but I've lived long enough to know that what we are and who we choose to be are two different things."

"And if choosing isn't enough? If I lose control again?"

"Then at least you'll have tried to be something more than what you believe yourself to be."

I stare at my hands, which have taken so many lives. I want to agree with her, but I don't know if I can. "It doesn't matter. Hannah will never trust me now. Rebecca made sure of that."

"Rebecca told her the truth. What Hannah does with it is her choice."

"Her choice will be to stay as far from me as the binding spell allows."

Elizabeth sighs, moving toward the door. "Perhaps. Or perhaps she'll surprise you."

I shake my head.

"Julia... Hannah has affected you more than anyone has since Charlotte, and you're determined not to see it. Charlotte loved and trusted you, and—"

"Don't," I say, the word barely coming out.

"Do you think she was wrong to love you?"

"Of course I do."

Elizabeth's brow furrows. "That's too bad. Because I think she saw a part of you that even you don't know exists. And I think Hannah might be willing to see that part of you, too."

There's a pause. Somewhere beyond the stone passageway, the grandfather clock ticks on.

"It's a quarter to six," Elizabeth says. "If you want to break this spell before your time runs out, you're going to have to convince a woman who's currently terrified of you that she can trust you. It's the only way."

I stare at her. Does she realize how impossible that sounds?

Knowing Rebecca must be checking the time and smiling makes me flex my fingers, itching to blast something to dust.

Elizabeth turns to leave.

"How the hell am I supposed to do that?" I blurt, and there's no masking the panic in my tone. How can I convince Hannah to trust me when I cannot even trust myself?

She looks back over her shoulder, a crease between her eyebrows as she studies me. "Surrender requires vulnerability. If you want Hannah to surrender her heart, you might need to surrender yours first."

I scoff. That advice is about the furthest from useful she could get. I never asked for Hannah's heart.

"And clean this room up," she says as she climbs the stone steps. "I want everything back in its place."

I scowl after her.

Elizabeth has always been fair and trusting toward all witches who join our coven. She tries to find goodness in everyone, even the cruelest among us. But she does not understand what it's like to have darkness written into your soul. To know that every relationship, every connection, every moment of tenderness is a prelude to destruction.

Soon, Hannah will be trapped with me forever—a slow death sentence for a girl whose only crime was burning the wrong book.

Rebecca has created the perfect prison, one where I'm forced to watch another woman I...yes, a woman I care about...waste away, knowing I'm the cause but powerless to stop it.

I try to imagine a future where Hannah and I could coexist. Is it possible? Is there a way she could remain in my life without wasting away?

But all I see is Charlotte's corpse, and suddenly it's Hannah's empty eyes and gray skin in her place. The vision is so vivid I can feel it—Hannah going cold beneath my lips, her pulse weakening until it stops, that terrible moment of realization that comes too late.

My insides lurch. I splay my hand against the wall to steady myself.

I cannot survive watching another woman die because she was foolish enough to trust me.

Maybe that is my real curse. Not the binding spell, but the certainty that I will destroy anyone who gets too close. And maybe Rebecca understood that all along.

I seize the grimoire once more, determined to find a way out. I have to keep trying until our time is up. Not because I believe Elizabeth's platitudes about choice and destiny, but because watching another woman waste away at my hands is a torment I will not survive twice.

26

HANNAH

THE GRANDFATHER CLOCK STRIKES six by the time I get up the nerve to enter the parlor again. Only an hour until the moon sets. An hour to convince Julia to surrender, which I'm willing to bet is something she's never done before.

Julia is in one of the wingback chairs, a stack of ancient books beside her, one of them open in her lap with symbols written across the page. She's concentrating so hard she doesn't see me, so I lean against the doorframe to watch her for a moment.

Her profile is striking in the firelight—the sharp angles of her cheekbones and jawline, her neck, the straight line of her nose. Her thick hair is tucked behind her ear and her ankles are crossed, making her look so normal. She's running an elegant finger down the page, her lips moving silently as she concentrates. My fingers ache to touch her and smooth the crease between her brows.

The room is peaceful, just her and the crackling fire, which has been rekindled with more wood. I picture myself sitting beside her and picking up my own book, the two of us reading under the warm glow while frost builds outside, catching each other's eye and smiling.

A whole other life that will never happen.

Why did that image come to mind, anyway? Julia is not that type of person. She and I could never be on those terms.

I watch her fingers move across the pages with surprising delicacy for someone so deadly—those fingers that were inside me a short while ago. My thighs clench at the memory. I'm still tingling between my legs, wanting more.

I trace my gaze down the swell of her breasts and the curve of her waist. Is there anyone more beautiful in the entire world?

My breath hitches as I try to keep my composure. Slowly, over the course of the evening, I've become insatiable for her. Even the simple flex of her forearm as she turns the page makes my mouth dry.

I shut the parlor doors and lock them, and the click makes her look up.

Our eyes meet across the room, and the air changes, the temperature seeming to rise several degrees.

The firelight throws shadows across her face. Her wintry eyes pin me in place, and her parted lips remind me of her bruising kisses. My skin prickles with the memory of what we did in the forest.

If I'm not mistaken, there's a flash of that look on her face now. Like the memory is tormenting her, too.

Good. Let her want me until she can't take it anymore.

The air is thick. It feels like an invisible wall is pressing at my back, forcing me closer.

I can see her fighting the binding spell's pull too, gripping the edges of the book in her lap with white knuckles.

"Find anything?" My voice comes out strained.

She blinks and looks down at the book. "Rebecca was thorough."

The defeat in her tone makes my chest squeeze. I've never heard her sound so human.

I walk over, my bare feet silent on the Persian rug, my heart pounding.

Riley would be horrified at what I'm about to do. Dean would drag me out of here. But they're not the ones bound to her. They don't understand this pull inside me. Being close to her is the only thing my body wants, and it's the only way out of this.

So I keep walking closer. "Julia."

She meets my gaze, and the rawness in her eyes catches me off guard. For once, there's no predatory confidence, just a woman facing the possibility of losing everything.

I swallow hard, summoning bravery. "I'm ready to try again. To trust you fully this time."

Her eyes widen in surprise. Then her brow furrows, and she searches my face. "After what Rebecca told you?"

"*Because* of what she told me." I move close enough to catch her scent, which sends a comforting trickle through my veins. "I understand what I'm risking now, and I'm choosing it anyway."

"Then you're either incredibly brave or incredibly foolish."

"Maybe I'm both. But...I'm also incredibly tired of being afraid." It hits me that I'm not afraid of her anymore, which doesn't make sense, given all I've learned. Then again, maybe it makes perfect sense. "Of everyone in my life, you're the only one who's been honest about who you are. Riley lied. My parents pretended to care when they didn't. At least you were honest from the moment we met."

Julia closes the book and lays it on the pile, her movements slow. "Honesty is no reason to trust me, pet. If we attempt this again and fail—"

"I'm positive. But I need something from you." My pulse quickens. This is the gamble. "I need something real."

She goes very still.

I take a breath, steadying myself. "I want us to have sex, and not just for the purpose of feeding. You can feed on me at the end, but I need this if I'm going to trust you fully."

I'm not being entirely truthful about my revelation, but this is necessary. She needs to think this is about me surrendering and trusting her enough to let go. If she knows I'm trying to make her surrender too, she'll get her guard up even more than it already is.

"That is not what I am, Hannah." Her voice wavers, and she breaks our gaze.

She's afraid of what she feels. Which means she feels something. If I can make her want me so much that she lets me take control...

"I'm not asking you to change who you are." I close the distance between us, standing over her. To have her seated like this, looking up at me, feels like a reversal of how things have been all night. My stomach flutters as my body recognizes what could happen if she agrees.

"What, then?" she murmurs.

I run my fingers through her hair, toying with the tangled strands. She goes still beneath my touch.

Her hair is softer than it looks—thick and silky, smelling faintly of smoke and that apple-cinnamon scent I've come to crave.

I let the strands slip through my fingers slowly, watching the way her breath hitches. The sound is barely noticeable, small and involuntary, but it's there.

I do it again, this time letting my nails scrape gently against her scalp. "In the forest, I couldn't surrender fully because it was just about the feeding. About you taking my life force. You were still clothed, and...I need more than that."

Her chest rises and falls more rapidly as I stand over her, combing my fingers through her hair. One more step and I'd be right in her lap.

She searches my face. Her tongue darts out to wet her lips, and I suppress the desire to lean in.

"I can't surrender to a sanguine witch," I say, "but I can surrender to you."

She scowls at the fire, a muscle in her jaw jumping. "You're a fool if you think there's a difference."

I reach out and trace along her jawline, angling her face back toward me. She doesn't pull away. "Tell me you don't want me, Julia. Tell me that when you touched me in the forest, it was only about feeding."

Her pupils dilate. "Very well. But I—I don't know what you would have me do if I'm not to feed."

My pulse quickens until I feel it in my throat. Has Julia never had sex except to feed?

All this life experience, and she's never had an intimate encounter that wasn't about her magic. She's never seduced for pure passion or touched someone just to feel them. She's never had someone pleasure her because they want *her* instead of her magic. She's never just been a woman wanting another woman.

The realization puts a surprising ache in my chest. I'm not just asking her to surrender—I'm asking her to be vulnerable in a way she's never been before. To let me see her as something other than a sanguine witch.

I thought I was the inexperienced one, but in this, she's more innocent than I am.

No wonder she looks afraid.

"Let me show you." My voice comes out breathy, betraying how much I want her.

Before I lose my nerve, I straddle her lap—one knee on either side of her thighs, my arms caging her head as I grip the back of the chair.

Her breath hitches as she looks up at me. I swear I can feel her heartbeat from here, racing as fast as mine.

Seeing the hungry look on her face and knowing I can affect her like this makes me dizzy with want.

Her eyes drop to my mouth, and her lips part.

I bend down and bring my lips to hers, savoring her sweet taste.

Her mouth opens for me, and her hands glide up my waist to hold me.

She leans forward as if to get up, but I press into her harder, pinning her with my body. I trace her lower lip with my tongue, and she lets out a soft sound that sends heat straight to my core.

I break the kiss and pull back enough to look at her. "Tell me you want this," I whisper.

Her chest heaves against mine. Her eyes are wide, her lips full with that freshly kissed look.

She dips her chin in the smallest of nods.

I might be imagining it, but I swear she's already starting to surrender.

And once she does—once she comes apart for me—we'll both be free.

Or so I hope.

27

JULIA

HANNAH'S WEIGHT ON MY lap is driving me to madness. It's hard to believe this woman who once looked at me with fear is now writhing on top of me, claiming my mouth like she's trying to devour me. Her tongue flicks over mine, and when she rocks her hips against me, it's everything not to throw aside my promise and begin the feeding incantation.

My magic stirs restlessly beneath my skin, confused by the pleasure without purpose, the touch without taking.

In all my years, all my feedings, no one has ever asked me to be with them without my magic. They wanted the power, the intoxication, the dark thrill of being consumed. But Hannah wants...what? I don't understand why she insists on this. What's the point of this intimacy if I'm not going to fill my magic in the process?

But if this is how I get her to surrender enough to break the spell, so be it.

I grip her waist and kiss her back hard, running my tongue over her lips. Somewhere during the evening, my desire for her has turned into something painful. Every brush of her lips sends fire through my veins, and every sound she makes deepens the ache between my legs until I cannot think.

Her hands tangle in my hair, tugging hard enough to make my breath hitch. She swallows the sound with a deeper kiss, and I can't help the way my back arches to meet her.

What is she doing to me? Making my body move without my permission, making my breath catch and my insides ache with desire. I'm Julia Moreau. I do not lose control. I do not let anyone reduce me to trembling need, no matter how beautiful. But her hands in my hair, her tongue in my mouth...

This is dangerous. A traitorous part of me wants to be touched without the excuse of hunger, to matter to someone beyond what my magic can do for them.

"You're thinking too much," Hannah murmurs against my mouth, her breath hot. "Let go."

She grinds down against me, the friction through our clothes making my thoughts dissipate like scattering dust. And as she trails her lips down my throat, nipping at spots that make me shiver, the confusion roaring inside me falls away. All that matters are her lips and hands.

She pulls back to look at me, her eyes wide and wild, her lips swollen from our kisses. No one has ever looked at me the way she does, with a hunger that matches my own.

"That's better," she whispers.

Before I can deny whatever she thinks I'm feeling, she rocks back and grabs the hem of that tiny shirt of hers. She pulls it over her head, revealing her perfect breasts and hard nipples. Her smooth, pale skin isn't full of goosebumps this time, but she's marked by my fingers and the rough tree bark from earlier. This evidence of what we did, of the way she begged and moaned for me in the woods, makes something desperate roar back to life inside me. I want to mark her again. I want to bite her perfect skin until she's gasping my name.

Without taking my eyes off her, I extend my hand toward the parlor doors, sealing them with a rune. Of course, nothing will truly keep Elizabeth out of a room in her own house, but it will be enough to deter her and to stop the others from entering.

Hannah glances at the door, her chest heaving as she watches red marks seal us in as if by a molten blade.

"Undress for me," I command. I want to savor this, to see every inch of skin she reveals for me.

She hesitates for the briefest moment, then stands, removing her bottoms so she's naked in front of me once more.

"Your turn," she whispers.

She reaches for my bodice, and I catch her wrists, stopping her. The movement was instinctive, my body reacting before I thought about what I was doing.

Hannah goes still, holding my gaze. "Trust me."

The word prickles my ears. *Trust.* I have never granted anyone such power.

Every instinct screams at me to get to my feet and back her against the wall, to pin her wrists above her head and show her who's in control. I could have her on her back in seconds, legs spread and bound by magic, perfect lips begging. The urge to dominate her is so strong that magic crackles between my knuckles.

But something challenging in her gaze makes me stay seated. She is daring me to let this happen...and I hate how much I want it.

Slowly, I force my fingers to uncurl, releasing her wrists.

My pulse is racing. This simple act of letting go feels like stepping off a cliff. Every second I allow her to continue is a second I'm not dictating what happens next, not protected by the armor of dominance.

But when she smiles—not triumphant, but something softer—the unease inside me loosens, and I let her reach forward once more. Her hands are gentle as she finds the small hooks down the front of my bodice. One by one, she pries them free until the whole piece relaxes.

She eases it open, sliding her hands around my waist as she pushes the cloth back.

With only my blouse and chemise between her skin and mine, her touch is like fire, making me burn and ache everywhere.

She kisses me, slow and deep, then pulls back to unbutton my blouse next. When the cool air meets my skin, she pushes it back over my shoulders, her hands following. Only my chemise is left.

She traces the curves and planes of my body like she's memorizing me. I shiver.

Never has anyone touched me like this. Charlotte worshipped my power, but Hannah touches me like...

I don't know.

I don't understand her.

My heart pounds as she reaches for my chemise and tugs upward.

I lift my arms, letting her remove it, aching to feel her soft touch on my bare skin.

I'm more exposed than I've ever been. Not just my skin, but something deeper that I've kept locked away since Charlotte's body went cold beneath me.

God, I don't deserve Hannah's gentle hands, her wanting eyes, the way she caresses me. What if this ends the same way? What if I let Hannah touch me, not for feeding but for pleasure, and I destroy her anyway? She is the one person who has dared to see me as a woman instead of a sanguine witch, and I don't know if I can be that for her.

"Beautiful," Hannah breathes, and before I can process the compliment, she lowers her mouth to my chest.

The wet heat of her tongue on my breast makes me arch, a sound I don't recognize leaving my throat. She takes her time, lavishing my breasts with attention until I'm panting, my fingers tangled in her hair. When she grazes her teeth over the sensitive peaks, molten heat rushes through me. I'm so ready for her that every brush of her tongue feels like torture.

When did pleasure become something I am allowed to receive instead of just take?

"Hannah—"

She raises herself up and captures my mouth again, swallowing my protest. Her hand slides between my legs, rubbing through my trousers, and pleasure surges through me at her touch.

My face is hot. Sweat prickles the back of my neck. This is mortifying. I don't respond like this. I'm the one who makes others writhe and beg. It must be magic at play, all these manipulative spells stripping away my defenses and turning me into someone desperate.

Or maybe it's not magic. Maybe it's just Hannah, whispers an annoying voice at the back of my mind.

I need to regain control. I massage her breast, pinching her nipple until she gasps. I run my other hand up her thigh and between her legs, and the wetness I find there makes us both moan. I trace circles that make her tremble, then slide inside, feeling her clench around me.

"Julia," she gasps, her head tipping back.

She rocks against my hand, mesmerizing in the way she moves and the sounds she makes. When I rub my thumb over her pearl, she cries out, her grip digging into my shoulders.

Her breasts bounce as she rides my fingers, her thighs hot through the material of my trousers.

But the facade of control is brief, and too soon, she's sliding off my lap. I grab her to pull her back, but she resists. Instead, she sinks to her knees between my legs, looking up at me with greedy eyes.

She slides her hands up my thighs and begins unbuttoning my trousers.

I watch her, dizzy, breathing hard. I don't stop her.

When she tugs my trousers down, I buck my hips to let her, and the next thing I know, I'm completely naked.

"Spread your legs for me," she says, throwing my own words from the forest back at me.

I open my mouth to tell her to take that back. I am the one who consumes, not the one who gets consumed. But as she looks up at me with those devastating eyes, I can do nothing but give in.

The smile that curves her lips is absolutely wicked. When did she learn to look at me like that? When did the innocent girl from the backyard become this creature who makes me burn before she's even touched me?

She leans in, her breath ghosting over where I'm aching for her, and I have to grip the chair to keep from grabbing her head and directing her mouth where I want it.

A desperate sound leaves my throat, and all I can think is "*yes.*" I need her mouth on me more than I need my next breath.

She looks up at me one more time, holding my gaze as she leans in.

Do I stop her? If I let her pleasure me like this, there will be no more pretending this is just about breaking the spell. I need to take back control before it's too late, before she reduces me to something weak and desperate and—

Her tongue slides over my center, and coherent thought abandons me entirely.

28

HANNAH

I DRAG MY PALMS down Julia's waist and along her inner thighs, savoring the silky texture of her skin. The sight of her naked body is more than I can bear—her full breasts, the curve of her waist, the warm glow of her skin in the firelight.

I open her legs further and glide my tongue up her center, slow and firm.

She makes the sweetest sound, her thighs trembling. Her fingers thread through my hair, her touch sending a shiver through me.

Her taste and scent are driving me wild. I want to devour her like she's the first meal I've had in months. But I hold back, taking this slow.

"I've been wanting to taste you all night," I whisper against her inner thigh. I ghost my breath over her center, teasing her, drawing this out.

Her fingers tighten in my hair, and she whimpers incoherently.

I push her legs further apart, draping one over the chair's armrest. Her breath hitches, and for a moment, she tenses. But as I part her folds with both hands and lick her again, she tips her head back, moaning louder this time.

I swirl my tongue, exploring her, testing what makes her thighs quake and involuntary sounds burst from her lips.

She tastes so sweet I can't stand it.

I crawl closer, burying my face between her legs, and close my mouth around her. I lick and suck until I can't help the hungry, desperate sounds that come out of me. I'm being messy and sloppy, but I'm too drunk on her taste to care.

She gasps and writhes, and I grip her thighs tighter to hold her still.

"Oh—oh, that's—" she stammers, her chest heaving.

She clenches her fists like she's trying to stop trembling. Clamps her jaw shut as if forcing herself to be quiet.

She's giving me her body, letting me touch and taste her, but she's fighting the pleasure. Or maybe she's fighting the vulnerability.

Every stroke of my tongue makes her fight harder. Her chest rises and falls rapidly, a sheen of sweat glistening on her skin.

I tease her opening with two fingers. "You want me inside you?" I whisper.

She nods, and as I slide into her, the moan that bursts from her lips is so sexy it makes my core clench.

I never thought I would see Julia Moreau this undone. She's at my mercy, panting hard, her legs trembling. I stroke her inner walls while flicking my tongue relentlessly.

Goosebumps rise up her legs. She whimpers softly.

I thrust into her harder and increase the pressure of my tongue, savoring the way her breathing becomes ragged.

Her grip on my hair tightens. Her moans become breathy. "Hannah…"

I watch her face, relishing these precious minutes where the mask she presents to the world is starting to slip.

Her eyes are shut tight as she rocks her hips against my hand and mouth. Her lips are closed, her nostrils flaring as her breaths quicken. There's a crease between her brows.

She's fighting hard. She's letting me pleasure her, but pleasure isn't enough. The binding won't break if her surrender is only physical.

And *I* don't want her surrender to be purely physical. After all we've been through, I don't want this to be something she's just doing to break a spell.

I pull back.

Julia's eyelids fly open. "No," she gasps, her hips chasing my mouth. "Keep going."

I kiss her inner thigh. "Julia..."

Her brow pinches.

I lock her gaze. "I want you to let go completely. Not just your body. All of you."

She stares down at me, breathing hard, panic flickering behind the haze of desire. "I am letting go."

"No, you're not." I kiss her thigh. "You're still holding back. You're hiding behind the sensations."

"I'm not—" Her voice catches.

I stroke her soft skin, keeping my voice steady even though I'm afraid to push her too hard. "You're still trying to control what you feel. What you let me see."

Her jaw clenches. "What do you want from me?"

"I want you to stop being afraid of wanting me without magic or curses forcing your hand."

"Hannah..." It's half plea, half warning.

My heart is pounding so hard I can barely breathe. I know nobody has coaxed total surrender out of Julia Moreau before, but we need this if we want to unbind. *I* need this. I need to know I'm not just someone to feed on.

My throat tightens, but I make myself say what terrifies me most. "I care about you, Julia. You've changed me and made me braver. You've shown me a part of myself I didn't know existed." I hold her gaze, letting her see my want, fear, and hope. "Tell me you want this too. Not because you have to break a spell. Tell me you want me because you want me."

29

JULIA

WHEN HANNAH PULLS BACK, I want to scream.

But her words make me freeze, a cold sensation flooding my veins.

I care about you, Julia.

My chest heaves as I look down at her, my whole body aching for release. She looks back at me with those deep blue eyes.

What the hell does she think she's doing?

She licks a slow, torturous circle, keeping me on the edge. Draws her fingers out, then in. Molten heat blazes through my middle. The pleasure is maddening, but she won't finish it.

"Tell me what you're feeling," she whispers.

I'm trembling. I tangle my fingers in her hair, trying to guide her mouth, but she resists.

Damn her. She is going to keep me here, teetering on the edge, until I...

Realization crashes over me like cold water.

Surrender.

This is not some game of torture she's playing. She is trying to make me surrender in her own way.

Does the binding spell require *me* to give in completely? Both of us, perhaps?

My heart skips a beat as the pieces slot together. The spell has been behaving strangely these last hours, tightening and loosening in response to something I could not identify. It was *me*. *My* surrender. Whenever I softened to Hannah, the spell hummed, coming closer to snapping.

She is trying to guide me back to that place. This clever, infuriating woman has figured out what Rebecca's spell needs and is doing everything to take me there.

I should be furious. I should push her away, reclaim control, remind her who holds the power here.

But her words echo in my head. *Tell me you want me because you want me.*

My heart squeezes. Does she fear she's no more than a body that feeds my magic? Is that what I have led her to believe?

Of course I have. I've made it clear that I take what I need and discard people when I'm finished with them. She has no reason to think she is any different.

But she is. This woman with the autumn-colored hair and infuriatingly stubborn heart is different from anyone I have ever met, and I want to keep her. I want her, not because of a spell or my magic, but because she has made me feel something I thought I buried a century ago.

A terrifying truth settles over me: I want to tell her this. I want to admit that this moment with her between my legs is not about using her body to feed my magic, nor about breaking spells. This is happening because we want each other.

I wet my lips, the words sticking in my throat. Can I admit that what I feel for her has grown beyond necessity? If I surrender to her and let her know I've come to care for her, I am giving her the power to hurt me.

I could stop this and push her away. I could protect myself the way I always have, by refusing to let anyone matter.

But as I look down at her messy hair, swollen lips, and those beautiful eyes that see too much, my heart stumbles over itself.

I do not wish to protect myself from her. I'm tired of being alone and safe and feared. For once, I want somebody to see a different part of me.

"I'm yours, Hannah," I whisper.

It's all I have. All I can bring myself to say. And I hope it's enough.

The words hang in the air between us. My chest heaves as the truth settles over me—the realization that I mean it.

Her eyes light up, a flash of triumph and tenderness.

My heart beats faster. Perhaps I should not have said that. It makes me weak and—

Her mouth finds my center again, her tongue beating a relentless rhythm, and my doubts scatter.

I gasp, sinking lower in the chair. I keep my eyes open this time, watching her pleasure me.

Her tongue moves fast, gentle yet firm, then disappears as she closes her lips over me. Her fingers glisten as she pulls them out, and when she thrust them back in, she curls them, stroking my inner walls. Her other hand reaches up to tease my nipples, and the combined sensations are almost too much.

"Oh God—Hannah—I—"

I let go of her hair and grab the armrests, needing something to anchor me because I'm about to come apart. My whole body is trembling, heat spiraling up from where her mouth works against me, spreading through my limbs like wildfire.

I've taken pleasure countless times through feedings and intimate rituals, but this is so different.

Goosebumps ripple up my thighs. She pulls her fingers out and thrusts her tongue inside me instead, making me gasp. She closes her lips over me, and the moan that vibrates through her sends me over the edge.

I arch my back. I cover my face with both hands, suddenly unable to bear her seeing me so undone and vulnerable.

Pleasure rips through me like something breaking free after being caged. I cry out, the sound filling the room, and I can't stop the waves crashing over me as her tongue works me through every tremor.

When she finally stops, I'm gasping, still covering my face because I don't know how to look at her now. I don't know how to face what just happened between us.

I gave her words I've never given anyone. I am fully hers, and I cannot take that back. What happens now? I have to go on with my life knowing this woman has power over me? The vulnerability is staggering, and every instinct screams at me to take back control.

When I open my eyes at last and lower my hands, I find her sitting back on her heels, watching me. Her mouth is wet, her expression soft.

The binding spell still has its hold on us, which means we aren't done. It must be Hannah's turn to surrender to me.

Good. I need to remind her—and myself—that I am not some lovesick fool who's lost all her teeth.

Hunger surges through me. It's the familiar need to feed, yes, but also something else. I want to unravel her the same way she unraveled me. I want to see her fall apart the way I did. I want her to understand exactly what it means to open herself to me.

"My turn," I growl.

30

HANNAH

J ULIA GRIPS MY SHOULDERS and pushes me back. I let myself fall onto the rug in front of the fireplace, her on top, and for a moment, I just stare at her, taking in how unbelievably beautiful she is.

Something shifted between us when she surrendered. I could see in her eyes that she wasn't just saying the words. She meant it.

But now, as she pins me down with this hungry look in her eyes, it's clear my moment of asking her to surrender to me is over. All I can hope is that it was enough. That after she drinks her fill of me, the binding spell will be satiated.

"You must feel smug, getting me to say those words." Julia pins my wrists above my head with one hand, her hair falling down and forming a curtain around our faces. Her voice is low. "But don't forget where you belong, pet. Spread out under me, at my mercy. You got what you wanted, and now I get my end of the bargain. You're going to let me take from you until I'm satisfied."

The firelight dances across her face, highlighting the feral gleam in her eyes. This is the Julia I met in my backyard—dangerous, powerful, wild. There's something even more intense now, like all this time we've spent together has only made her hungrier.

It ignites a blazing fire deep inside me.

When did I start finding Julia's threats seductive instead of terrifying? When did the thought of her power start making me ache with want instead of fear? I should be fleeing, horrified by what I'm becoming. But as Julia's eyes lock onto mine, predatory and possessive, all I can think is how much I want her to look at me that way forever.

"Take me," I whisper, and I'm sure my tone betrays that I've never wanted anything more.

"I'm going to *devour* you." She hooks two fingers under my chin like claws. "Every drop of pleasure, every gasp, every tremor. You gave yourself to me so beautifully in the forest, and now I'm going to take everything—slowly, thoroughly, until you're shaking with how good it feels to feed me."

My pulse races, and that intoxicating rush of fear and arousal makes my head swim. Somewhere between the forest and this moment, she's become the only thing I want.

She kisses my neck roughly, trailing downward. At my breasts, she sucks and bites until I'm arching beneath her.

With her free hand, she reaches between my legs. She teases me, circling but never quite touching where I need her most. I rock my hips, trying to guide her, but she just smiles that wicked smile I've come to crave.

"So impatient," she purrs. "You made me wait. Now it's your turn."

"Julia—" Her name comes out broken.

"Beg for it." The command is softer than usual. Her eyes search mine, like she needs to hear it. She needs to know that I meant what I said: I want her for who she is.

I tug at her hold on my wrists, my whole body aching for her. "Please touch me. I need you, Julia."

Only then does she slide her fingers between my folds, and the relief is so intense I cry out. I'm already soaking wet, my desire having pooled there while I was pleasuring her. The evidence of my arousal makes her eyes gleam.

"You're practically dripping just from tasting me," she purrs, gliding her fingers up and down. "Did you like kneeling between my legs? Thrusting your tongue inside me?"

I nod.

"Good. Because I expect you to do that for me again and again."

My heart skips. She's talking like there will be more of this. Like tonight isn't all the time we have together.

She toys with me with expert fingers, building me higher while beginning to murmur the feeding incantation. Every cell in my body tingles as her power trickles into my veins.

I moan, rocking my hips, desperate for a release.

She takes her fingers away to examine them. They've turned as dark as shadows from feeding and are glistening with my arousal.

She pushes them into my mouth, making me taste them. I suck on her fingers, swirling my tongue around and between them. The way her eyes glint makes me burn.

As she brings her hand back down and her fingers enter me, I can feel my life force beginning to flow into her. It's different this time—deeper, more intimate. The pleasure and feeding intertwine until I can't tell where one ends and the other begins. Every slide of her fingers sends waves through me while feeding her magic in a continuous cycle of give and take.

The incantation grows stronger on Julia's lips as she moves her fingers, and I'm climbing higher, the pleasure building to an unbearable peak. My vision blurs at the edges, that familiar darkness threatening to creep in as my life force drains.

But then—

Julia's movements falter. Her fingers are still inside me, but the incantation dies on her lips. She breathes hard, staring down at me with something new there: fear.

"Hannah, I'm going to hurt you."

She lets go of my wrists and tries to pull away, but I wrap my legs around her waist, keeping her close. The feeding has stopped, leaving me aching, but this moment feels more important than any physical release.

"Julia." I reach up with both hands, cupping her face, forcing her to look at me. Her winter-blue eyes are glossy and vulnerable in a way that makes my chest ache. "I'm not Charlotte. And you're not the same person you were then."

"You don't understand. When feeding feels this good, I lose control. I cannot stop myself from taking everything."

"I trust you, Julia. I know you can stop because you've done it before."

"I've only been able to stop because I have to. Because of the binding spell."

"The spell is still there. You're safe. But I think you can stop because you want to, not because you're forced to."

Something shifts in her expression. Her eyebrows pull down, like she's letting herself hope.

"Keep going," I breathe, rolling my hips against her hand. "I'm not afraid."

She searches my face for a long moment, then begins stroking me again, slower and gentler. The incantation flows from her lips like a prayer rather than a demand.

Dark tendrils bloom from her skin and snake toward me, wrapping around me and holding me to her.

I keep my hands on her face, maintaining eye contact as the pleasure builds. The feeding resumes, but it's calmer, more controlled, more careful.

"Just like that," I gasp, my every muscle coming alive. "Don't stop."

She kisses me deeply, letting out a sigh into my mouth.

The slowness awakens something new inside me. The desire is just as fierce, but it's so different from before. The tendrils of magic tighten around me, awakening every cell in my body. A flutter builds in my chest, and then my belly, until I reach a peak and there's nothing left to do but freefall.

She gives one more slow stroke, and my climax crashes over me like a wave. I cry out. Julia stops kissing me to watch my face, and I hold her gaze as my body convulses with ecstasy. My essence flows into her, and relief floods her features as she realizes she's in control, and she's not destroying me.

The air shimmers, like heat rising from summer pavement. The fire flares brighter. Shadows writhe on the walls. My chest grows hot, something deep inside me pulsing like a second heartbeat.

Julia's eyes widen.

"Do you feel that too?" I whisper.

She nods.

My heartbeat quickens. "Is it the binding spell?"

"I—I believe so."

The warmth expands, radiating from where the binding has lived all night.

"Kiss me," I whisper, pulling her face toward mine.

The words spill out, almost frantic. I just want her lips on mine one last time before the spell that's been keeping us together breaks.

She does.

The kiss is desperate, but I no longer feel my essence draining. She's just kissing me for the sake of kissing me.

The room warms, like the sun is rising. Every cell in my body hums with energy. The spell strains inside me.

"What have you done to me?" Julia whispers against my lips, her words so broken and vulnerable I can hardly bear it.

I open my mouth and deepen the kiss, holding her face gently between my palms.

She slides her hand up my waist, chest, and neck, stopping to cup my cheek. For once, her touch isn't rough and possessive, but careful.

The heat intensifies until it's unbearable. Light bursts behind my closed eyelids. The spell pulls at my chest, wanting me to be flush against her. It brings me closer, closer, until I can't get any closer without being *inside* her. And then—

CRACK!

The sound echoes through the room like thunder. The binding breaks in my chest like a rope snapping under too much tension. The force of it makes me arch, crying out into Julia's mouth.

She bites back a cry too, gripping my shoulder so tight it hurts.

The windows rattle. The fire surges, threatening to reach out of the hearth and burn the house down.

Abruptly, the room falls silent.

I go limp, too exhausted to move. I can only lie there as Julia collapses next to me, her body warm and comforting against mine.

We stare at each other in shock, breathing hard.

The fire has settled back to normal, crackling softly. The shadows on the walls grow still again. Everything feels too quiet after the explosion of magic.

"We broke the binding," Julia finally whispers.

"Yes." The word barely comes out.

I wait for relief to flood through me. For the joy of being free.

Instead, there's just...emptiness. It's like something has been surgically removed from my chest, leaving a hollow space where it used to live.

Which is ridiculous. We severed a curse that would have bound us until death.

Then, to my surprise, Julia smiles. It's not her usual smirk or sneer, just a genuine, pure smile that transforms her whole face. It's the most beautiful thing I've ever seen in my life.

She leans closer and kisses me.

It's different from before, gentle and unhurried. No teeth, no bruising pressure. She tilts her head to fit us together better, and her hand comes up to cup my cheek with a tenderness I didn't know she possessed, her thumb stroking my cheekbone. I kiss her back just as carefully, hardly daring to move and shatter the moment.

When she pulls back, we both freeze.

Her eyes widen as she realizes what she's done.

We just kissed. Without any spell forcing us together. Just her lips on mine because she wanted them there.

I search her face, looking for regret or horror. But all I see is the same confusion I feel.

Should we be pulling away from each other, embarrassed by what the spell made us do? Because instead, that kiss feels like the most real thing that's happened all night.

I wait for her to say something. To acknowledge what happened between us and reaffirm that she meant what she said.

But she just lies back down next to me and stares at the ceiling, her jaw tight.

I'm suddenly hyperaware of our nakedness, of the marks covering our bodies, of the lingering taste of her on my tongue. The spell is gone, but I still want to be close to her.

"So." My voice comes out too high. "That's it, then. We're free."

"Yes." She spots her discarded clothes and summons them with magic. "Free."

The word hangs between us like a question neither of us knows how to answer. Without the binding spell, what are we? What do we want to be?

Julia pulls on her chemise, still not looking at me. "I suppose I wasn't the only one who needed to surrender."

My face heats up. Of course she figured out what I was doing.

She doesn't say anything else, and the silence feels worse than an argument. Is she angry? Does she regret what she said?

Through the window, the sky is brightening from black to deep purple. Dawn is coming. We broke the spell just in time.

So why does the thought of leaving this room make my chest ache worse than the binding spell ever did?

31

JULIA

I FIND REBECCA STANDING on Elizabeth's terrace as dawn breaks, painting the frost-covered gardens in gold and pink. She's wrapped in a maroon shawl, cradling a steaming cup of tea between pale hands, looking every one of her hundred and forty years.

She doesn't turn when I step outside, though I know she senses me. The morning air bites at my skin, which is still sensitive from Hannah's touch. I can still feel the ghost of her fingers in my hair and her breath on my neck.

We parted ways in the parlor, each of us needing to resolve our unfinished business: me with Rebecca, her with Riley.

So, here I am, knowing what needs to be said but unsure how to phrase it.

"The binding broke," Rebecca says to the sunrise. Not a question.

"It did."

"And yet you're still here instead of disappearing into the wilderness." She sips her tea. "Is the girl still alive?"

I bristle at the implication, but I deserve it. "Yes."

"Surprising." Her tone might be as close to approval as I'll ever get. "I expected to find her corpse by morning."

"As did I," I admit.

I move to stand beside her at the stone railing, leaving a careful distance between us. Below, Elizabeth's gardens sprawl in geometric patterns, everything controlled and contained.

"I took your sister from you." My words come out steady, though my throat tightens around them. "I cannot undo that."

Rebecca looks at me sharply. I see Charlotte in the shape of her eyes and the curve of her mouth, and it's a punch to the gut I was not prepared for.

I make myself hold her gaze. "I understand now what I stole from you. Her life, her future, *your* future. And I—" I swallow, my voice wobbling. "I deeply regret it."

Rebecca's hand shakes, her knuckles whitening around her teacup. For a moment, I think she might throw the tea in my face. I wouldn't blame her.

"Do you know what has tormented me the most? It wasn't finding her body, cold and alone, or sorting through her belongings, or spending years learning dark magic while vengeance burned a hole in my gut." Rebecca sets the teacup down hard enough that it cracks, tea spilling across the stone. "She died thinking you loved her as much as she loved you, and I've had to live knowing you didn't." Her voice breaks. "She had stars in her eyes whenever she talked about you, Julia. She was infatuated with your power. She thought the two of you were forever."

The words pierce me like daggers. My throat is too tight to speak.

"She wrote poems about you," Rebecca continues. "About the love you shared, and how lucky she was that you'd chosen her. The last one was two days before she died. She said she'd never been happier. Did you know that?"

Good Lord. I grip the railing to stay upright. I had no idea Charlotte romanticized our feeding sessions like that. The part of me that's still twenty-three and arrogant wants to argue that she knew what she was getting into, and she offered herself willingly. But that's a lie I've been telling myself since it happened, and I'm finished with it.

"I burned them all," Rebecca whispers. "I couldn't stand to read her joy when I knew what you'd done to her."

Good. They should be burned. Those poems were written by a girl too enraptured to see she was being consumed.

I wipe my stinging eyes. God, I was so naive and reckless. I deserved every bit of vengeance Rebecca hurled at me.

"And in the wake of it all," she snarls, "you ran."

"I couldn't face what I'd done," I say, my voice broken. "I ran from you, from the truth of what I am, from anything and everything that would remind me of her."

Rebecca scoffs.

"I did care for her," I say, though the words feel inadequate. "In whatever way I was capable of then. It wasn't enough, but it was real."

"Real?" Rebecca lets out a bitter laugh. "You fed on her for months, Julia. You watched her waste away, and you kept taking."

"I was immature and drunk on power. I thought I could control it. I—" I shake my head. "It does not matter what I thought. I was wrong."

She glares at me, her expression glacial.

"You won, Rebecca." The admission burns my throat. "The binding spell forced me to face what I am and what I'm capable of, and I hated every moment of it. I had to watch the same pattern threaten to repeat."

She faces me, one eyebrow raised. "You've grown to care for the girl."

I think of Hannah's trust, and the way she looked at me even after learning what I'd done to Charlotte.

When she first offered herself to me back at her house, I feared she would meet the same end. It seemed like the only possible outcome. But Charlotte only loved my power. She loved what I could give her, and what we had never extended beyond that. But Hannah...

I stop that thought before it can complete. I will not admit this to Rebecca. What happened between Hannah and me is none of her concern.

Instead, I say, "I cannot bring Charlotte back, and I cannot undo the pain I caused you. But I want you to know that her death changed me, even if it took your curse to make me understand how."

Rebecca's exhaustion is plain in every line of her face. It's not just tiredness, but the bone-deep weariness of carrying hatred for over a century.

"I don't forgive you," she says finally. "I may never forgive you. Charlotte was my sister and best friend, and you took her from me."

"I know." I expect no forgiveness, and I will not ask for it.

"But I'm so damn tired of hating you, Julia. I'm tired of letting what you did consume me the way you consumed her." She laughs bitterly. "Do you see the irony? I've spent a hundred years letting you feed on me in a different way. My anger, my grief, my entire *life* has been about you."

She balls her fist as if she's about to strike me with magic.

"I dedicated my life to planning revenge, perfecting the binding spell, and ensuring that journal was never lost, knowing that if you ever awoke, I was going to make sure you suffered. And now that it's happened..." She frowns into her tea leaves like she's reading the future.

"It doesn't bring her back," I finish.

She turns the cracked teacup, examining the damage. "Revenge hasn't filled the hole Charlotte left. It just made it deeper. I thought seeing you broken would heal something in me. But you're standing here, and Charlotte is still gone, and I'm still the witch who wasted a century on hatred. So I'm choosing to stop. Not because you deserve it, and not because I forgive you, but because I refuse to let you destroy the remainder of my life the way you destroyed hers."

I nod, unsure what else to say.

She sighs heavily. "Perhaps I can rest knowing you now understand what it means to risk losing someone you—" She pauses, giving me a meaningful look. "Someone who matters."

Heat creeps up my neck, but I don't deny it.

We stand in silence as the sun climbs higher, burning off the frost. The light is almost painful after the long night.

"I suppose I'll see you at coven circles," Rebecca says.

"If you'll have me."

"That's not up to me." She steps back, looking me up and down with calculating eyes. "Don't expect us to be on good terms. If you return, the best I can offer you is neutrality."

"That's more than I deserve."

"Yes. It is. But I'm not doing it for you. I'm doing it for myself and what's left of my life." She walks past me to go back inside, then pauses. "Charlotte loved easily. She was soft and trusting, and she would have forgiven you even as she was dying, because that's who she was."

The words hang in the cold air.

"But this girl isn't like that, is she? Hannah sees exactly what you are. The monster, the killer, the creature who can't help but consume everything she touches. And she's choosing you anyway."

My throat tightens. Indeed, Hannah is nothing like Charlotte. Charlotte made me feel powerful. Hannah makes me feel human.

"I wonder if it's better or worse that Hannah sees through you," Rebecca muses. "Charlotte died believing the lie that you loved her and were worthy of her devotion. At least she had that comfort. But Hannah knows the truth. She knows what you did to my sister and knows you could do the same to her. And she's foolish enough to still want you." She shakes her head slowly, pulling her shawl tighter. "Maybe that makes her braver than Charlotte. Or maybe it makes her more broken. Either way, I hope you see what's happened here, Julia. You didn't become a better person. You just finally got caught and forced to face consequences."

The words are a slap, sharp and stinging, because they're true.

The door closes behind her with a click, leaving me alone with the dawn. A strange, hollow feeling lingers in the air as our vendetta ends, not with violence, but with exhausted acceptance.

Rebecca is right that Charlotte was soft and trusting. She believed the best in everyone, and she deserved so much better.

Now, there's Hannah, who's been guarded since we met, unwilling to be vulnerable. She sees exactly what I am and has seen me at my worst. And she still bared her soul to me. Is that courage or self-destruction?

I gaze out beyond the garden, where the forest leads to a wide world I have yet to explore.

The binding is broken. Nothing holds me here except my own choice. It's time to do the noble thing and let Hannah move on. Time to let her find someone who won't drink her essence and bring her to the brink of death with every feeding.

32

HANNAH

RILEY IS IN ELIZABETH'S kitchen, washing teacups like it's a normal morning and she wasn't nearly killed in a feeding ritual a few hours ago. She's scrubbing each cup with unnecessary force, the porcelain clinking against the sink basin.

"Can't you use magic to do that?" I ask from the doorway.

She doesn't turn around. "Aunt Rebecca says it's character building to do it manually."

I step into the kitchen, hyperaware of how different everything feels without the binding spell. My chest feels empty, and after what we did, my body is a map of evidence. The bites, bruises, and scrapes might as well be fluorescent.

I'm marked, inside and out.

"You okay?" I ask.

"I'd feel better if I could blast that bitch with a jet of fire, but Elizabeth wouldn't let..." Riley turns, and her words die as she takes in my state.

The cup in her hand shatters.

Tiny fires crackle around her fingers as the porcelain shards scatter across the floor.

She stares down at her hands like they've betrayed her, then huffs and clenches her fists, looking up at me. "Hannah, what did she do to you?"

"What I wanted her to do," I say, steady and certain.

Riley flinches like I've slapped her. "You don't mean that. It's the binding spell talking, or sanguine magic—"

"The spell broke at dawn." I move closer, stepping through the broken porcelain. "I'm here because I want to be. Everything that happened between Julia and me, I chose."

I'm close enough to catch her familiar lilac scent beneath the dish soap. It smells like something from the distant past, no longer my source of comfort but a memory of the life I used to have.

Riley's eyes search mine, probably looking for the girl she knew, who read poetry and blushed at compliments and cried during movies. That girl would never have begged a dangerous witch to claim her on a forest floor, and would never have offered her life force repeatedly.

But that girl also got abandoned over and over, and always wondered what was wrong with her that made people leave.

"You've changed," Riley whispers, and it's not quite an accusation but close.

"Yes. Haven't you?"

She looks down at her hands, where little flames dance between her fingers, and which bear the scars of her magical awakening. "I spent twenty years trying to be normal. Good at sports, good grades, good daughter. But I was so desperate to fit in that I never asked if normal was what I wanted. Then I woke up and my life was literally on fire, and I had to choose between trying to suppress it or accepting that I'm different, and being different is what makes me special."

My eyes sting, and my throat is too tight to speak, so I just nod.

"I chose the fire, Hannah. I chose power and danger and a lineage of women who don't apologize. And it meant losing you, but—" Her voice finally breaks. "But I'm not sorry for becoming who I was meant to be. I'm only sorry I couldn't bring you with me."

"You didn't even try," I say, barely audible.

"Because bringing you would have meant watching you burn." She lifts her hands, and the fires blaze hotter, the heat stinging my face even from a distance. "I can't protect you from this."

"I know I don't understand what it's like to discover you're a witch," I say, "but I know what it's like to have everything change overnight, and to realize the world is completely different from what you thought. I know what it's like to have everything you thought was real turn out to be a lie."

Riley looks away, blinking back tears. "I never wanted to lie to you."

"What we had was beautiful." I reach out and take her hand, feeling the buzz of magic beneath her skin that was never there before. "I'll always love you. But things are different now, and neither of us can go back to who we were."

"She will destroy you, eventually," Riley says quietly.

"This isn't about her."

She lets out a cold laugh and pulls her hand away. "Keep telling yourself that."

I bite my lip. In truth, I don't know where Julia and I stand. We might never see each other again after this. Or maybe...

Well, this isn't the moment for hopes and wishes. I don't have to explain this to Riley.

So I back up, ready to go. "Bye, Riley. I want you to be happy. With your magic, with your coven, with whoever you become. You deserve that."

"So do you," she says softly. "Even if your happiness looks like something I don't understand."

I nod. This goodbye is both better and worse than her text message. Both easier and harder.

As I return to the foyer, I catch my reflection in one of the mirrors. I'm a mess of tangled hair and bruises, with shadows under my eyes that weren't there before. But instead of defeat, I see courage. I see a new version of myself, bold and unafraid.

Rebecca passes me going the other way, and she scans me up and down with a cold, mistrustful look. I stare right back.

As she enters the kitchen, I hear Riley say to her, "Teach me the binding spell. I want to know how to trap monsters."

Rebecca laughs. "The best way to trap a monster is to become one they fear."

I leave them behind to go find Julia, my stomach twisting at the idea of my ex learning spells from a woman who imprisoned someone in a journal for 118 years.

But that's none of my business.

Whatever Riley's future in the coven entails, I know she'll be good at it. She was always good at everything she tried. Soccer star, honor student, girlfriend.

Now she'll be good at magic too.

I just won't be there to watch.

Julia is gone.

I realize it as I travel from room to room, the house's emptiness slowly settling over me. The air doesn't hum with her presence anymore.

But I call anyway. "Julia?"

My voice echoes through the vast house, bouncing off high ceilings and antique furniture, getting swallowed by velvet drapes and Persian rugs. The answering silence mocks me.

"Julia!" Louder this time, more desperate.

Nothing.

I move through the rooms like I'm searching for a ghost. The parlor, the sanctum, the upstairs bedrooms.

That hollow feeling expands in my chest until I might collapse inward.

At last, Elizabeth pokes her head out of her bedroom, dressed for the day in jeans and a T-shirt. "She left, dear."

The words land like a punch.

"When?" My voice sounds thin and fragile, nothing like the person who stood in the kitchen just now telling Riley I'd made my choice.

"A few minutes ago. I saw her out the window, crossing the yard."

The breath leaves my lungs in a rush.

I whirl around, thunder down the steps, and burst out the front door.

"Julia!"

The morning air is cold against my skin, raising goosebumps on my bare arms.

I head for the forest where I surrendered to her. That's where I left her cloak, so maybe she went to get it. Branches catch at my clothes and hair as I run, but I don't care. I need to find her. I need to see her one more time and—

What? What do I need?

I don't know. But this ache in my chest is unbearable.

The oak tree looms ahead, ancient and indifferent to my pain. The memory of what we did here crashes over me—her fingers inside me, her body pressing me against the tree and into the earth, the exquisite edge between pleasure and pain and something darker.

Her cloak is gone. She's already collected it and left.

"Julia!" I scream it this time, my voice ragged.

The trees absorb the sound, giving nothing back. Even the birds are silent.

She's really gone.

I sink to my knees. The ground is still disturbed from what we did here.

I press my hands against the cold dirt, feeling for some trace of her magic, some lingering warmth, some proof that tonight was real.

There's nothing.

My chest heaves. What did I expect? A formal goodbye? A tender morning after? An exchange of phone numbers like this was a normal hookup?

The laugh that escapes me is half hysterical. Julia doesn't do normal. Julia is a century-old witch who just broke free from a curse that bound her to me, and of course she ran.

Just because she showed vulnerability doesn't mean she's changed her fundamental nature, and just because she made me feel seen doesn't mean she wanted to keep looking.

I should be relieved. This is for the best, and deep down, I know that. I have to go back to real life now: go to work, where I'll shelve books and recommend cozy mysteries to cheerful customers, and pay bills I can barely keep up with, and set up coffee dates with friends who will surely notice I've changed. In time, my body will recover, and the marks will fade, and...

Well, I know the memory of her never will. The feeling of surrendering to her, of craving that dangerous edge between pleasure and destruction, is carved into my soul now.

I touch the tender bruises on my throat where she grabbed me early in the night. Beyond these marks, she's changed something in me that I can't reverse.

And then she left.

Like everyone in my life seems to do.

It's time to accept that this brief and intense part of my life is over. Julia is gone, and I have to live with that.

It's time to go home.

My house looks the same as when I left it. Same overgrown grass, same empty driveway, same firepit with disturbed ash blown across the backyard. But I'm not the same person who lit that bonfire yesterday.

God, was it really just yesterday?

I let myself in through the back door and kick off my shoes. The house is deafeningly silent. No TV left on, no signs of life, just emptiness waiting to swallow me whole.

The floorboards creak under my feet as I shuffle like a zombie toward the couch, where I summon my very last drop of energy to call in sick to my 10 a.m. shift at Book Nook.

I pass out before I even put the phone back down.

It's mid-afternoon by the time I wake up, groggy and aching, and try to go through the motions of normal life. I shower off the dirt and sweat and evidence of the night, avoiding looking at the marks all over my body. I make coffee with shaking hands. Sit at my kitchen table and stare at nothing.

There's no binding spell squeezing my chest, no magical presence making the air electric. Just me and the quiet.

This is what I wanted, isn't it? Freedom. My life back. University next year, a chance to start my life for real.

So why does it feel so awful?

I try to eat toast and nearly choke on it. Try to watch TV but can't focus. Crawl into bed to try and sleep more, but every time I close my eyes, I see her face as she admitted she was afraid of hurting me.

This is for the best. We're too different. She's a century-old sanguine witch who feeds on life to survive; I'm an ordinary twenty-year-old who just wanted to get over a breakup and start a career. We make no sense.

But my fingers keep tracing the marks she gave me. My body keeps remembering the weight of her on top of me, the sound of her coming apart, and the way she looked at me when the binding broke—surprised, uncertain, almost hopeful.

So why did she leave?

I keep reminding myself that I'm better off without her, but it's increasingly hard to convince myself that what we had was forced there by magic and spells.

If that were true, shouldn't these feelings have gone away? Why do I miss her so much?

Maybe I don't want to be normal anymore. Maybe I liked the danger and darkness and Julia's terrible, wicked beauty.

The temperature drops as the sun begins to set, casting the house into amber and shadows.

I should eat, and call Dean, and do *anything* except sit here wishing last night ended differently.

I force myself to stand, my legs stiff from sitting too long. The house is freezing because I forgot to turn the heat up when I got home.

I kneel in front of the hearth to light the fire, which also reminds me of her since this is the first place she fed from me. *God dammit.*

As I reach for the kindling, something moves in my periphery.

My heart jumps.

I leap to my feet, peering out the window into the backyard.

Past the dead grass, past the ash and debris strewn across the lawn from last night, a shadow moves in the forest.

And there, standing among the skeletal trees and the carpet of orange leaves, is Julia.

33

JULIA

I TOLD MYSELF I'D leave her be.

I made it an hour from Elizabeth's before the hunger dragged me back—not the binding spell this time, nor the familiar hunger for life force, but something else I have no name for.

A tracking spell proved easy this time, now that her essence flows through my veins.

The forest behind her house welcomes me like an old friend as I stalk through the shadows. There's a trail here, slick and well-trod from people and animals. A man jogs past within arm's reach, his life force warm and inviting. The old Julia would have taken him without hesitation. But he is so dull and tasteless compared to what I'm craving.

I can see Hannah through her windows. She shuffles around her house with a solemn, listless energy. She sits for an hour at the table, not moving, not eating. Lights turn on and off as she travels from room to room. Over and over, she touches the marks I left on her skin and examines them in her reflection.

She's trying so hard to return to normal. Poor, sweet Hannah. Does she understand that I've ruined her? That she now belongs to something darker than her ordinary world can offer? Everything I awakened, every boundary I pushed, every moment she begged for more changed her irrevocably.

I ought to feel guilty. Elizabeth would say I should. Rebecca certainly would.

But I know what she's feeling. That struggle between what we should want and what we actually crave.

I could help her with a memory charm. I could make her forget me and all that's happened.

But why should she be allowed to forget while I have to live with the memory of what we did?

No. I cannot let her go. This woman looked at my darkness and wanted me anyway. She saw me make enemies wherever we went, from Rebecca to Maya to Riley, and she didn't run. She showed me pleasure I never knew possible and even brought me to surrender.

My heart beats faster as I creep through the trees, stepping close to the fence that divides her yard from the woods.

I thought once the spell broke, this obsession with her would fade. But she's not just a feeding source, soft and supple and begging to be consumed. She fights me even as she submits. She makes me work for every surrender. And somehow, she makes me want to be more than a parasite.

At last, Hannah's head snaps up, and our eyes meet through the glass.

Neither of us moves.

A sanguine witch's hunger never goes away. It just finds new shapes, new desires. I still need to feed, and without the binding spell's protection, taking from Hannah would be more dangerous than ever.

But I've come to crave more than her life force. I want to know what sounds she'll make when I feed from her without a spell compelling us. I want to know what she'll let me do to her and what she'll do to me. I want to see how much deeper into darkness we can go together.

Abruptly, she disappears from view.

Is she going to pretend she didn't see me? Call for help? Run?

Maybe she's done with me now that we're unbound. Maybe she doesn't want the risk of feeding without the binding spell to protect her.

But then, the door opens.

She stands silhouetted in the doorway, warm light spilling around her. She's wearing soft clothes, her hair loose, those marks I left still visible on her neck.

She doesn't look afraid.

You might also enjoy...

How to Flirt with a Witch

From Fan to Forever

The Road Trip Agreement

Snowed In With Summer

Striking Gold

Don't miss Tiana Warner's next book! Sign up for her newsletter and get a free Sapphic Cozy Fantasy novelette:

tianawarner.com/newsletter

ABOUT THE AUTHOR

Tiana Warner is a multi-award-winning sapphic romance author and outdoor enthusiast from British Columbia, Canada. She is passionate about animal welfare and volunteers with local dog rescue organizations. You can often find her cuddling a foster dog, riding her horse Flynn, or exploring nature.

Instagram @tianawarner
TikTok @tiana_warner
Website tianawarner.com

www.ingramcontent.com/pod-product-compliance
Lightning Source LLC
Chambersburg PA
CBHW031957050726
47590CB00006B/1943